S0-ARS-868

WHICH DOCTOR
killed Martin Sandeman?

DR. PHILIP AINSWORTH
The visiting American, who seems eager
to avoid questions about his past?

DR. FRANCIS HENCHARD
Senior psychiatric consultant, who
had been treating the missing boy for
quite some time?

PROF. CYRIL PEMBERTON
Chief of the Children's Hospital, who
treats the murder as an everyday event?

DR. WILLIAM RUTHERFORD
Sandeman's arch-rival, who argued with
the victim on the night of the murder?

DR. JULIAN GARSIDE
Who returned—coincidentally?—
from study leave in America on the
very day of the murder?

DR. JOHN CRISP
The junior member of the staff,
who is all too obliging?

Also by Edward Candy
Published by Ballantine Books:

BONES OF CONTENTION

WORDS FOR MURDER PERHAPS

WHICH DOCTOR

Edward Candy

BALLANTINE BOOKS • NEW YORK

The Paediatric Section of the Royal Society of Medicine could not have met under the auspices of the Department of Child Health in the University of Bantwich in April 1952, because the latter august institution, unlike the former, is only a figment of the author's imagination.

The Bantwich-Bannister Children's Hospital, its medical and nursing staff, and all the events related in the following pages are also purely imaginary. Any resemblance between them and real persons and events is purely coincidental.

Copyright © 1954 by Edward Candy
Copyright renewed 1982 by Edward Candy

All rights reserved under International and Pan-American Copyright Conventions. Published in the United States by Ballantine Books, a division of Random House, Inc., New York, and simultaneously in Canada by Random House of Canada Limited, Toronto.

Library of Congress Catalog Card Number: 83-25365

ISBN 0-345-32082-4

This edition published by arrangement with Doubleday & Co., Inc.

Printed in Canada

First Ballantine Books Edition: August 1985

*To
Michael, Edward,
and
Johnny*

PART ONE

NOCTURNAL

One dies! Alas! the Living & Dead!
One is slain & One is fled.

WILLIAM BLAKE

ONE

Of course they should have been asleep.

"Get into bed!" Tom said.

"Is it Sister?"

"It's a lot of them," Tom said. "Get in quick: there'll be a bloody great row if they catch you."

The vernal moon, remote, impersonal, austere, came up behind the cypresses and steeped the balconies in a candid radiance. Distantly motor horns and train whistles announced the presence of a town beyond the cypresses: a radiance altogether more rosy to the east showed the casual watcher where the immense furnaces of the Bannister works blazed unremittingly through the April night. The casual watcher was however lacking: the balconies, starved of star-crossed lovers, housed to the right a distressing clutter of ladders and paintpots and to the left two beds widely separated, each occupied by a child ostensibly asleep.

The two balconies formed an acute angle. Between them stood the squat tower of the administrative block. The drive ran its course flanked by the discreetly pessimistic cypresses and spent itself in a small semicircle of gravel at the front steps. Over the steps a lamp burnt without conviction; it was the unstinting moonlight that illuminated the name over the door and announced this to be the Bantwich-Bannister Hospital for Children, 1891. A riot of bas-relief depicted suffering childhood succoured

3

by the captains of industry, but so solid and impenetrable was the door beneath that there seemed little hope of this admirable purpose ever reaching fruition.

To the left and right of the door were windows, closed and shuttered. Beyond them balconies—a modern addition—streamed vaguely away, each overlooking a strip of lawn and flowers, each incongruously proclaiming the value of good fresh air to the aromatic compound of soot and damp that Bantwich endlessly exuded to an offended sky. The balconies, being a tribute to the influence of nature, were pari passu an invitation to the ineptitudes of man: the pastel paintwork was apt in the course of one year to become dishearteningly grey. Since Sir George Bannister and his colleagues on the Regional Hospital Board were well disposed, and since Professor Pemberton of the Bantwich University Department of Child Health was a man much given to expounding the importance of first impressions, the early summer was often dedicated to obliterating the depredations of unflagging local industry with a fresh coat of paint. Hence the pots, brushes, and ladders, and the half-delectable, half-nauseating smell that greeted the casual watcher, thus belatedly arriving upon the scene.

He had hardly observed the cypresses, the balconies, the moonlight: the legend over the lamp was for him redundant. He was hungry, tired, and in a temper verging upon the bearish. His stubby fingers explored the door, found a handle, turned it, and met with firm resistance. He knocked, using his bare fist upon the wood, once, twice, and again. Nothing whatever happened. He retreated and looked round. On the left-hand balcony two small boys were sitting upright in their beds looking at him. He waved, out of a habit of mild indulgence to the young, and then prepared for a further assault upon the building. But one small boy, the nearer of the two by the length of the balcony, beckoned to him. Fabian Honeychurch hesitated a moment, then picked his way through a barricade of daffodils and stood on the lawn.

"There's a bell," said the boy, pointing.

There was indeed a bell, shyly concealed at the side of the door in the happiest fin-de-siècle mode: dressed up in fact in a little wreath of ivy leaves.

"Thank you," said Honeychurch. "I didn't see it."

"The regulars have keys," said the boy. He added hopefully, "You're only here for the weekend, aren't you?"

"Yes, I am," said Honeychurch, "and what's more, I've nowhere to sleep. My secretary seems to have forgotten to make a hotel booking. Do you think I could stay here?"

The boy looked thoughtful. He shook his head.

"The beds are too small. We only take boys up to ten and girls up to twelve. You're more than ten."

"Quite a lot more," Honeychurch admitted. "Still, I'm going to try. I'm extremely tired. Why aren't you asleep?"

The boy's glance was wary. Evidently this question was familiar to him.

"It's the moonlight," he said finally. "It keeps Teddy and me awake."

Honeychurch looked along the balcony. "Is that Teddy? Why are you so far apart?"

"Sister said we talked too much. Anyway, we'll be in the ward tomorrow; they're going to start painting this side after the weekend. It was meant to be done in time for the meeting, but the painters were too slow. The professor got in an awful rage about it."

"It does seem rather a pity." Honeychurch, looking away from the smeared grey surfaces around the child's bed to the gleaming walls far over on the right, conceded the point. "I can quite imagine the professor would be annoyed."

"Do you know the professor?"

"Yes, indeed. We have been acquainted for many years."

"You look old enough to be a professor yourself."

"As a matter of fact, I am one."

"Go on," said the boy, admiringly. "Are there any more of you coming?"

"Several," said Honeychurch. "Now I'm going to ring that bell."

"I don't suppose anyone will answer it," said the boy.

After three unavailing peals had brought home to Honeychurch the extent of his young friend's local knowledge, he returned disconsolately to the balcony.

"Are you really a professor?" said the boy. "You don't talk like one."

5

"It takes all sorts to make a world," said Honeychurch weightily. "Is there any other way of getting in?"

"You could go back down the drive," said the boy, not without a certain malicious pleasure, "and then walk a long way down the road to the Outpatients' Entrance. Or you could turn right at the gates and go up the hill to the Residents' House. Any of them would lend you a key."

Honeychurch looked at the low brick wall that separated him from the balcony.

"Could I come in your way?" he asked.

"What, into the ward?" said the boy without much surprise. He looked doubtfully at Honeychurch's massive form, megalithic in the moonlight. "Can you climb? Aren't you too old?"

"I don't think so. I'll heave my case over first." Honeychurch suited the action to the words and then propelled himself over the parapet. Once within, he dusted his clothes and bent to retrieve his suitcase.

"There's a lot of them in the ward," said the boy. "You'd better stay here until they've gone. What's your name?"

"Fabian Honeychurch. What's yours?"

"Tom Bryant. He's Teddy Bannister." The boy indicated his companion in the other bed. "He's gone to sleep. Well, of all the—! And tonight of all nights!"

"What's special about tonight?" Honeychurch asked, cautiously approaching a window opening on to the ward.

But Tom was frowning and had laid a finger on his lips.

"I can hear Sister Starke," he said in a fierce whisper. "She's got ears like a hawk."

Has a hawk ears? Honeychurch wondered and peered through the window. "They," as Tom collectively called the adult enemy, were certainly in the ward, and there were certainly a lot of them: two nurses, one sister, one young and two rather older men in white coats, a young woman ditto, brandishing a notebook in the time-honoured style of the female medical student, and a porter noisily manipulating oxygen cylinders. All eight of "them" were standing round a cot enveloped in the plastic drapes of an oxygen tent. Much talk was going on and this, like the porter's operations, was conducted considerably above whispering level. Indeed, it seemed quite heated.

He looked round. There was no comment from Tom, who lay now with an arm thrown over his head and his knees showing up bonily under the bedclothes. From force of habit, Honeychurch listened for a moment to the boy's regular breathing, glanced at the other child and looked back into the ward. There were swing doors giving access to the balcony: he picked up his suitcase and resolutely pushed them open.

The sides of the ward were in deep shadow. Only two lights were on: one on the nurse's desk at the far end and the other over the cot where seven people—the porter had gone away—still stood. Possessed by some curious unwillingness to be seen—almost, he wryly thought, as if he were the undoubtedly graceless Tom choosing a bad moment for an escapade—Honeychurch hovered bulkily by the doors. One face in the group was familiar: Martin Sandeman had been one of his own clinical assistants some three years ago. Indeed, it was Honeychurch himself who had passed the promising Dr. Sandeman on to Professor Pemberton with the unholy reflection that these two should suit each other down to the ground, sharing as they did the dubious distinction of being repulsive to Honeychurch and therefore to all right-thinking men. Sandeman was not much altered: the same well-oiled hair that refused to lie flat surmounted the same pale features, the same pale eyes: he wore the same sort of shoes, Honeychurch noted with distaste—flamboyantly piebald in decoration, subversively suede in texture.

The other faces meant nothing to him, and even as he was scanning them the group broke up. Sister had sent the two nurses packing, the medical student had wandered down the ward and was writing something in her nice new notebook. The younger of Sandeman's two companions, a tall youth with the look of constant anxiety common to all house physicians, was showing something on the infant's chart to the last of the three—a short, stocky individual, Honeychurch saw, with thinning dark hair, a round face of pleasing expression, and a voice raised at present in evident annoyance. Honeychurch drew nearer; a nurse saw him and stifled a scream. Sister saw him and advanced awfully down the ward.

"Who are you?" she demanded. "What are you doing here? If you're a parent, you should have gone to the waiting room. If you've come about the oxygen tent, you should have been here an hour ago."

Honeychurch put down his suitcase with a certain weary exasperation.

"I am not a parent." He spoke in the measured tones of one offering precise information on subjects that matter. "Nor have I come to do anything about the oxygen tent. I am Fabian Honeychurch, and I am in Bantwich for a meeting of the Paediatric Section of the Royal Society of Medicine. My hotel booking would seem to have miscarried."

"The meeting is tomorrow," Sister Starke said firmly. "You have come a day too early. And how did you get in?"

"By the balcony," said Honeychurch. "After I'd rung the bell a great many times and knocked repeatedly. Now if you'll kindly tell me how to get to Pemberton's room and arrange a little food for me—"

Sister drew herself up and remarked that this was a hospital, not an hotel.

"Rubbish," said Honeychurch tartly. "My dear lady, I have travelled one hundred and forty miles since afternoon tea, I detest the industrial Midlands, and I abominate cheap hotels. I cannot find a room in any place where I would put an atom of faith in the sheets or the cooking. If Cyril Pemberton cannot be found, then someone else must be, for I don't intend to budge until I see some prospect of food and rest. Is that clear?"

By now the cluster around the cot had broken up entirely and drifted, impelled by a common interest, towards the contestants in this altogether uneven battle. Honeychurch possessed seventeen stone of unshakable confidence in his own right to be taken seriously and felt no need of an ally; he was provoked to even more marked irritation by the advent of Sandeman, who would undoubtedly recognise him and assume control of the situation. To be beholden to Sandeman was a contingency decidedly to be avoided. Honeychurch turned on his heel and strode down the ward to the crucial cot, picking up the discarded notes and casting a speculative eye on the child within. He beckoned the house physician to him.

"Evening. My name's Honeychurch." He nodded his

head in the direction of the infant. "What's all the trouble about? What's your name?"

"I'm Crisp," said the young man, evidently in some distress. "Are you Professor Honeychurch from Great—" He cast a hunted look towards Sister Starke.

"Sandeman will explain to her," Honeychurch said kindly. "Pretty sick, eh?"

"Yes. Yes, she is." Crisp spoke in a sort of ferocious undertone. "It started as a straightforward bronchopneumonia, but it hasn't responded to penicillin and sulphonamides, and she's gone right downhill in the last hour or two."

"What's wrong with Terramycin?" said Honeychurch, beginning to feel a little less tired. "You've got the stuff, haven't you?"

Crisp waved his hand in a wildly uninformative gesture.

"Well, you see, sir, she's in one of Rutherford's beds."

"Who's Rutherford?" Honeychurch asked suspiciously. "That chap over there who doesn't care for Sandeman?"

"Yes, that's him. You see, we're doing a controlled experiment with Terramycin, and this child's one of the controls. So she's not supposed to have it. Oh Lord, they're at it again."

They were coming back to the cot, talking with a concentrated fury of dislike. It was immediately clear that Rutherford, though blessed with beds of his own, was still subordinate to Sandeman: that Rutherford, controlled experiment or no, intended to treat the gasping baby in the tent with Terramycin, and that he was asking Sandeman for his sanction. What was less immediately comprehensible was that Sandeman had apparently agreed. This, it seemed, was not enough.

"You'd better prescribe it yourself," Rutherford said, looking not incuriously at Honeychurch.

"My dear Rutherford!" Sandeman's specious endearments grated, as always, on his late chief's nerves. "What a ridiculous suggestion! You've heard my opinion. I think you're perfectly justified in taking this case out of the series. I quite agree you can't let the baby die in order to prove a point."

"You agreed with me once before on a similar occasion," Rutherford said quietly. "In case you think you can get away with it again, just remember there are witnesses this time."

"Dr. Rutherford," said Honeychurch, rather to his own surprise, "if you know where Professor Pemberton is to be found, would you be good enough to take me to him? Evening, Sandeman."

"Good evening, sir," said Sandeman. "I'll take you to the professor myself if you'll allow me. Rutherford"—he contrived to make his voice extraordinarily insulting—"has his work to do."

Honeychurch would have judged Rutherford, on the basis of face, figure, and manner, a placid and reasonable individual. Yet he remarked with considerable approval the prompt reaction of rage in the man's eye as he turned away.

"Thanks very much, Sandeman," said Honeychurch affably, "but I'll wait for Dr. Rutherford. It won't take him more than a minute to write up the Terramycin, and I shall enjoy making his acquaintance. After all," he added with a smile of pure sweetness, "I really know you quite well already, don't I?"

TWO

Whatever architect had been responsible for the lesser amenities of the Children's Hospital had clearly devoted much time and labour to designing an appropriate entrance to the medical ward. Honeychurch turned as he left for a last glance and found the view partly blocked by another inscription, coyly ogling the sick child with WELCOME TO BANNISTER WARD, A FAIRY LAND FOR SICK CHILDREN. Around it, stone cherubs of a suspect corpulence disported themselves in a welter of cumulus clouds. Honeychurch stared upwards, and Rutherford seized his opportunity to stare at Honeychurch.

It had been from first to last a curious evening, starting tamely enough with a book by the fire and a pile of notes waiting to be finished by his side; changing to an unwonted outburst of energy when the telephone rang; moving to a familiar climax with the appearance of Sandeman—as usual in a foul humour loosely disguised under his veneer of unctuous politeness. And now by way of *deus ex machina*, Honeychurch, legendary, pontifical, and somewhat resembling Father Christmas in his person and mode of entry, had arrived most opportunely and snatched him away before he could lose his temper—which would have been pointless and foolish, since the whole sorry story of his relationship to Sandeman was drawing so rapidly to its close.

Honeychurch spoke. His voice was growly, ursine,

11

peculiarly pleasing. "There seems to be no end to the Bannister influence. If I heard correctly, there was even a Bannister on the balcony. Would he have been related?"

"That's the heir apparent to the Bannister millions." Rutherford held a second door open for him.

"Really to millions?" Honeychurch passed through, reluctantly lowering his eyes from the stone cherubs.

"Even with death duties. He's the grandson or great-grandson of the one who built this place. The current baronet believes in making concessions to what he calls the spirit of the times; he gets his medical care on the National Health Service."

"The boy could hardly do better elsewhere."

Rutherford shrugged. "It wouldn't make much difference. He's only had a very mild spell of chorea. I hope he was asleep when you came in," he added. "The professor likes them doped to the point of coma."

"He seemed to be asleep," Honeychurch said. "The other one was very much awake. A delightful child."

"Tom? Yes, he's a nice kid. He's been brought up in some sort of institution; not a bad one actually, but he's got rather beyond their means."

Honeychurch suffered himself to be led down a flight of steps. They were in the open air; surprisingly, in an orchard. Between the main building and the untidy huddle of odds and ends that housed laboratories and X-ray equipment a triangular space had been planted with apple trees. Near the path the trees supported a washing line: an orderly was taking down a row of napkins and humming under her breath.

"Little winding sheets," said Rutherford absently. "Isn't that what Herbert calls them? But probably it wasn't nappies he had in mind."

"Do you read Herbert?" Honeychurch looked at him in mild wonder.

"I read anything I can get my hands on."

"'When boyes go first to bed, They step into their voluntarie graves.' I'm particularly fond of that: but it's hardly a point of view that commends itself to the modern mind."

"Not to the modern medical mind, anyway; it does rather suggest we're wasting our time. Pemberton would hate it."

12

"Pemberton has not had the advantages of a liberal education," Honeychurch said heavily. "He believes that activity is a good thing in itself—a point of view to which no one in the seventeenth century could possibly have subscribed. I expect he keeps your noses firmly to the grindstone. How do you all survive it?"

"Speaking personally, I haven't," Rutherford said, wondering why he should reveal his own problems to a total stranger, but deciding that to do so was obscurely a comfort. "I'm leaving at the end of the month."

"Is that when your appointment ends?"

"Yes and no. It was a one-year appointment, renewable subject to satisfactory—you know the sort of thing. Senior registrar job, in fact. But I had a slight difference of opinion with the powers that be some weeks ago, and Pemberton has decided he can bear my loss with equanimity."

"I'm sorry to hear that," Honeychurch said and sounded as if he meant it. He added after a hesitation that was, in so large a person, the acme of delicacy, "Has he given you a testimonial?"

"I haven't asked him for one."

Honeychurch frowned disapproval, but his nod belied the frown.

"Do you want to go on with paediatrics? Pemberton's name carries considerable weight, you know."

"I know, and yes, I do. I've taken a long time to make up my mind: I wasted five years in the Army—no, not wasted; I don't altogether regret them—and now I thought I was all set to go ahead. It's disappointing, but there's nothing to be done about it."

"Forgive my impertinence," Honeychurch said, "but our friend Sandeman didn't have any part in this pother of yours, did he?"

That was, inevitably, where one landed oneself, confiding personal worries to an acquaintance of half an hour's standing; one could hardly reveal the full extent of Sandeman's part in the pother as a mere conversational gambit. Rutherford bent down and picked up Honeychurch's suitcase.

"As a matter of fact he did. But it's all settled now and not worth worrying about. Pemberton's house is at the end of this path."

13

"What's that? That enormous stucco wedding cake over there?" Honeychurch demanded, showing himself not unwilling to change a subject apparently distasteful. He waved a hand towards a building of a starchy whiteness almost incredible in this benighted city.

"That's the new Outpatient Department: it was built just before the war. The little shack on the left is the university Department of Child Health. Each of us has a cosy little room with running water and no curtains, so the professor has only to look through his study window to see who's toeing the path of duty. Rebellious spirits" —he glanced at Honeychurch—"have been known to steal out at dusk, leaving their lamps burning. Unfortunately, at seven o'clock in the morning a lighted window tends to create scepticism."

"You paint a terrible picture," Honeychurch said. "You confirm my very worst fears. I think you do well to leave this lesser purgatory. Have you any plans?"

Rutherford shook his head.

"You have no commitments, no family responsibilities?"

"None whatever."

"That of course makes a difference," Honeychurch said. "Is this Pemberton's house?"

They stood in the porch, looking at a knocker in brass depicting the ancient and dishonourable legend of the three wise monkeys.

"Hear no evil, speak no evil, see no evil: an extraordinarily negative morality," Honeychurch observed.

As if impelled by some external force, they turned towards the Department of Child Health. What had caught their attention was the switching on of a light on the first floor. A well-remembered figure approached the window and looked out over the orchard.

"Sandeman?" Honeychurch queried.

"Sandeman." Rutherford lingered over the name; then he was gone, leaving Honeychurch to the uncongenial task of interrupting Professor Cyril Stagforth Pemberton in the course of his evening's work.

The night was cold after the unseasonable mildness of the day, and in Pemberton's study the embers of a coal fire were emitting a faint disheartened echo of their former glow. Two armchairs disposed about the fire housed two

14

professors: two armchairs—one narrow, winged, and upholstered in relentlessly economical imitation leather, the other wide, deep, and covered with faded but still inviting velvet—were not more dissimilar than their occupants. Honeychurch nursed a glass of brandy as yet untasted and probably, he thought, not worth the tasting. He was beginning to feel stupid with fatigue: and still Pemberton talked. By some ten years he had preceded Sandeman as Honeychurch's assistant, and he had changed as little. A freak of nature had ordained that his skin and hair should be of identical colour and texture, and to this unedifying harmony he added a third component in clothes matched exactly to the prevailing scheme. In the course of time, a little more grey had been incorporated: that was all. Nibbling a biscuit with small predatory movements of his jaws, he talked; interminably, it seemed to Honeychurch, whose responses had long ago become purely automatic: indeed, he had the uneasy sensation of having been transformed into one of those clockwork robots designed to repeat some useless and unvarying action for an indefinite period, if only a passing wastrel will insert the necessary penny.

"Yes, there's some very nice work going on here. You know Sandeman?"

Honeychurch experimentally sighed. Pleased to find so much semblance of voluntary self-expression left to him, he assented to the proposition with warmth.

"An exceptional brain," said Professor Pemberton, chewing his way gingerly through his last biscuit. "He has an outstanding paper for you tomorrow evening. Of course we have some other good people. Porter promises well: Peebles is a steady worker. I'm sorry you haven't seen my wife, by the way. I always send her off to bed at ten; she has plenty to do all day with the children. Do you want that biscuit?"

Honeychurch relinquished his fragment of baked flour-and-water paste without regret. He tasted his brandy and with some difficulty avoided groaning aloud: but a mute resolve was forming within him. He would at all costs find an hotel on the morrow. Fleas, lice, bedbugs, the most nightmarish concomitants of an imagined epitome of low lodging houses, would at least spare him a repetition of this protracted insult to his demanding and unappeased flesh. Pemberton's wife was, he felt, decidedly to be envied. She was at least in bed.

Meanwhile her husband talked... punctuating the monologue with rapid sallies to the bookshelves in search of books and journals. By twenty past eleven Honeychurch's lap was liberally strewn with the effusions of the Bantwich school, that newly arisen comet in the sky of British paediatrics. For which, in a way, Honeychurch reminded himself, I might justly be held responsible: for did I not bring up Pemberton in the way he should go? Did I not direct Sandeman's first tottering steps along his chosen path? Yet what thanks, what credit do I get for it—and what, to be fair, do I want? He glowered lavishly at the unconscious Pemberton, half-seas under in a spate of articles on the respiratory excursions of the premature infant. Only, he told himself, to consign the aforesaid pair to a suitable limbo and go to bed.

With a becoming timeliness, Pemberton got up from his chair.

"Don't you bother; I'll find it in a moment. I can always lay hand on my journals."

He began to rummage in an as-yet virgin pile in a far corner of the room. Honeychurch sank back once more, beginning to feel that if the worst came to the worst an armchair might after all be slept in, if only Pemberton would keep quiet. But, no; he had emerged from a flurry of disturbed periodicals.

The nearest approach his face could make to the relatively extreme emotion of anger was made: he thumbed an exercise book with suppressed irritation and finally exclaimed: "Ainsworth! Yes, of course, I remember now. I lent him Volume II on the strict understanding he would return it before the weekend. Well, really! I can't have this sort of thing going on—journals disappearing, people showing no sense of responsibility. Perhaps he's still in the hospital. I'll just go over and see. Pity you missed seeing that paper. Very good bibliography, too. I shall only be a few minutes."

He had gone before Honeychurch could stop him. Indeed, Honeychurch himself had in a sense gone. Not, however, for long: his first uneasy dreams were broken by a knock on the door; his waking thoughts were crudely scattered by an unknown voice of plausibly Transatlantic timbre.

"D'you know where the prof is?"

"Which prof?" Honeychurch sadly enquired and tried to look as if he had not been asleep.

"Pemberton. Why, who else?"

"There are other chairs in other universities," Honeychurch pointed out with pardonable annoyance.

"Well, round here," said the newcomer, "when anyone says 'prof,' they mean Cyril Stagforth Pemberton. D'you happen to know where I can find him?"

"He went out a moment ago to look for one Ainsworth, I believe."

"Now that's what I call an astonishing coincidence," said the young man, for young and male he indubitably was, both facts being attested to by a variety of unsuitable clothing and a blue shadow under the jaw. "Just fancy," he added, with lush insincerity, "the affinity that must exist between our immortal souls. Right when Cyril Stagforth goes braying forth into the night in pursuit of one Ainsworth, one Ainsworth feels he cannot lay him down to rest without paying the prof a surprise visit. Though I must say," he added with a sudden descent into truthfulness, "I'm glad I've missed the old goat."

"Would you be secreting about your person," asked Honeychurch, "Volume II Part I of the *American Journal of Diseases of Childhood*, 1943? If so, you are right to be elated at Professor Pemberton's absence: he is much displeased. If I were you, I should return that inflammatory little publication and invent an excuse for being here. Then when he comes back, you can tell him that you restored his possession this morning and merely forgot to sign his little book. However, I shouldn't be talking to you like this. Presumably you work for him?"

"I work for him?" Ainsworth contrived to throw an alarming weight of emphasis on the pronouns. "Low as I may have sunk in this unappreciative world, I do not yet earn my living stooging for that God-awful washer of soiled diapers. No, I'm here on a fellowship provided by Tufkids Strained Foods Inc., Boston, Mass.: all I have to do is see what goes on and perform a few little antics of my own devising on the surgical side. It's not often I cross the prof's track."

"I should think that's just as well," Honeychurch said gently. "Where do you hail from—Boston, did you say?"

"Oh, I've been around. I did two years' surgical interne at Johns Hopkins. Then I went on to the Mayo Clinic. Then I came here."

"Did you qualify at Johns Hopkins?"

"No; I started at Cornell. Look, I'd better be going. I'll leave the journal like you said. Thanks for the tip."

"Cornell?" said Honeychurch, his interest suddenly aroused. "Do you know Eric Ziedermayr? And Jarvis Peterson?"

"Well, yes," said Ainsworth, arrested unwillingly on the threshold. Possibly he had heard footsteps as of an avenging but earthbound angel: certainly he was impatient to be gone.

"It's many years since I was last at Cornell," Honeychurch said. "Long before your time. But I won't detain you. We can talk about our common acquaintance tomorrow. No doubt you'll attend the meeting?"

"I wouldn't miss it for the world," said Ainsworth with conviction. "It'll give me a lot of quiet pleasure to see Martin Sandeman shooting off his mouth to a lot of elderly male wet nurses."

He was gone: Honeychurch had barely had time to note that Sandeman's unpopularity with his fellow workers seemed widespread when Pemberton erupted into the room, breathing accumulated wrath.

"Not a sign of him in the building: no one knows where he is. That's why I don't like having these independent workers in my department. It's impossible to keep tabs on them, and some of them don't seem to know the meaning of the word work. Taking an evening off during the week! What's that you've got there? What are you doing?"

For Honeychurch had lowered himself hugely to the floor before a bookcase and was delving in its depths. He emerged clutching a chastely bound periodical.

"I think you've been maligning Mr. Ainsworth," he observed. "Isn't this what you were looking for?"

Later, as he attempted to woo sleep in the tormenting embrace of the camp bed Pemberton had erected for him, it occurred to Honeychurch that he was only receiving his just deserts: it also occurred to him that Pemberton was a man of vindictive temperament and fully capable of designing this act of retribution while speciously regretting the unpreparedness of a spare room. His eyes closed: the camp bed trembled in its remote depths. Morpheus descended, albeit unwillingly, from the reluctant heavens.

Honeychurch slept. Pemberton slept. Ainsworth, Rutherford, and Crisp slept. Sandeman slept for ever.

THREE

He heard the owl: he wondered if anyone else had heard it. In all the seven weeks he had been in hospital he had never once heard an owl till now, but there were plenty of owls where he came from. He hoped he wasn't just going back there; that seemed too ordinary a thing to happen so late at night and so secretly.

Sitting up quickly in bed, he looked over at Teddy. Teddy had meant to hide his tablets under his pillow, but tonight Nurse Carter had stood over him and waited till he swallowed them. They had had a whispered conference after she had gone back into the ward: Tom thought he had read somewhere that if you kept on walking about after you took dope, you could stay awake for a long time. So Teddy had got out of bed and walked. He walked until Sister Starke came to do her round, and he was still awake when the fat man who said he was a professor came over the balcony. But getting into bed must have been too much for him, because he had been asleep and snoring when Tom looked at him again.

Tom got out of bed and shuddered when his bare feet touched the cold floor: he thought of his slippers, but knew it would be wrong to put them on. After all, he was meant to be walking in his sleep—at least, he thought he was. Perhaps he shouldn't waste time. All the same he lingered uncertainly by the parapet for a moment, wondering if even now he shouldn't try to rouse Teddy and tell him all about it. But mystifying Teddy was part of the adventure; and anyway, trying to wake him was like trying to wake the dead.

He slipped over the balcony and stood briefly in the moonlight: then he heard the owl again and started off down the drive. The gravel was unkind to his feet and got grittily between his toes. He wanted to bend down and pick a sharp bit out of the crease under his left little toe, but it wasn't far to go to the gates. He could stick the nagging, scratchy little pain that long.

And when he was halfway down the drive he heard a small scuffling sound in the trees on the left, and it was all he could do not to turn round and look. But he didn't, he walked on, conscious of a bounding pulse of excitement under his pyjama jacket. He hoped whatever was going to happen would be worth the trouble; if it were just a trick like the other times, he would be pretty angry. But he thought he knew what it would be. They had found his parents at last and he was going to come into his rightful heritage. There would be a pony, a sailing boat, and a cake every year on his birthday; all the things that Teddy Bannister took for granted and didn't even boast about. He wondered if his mother would be waiting for him at the gates, wearing a diamond necklace and carrying a box of chocolates: but by now he was at the gates himself and there was no one there at all. Two cars were drawn up at the kerb, one of them shiny, new, and long in the bonnet, the other battered and disreputable. Tom looked at them quickly and was shaken by a sudden doubt. Before he knew what he was doing he had looked back as if he expected help to come from that direction—if it came at all.

He saw someone leave the hospital by the front door and walk rapidly towards him: the fleeting illumination of his face in the moonlight was unrevealing. And then there was someone else coming out from the trees into the heavily shadowed drive. Then there was only one man again and a darker shadow than the rest lying on the ground at his feet. Tom jerked round, knowing and not knowing what he had seen. What happened to comic-strip heroes every day had happened to him—one man had killed another before his eyes, and he could guess who, too.

And now me, he thought. If he finds out what I've seen, I'm as good as dead.

Perhaps a child less well versed in the ways of heroism might have panicked, screamed, or run for his life. Tom used his head. There was only one place to hide, and he knew very well it might be dangerous—for there were two cars, and one of them belonged to the murderer. He heard soft sounds behind him, the muffled noises of a man dragging something heavy into the trees. Tom waited no longer; the doors were unlocked, and in a moment he was in the back of the older and nearer car. He crouched right down on the floor, clicking the door to behind him as quietly as he could. In the dark his heart throbbed and pounded like a machine. He curled himself up, instinctively aware that in occupying as small a space as possible he was increasing his slender chances of safety. Then he began to pick bits of gravel off his heels, thinking hard all the time. He heard footsteps coming nearer, and his stomach lurched in a new and beastly way: then he heard a smooth new engine starting up and felt suddenly elated. If the murderer had gone, he could slip back into the hospital and tell them what had happened; and at first they wouldn't believe him, they would be horribly angry. But sooner or later the body would be found and then they'd be sorry. Tom straightened up and immediately sank back again. It wasn't going to be easy as all that, for he had almost given himself away. Someone else was coming; someone was getting into this car. And if one man could kill another, what mightn't any man do? Wasn't it suspicious that this one had come so soon after the other? Might not the murderer have waited in the trees while somebody else went by?

The car was moving. Tom breathed as quietly as he could, wishing himself back in his bed: for that he was still in danger considerably more real than anything he had ever read he knew very well. And, looking back, he couldn't be sure. There had been such bars of shadow on the drive, it had been too dark even for him to recognise the face of the one who had been killed, though he had looked at him twice as long as the other. Had he made a mistake about the murderer because that was the one he had expected to see? There had been something—

He peered up at the back of the driver's head and knew

at once who'd got him. That was just as unlikely as the other, but everything was unlikely tonight, and he wasn't going to take any more chances. So he kept still and tried to guess where they were going. As soon as the car stopped he could get away and try to find a policeman. His picture would be on the front page of the newspapers, and his father and mother would see it and say proudly, "That's our boy," and come to Bantwich immediately to find him.

Cautiously he raised his head and looked up through the windows at tall buildings on either side. So they were still in the town; he hoped the car would stop soon because in towns there were always policemen even at night, but in the country it might take a long time to find anyone at all. He caressed his naked feet, feeling prematurely sorry for them at the thought of tremendous distances to be covered. And he saw with gathering anxiety that the buildings were thinning out: then there were no buildings at all, unless they were little ones that he couldn't see from where he crouched. He dared not stretch up any higher.

They went on and on; it seemed to Tom as if twenty miles stretched between him and Bantwich. Moonlight filled the car now, unbroken by trees or houses. He made himself as small as he could in the shadow cast by the door. Soon the hump of a hill rose on the left and the car was in the dark again. Silently and despairingly the child began to cry. He relaxed a little in the shadows and stuffed the woolly cloth of his pyjamas in his mouth to keep himself from sobbing aloud. But the car was making a fearful noise, leaping as if possessed over a road surface full of potholes; and when a sob eventually escaped him it was lost in the general din. Tears flowed thickly down his hot face; they tasted salt and pleasant.

The car turned abruptly and jerked into a sudden vivid light and then complete blackness. There was a silence during which Tom suspended altogether the necessary business of breathing. Then he heard two doors closing, first the door of the car, then a heavier but quieter one. A series of small noises followed that he couldn't identify.

He waited for what he thought was about ten minutes, though it was nearer two. Then he slid across the floor, opened the door and put his foot gingerly across the running board. By now he could see a bit in the dark: he saw that he was in a garage meant to hold two cars, but at

23

present there was only the one he had come in. The floor was stone and inimical to his feet: he withdrew and sat up on the car seat, looking round. There was one window, and it was small. He supposed he had better try to get through it. Summoning up his courage, he got out, shivered, and tried the garage doors. They were locked. Then he made for the window, but on the way he tripped and fell headlong over something on the floor.

For a moment he lay quite still. He wanted very badly to cry out. He explored his legs carefully with a fingertip and found several tender places and a sticky patch below the right knee. He got up: now he moved very slowly and got safely to the window. It was even smaller than he had thought, and when he reached up and felt round the frame there was no catch, only a fixed sheet of glass.

He crept back into the car, got on to the back seat and pillowed his head on his hand. He was past crying now, and soon he was past caring about his bruised shins, his grazed knee. He had been awake since four o'clock that morning, and most of that time he had been planning his now disastrously altered excursion. He slept, and if his sleep was disturbed by evil dreams, they left no trace on his wet and weary face.

PART TWO

DIURNAL

If they stand arm'd with seely honesty,
With wishing prayers, and neat integritie,
Like Indians 'gainst Spanish hosts they bee.

Suspitious boldnesse to this place belongs,
And t'have as many eares as all have tongues.

JOHN DONNE: *Satyres*

ONE

Forty years earlier the young Fabian Honeychurch had formulated a brief prayer for use on retiring after a more than usually hectic day. Please, he would beg divine authority, don't let anything more happen before breakfast. Let me get at least four hours' sleep.

It was this modest request for a little leniency on the part of Heaven that came unbidden to his mind when he woke the following morning; for the light streaming through the window had that limpid and tender quality that marks the medium-sized hours of early spring. Groaning, he pulled himself up and looked at his watch. It was, as he had suspected, just after seven. He speculated with misgiving on the likely course of events in a household inhabited by a young family under the patriarchal thumb of his host, and decided that early rising followed by cold baths and a slim meal of grapefruit or one of the more dynamic varieties of breakfast cereal was the least that he could expect. He hoped that his years and his position would spare him the greater indignities. He feared they would not.

But Pemberton entering the study at this moment was not the brisk, new-every-morning Pemberton of his recollections. The man wore only a dressing gown hastily pulled on over his pyjamas, and he had omitted to knock. Even for him this suggested unusual perturbation. Honeychurch sat up again in some alarm; the camp bed sank regretfully to the ground beneath him. He extricated himself painfully from the wreckage and looked an enquiry. But Pemberton had picked up the telephone and was dialling a number—and this without a word of explanation or apology. Honeychurch sat down again and searched himself for bruises; thoughts unutterable flitted through his outraged mind.

"I see you believe in getting the day off to a flying start," he remarked with some restraint.

But it was immediately plain that comment was unwanted and would go unheeded: Pemberton's face betrayed an emotion on altogether too large a scale for banter. It was natural for Honeychurch to be curious, admirable of him to refrain from asking questions. Catastrophe, whatever its nature, would declare itself soon enough; as soon, indeed, as a dilatory and befuddled operator inserted certain pegs in certain holes and enabled the news to break.

"Bantwich City Police?" said Pemberton. His hands were shaking: small drops of sweat had assembled on his forehead. "Professor Pemberton of the Children's Hospital here. I want to speak to whoever deals with"—he paused and then rushed on—"with homicide."

"Homicide!" said Honeychurch. It was some moments before he realised that he had spoken aloud. Pemberton still ignored him: a variety of distant noises indicated that someone who dealt with homicide was being found. Honeychurch sat still, conscious of tide upon tide of astonishment, incredulity, and—worst of all—mere curiosity, breaking over him. He looked at Pemberton: Pemberton looked back and saw him apparently for the first time, since his features now assumed the configuration proper to a smile and achieved only a grimace. He spoke again.

"Pemberton here, at the Children's Hospital. To whom am I speaking, please? May I have your name?" Even in his distress, Honeychurch noticed, the habit of carefully docketing his associates had not deserted him. "Well now, Inspector Grimshaw, something very unpleasant has happened here. One of my staff has been found dead in the grounds. He has been struck on the back of the head. The name's Sandeman. Yes, at once. And I'd be grateful if you'd make your arrival as inconspicuous as possible.

28

We've an important meeting here today. I shouldn't like any fuss. I shall expect you." He rang off.

Honeychurch said, with a guilty feeling of relief, "Sandeman has been killed? What an extraordinary thing! My dear fellow, I really am most distressed for you. Shall you not cancel the meeting?"

"Cancel the meeting?" Pemberton repeated mechanically. It was apparent that such an idea had never entered his head. "Good heavens, no! We're expecting at least three hundred visitors: I can't possibly disappoint them. Besides"—his voice sank to a reverent whisper—"Martin wouldn't have wished it. He'd have wanted his paper to be read."

The statement was irrefutable; nor had Honeychurch, feeling slightly sickened, any wish to refute it. He stood up abruptly.

"I think I'll dress now if you'll excuse me. Perhaps I could have breakfast with the residents. I won't trespass any longer on your hospitality. No doubt you have much to do."

"Well, if you're set on going—" Pemberton said with an obvious absence of regret. He looked at the camp bed. "You've done for that," he said.

"It will give me great pleasure to replace it," said Honeychurch. "Future guests might have to be turned away from your door because of my inordinate bulk. I cannot allow that."

Possibly Pemberton's recent shock had sharpened his none too acute perceptions: at any rate, he picked up the telephone again without replying.

"Put me through to Dr. Crisp."

Honeychurch began unobtrusively to fish for socks under a neighbouring bookcase.

"Crisp?" Pemberton was saying. "Where are you? Yes, well, stay there. I want you to get hold of all the staff— what's that? Yes, the unit staff, of course, and anybody else who was in the building last night. Mr. Ainsworth, for instance; he was certainly here." He frowned at Honeychurch, who was much engrossed in his shoes. "Tell them to be in my room in the department at nine sharp. Then come over here and take Professor Honeychurch back to Residents' for breakfast. Is Hobbs still with the body? Tell him to stay there until the police come. Now get off the line; I've got another call to make."

He dialled again.

"Can I speak to Dr. Henchard? Oh, is that you? This is Pemberton at the Children's Hospital. Has Thomas Bryant come to your place during the night? No? Well, he wasn't in his bed this morning. Sister has been on to the Laurel Homes, and he hasn't turned up there. I thought he might have come to you. No, there's no need for you to come up here. If you want to, of course I can't stop you. It won't do any good, though. Yes, all right, good morning."

"I beg your pardon," said Honeychurch, "but did I hear you say that Tom Bryant was missing?"

"I did say that. What do you know about Tom Bryant?" Pemberton's suspicious glance almost seemed to suggest that the boy might be concealed somewhere in Honeychurch's voluminous garments.

"I met him last night," Honeychurch said. "I thought him rather a nice child: I haven't spirited him away, though. Who is Dr. Henchard, and why has he a vested interest in Tom's whereabouts?"

"He's the senior psychiatric consultant to the Royal Bantwich Infirmary. The child was under his care before he was admitted here, and I allowed him to attend the clinic when he was over the worst of his nephritis. I knew no good would come of it," he added darkly.

"It's a strange coincidence," said Honeychurch, preparing to go as he saw Crisp coming past the window, "that the boy should run away the night Sandeman was murdered."

"Coincidence?" said Pemberton blankly. "Yes, I suppose it is. It must be, mustn't it?"

"Unless, of course—" Honeychurch began, and stopped. "Ah, here is Dr. Crisp. Good morning. I shall be delighted to have breakfast with you. Professor Pemberton will be fully occupied until he meets his staff at nine. By the way"—he discharged a parting shot—"I take it I am *persona grata* at that meeting? I was, after all, in the building last night. It might be as well to keep, eh—tabs on me."

* * *

It was a quarter to eight by the time Honeychurch emerged from Crisp's room, his toilet complete. The small, bleak dining room where the resident medical staff were fed at intervals from an unvarying menu was empty save for a sour-faced domestic transferring cups and plates from trolley to table, and making a formidable amount of noise in the process.

"Is there any chance whatever of breakfast arriving?" Honeychurch asked, after a moment's survey had convinced him there was not.

Crisp shook his head. "Not before a quarter past."

"Well, in that case, I suggest we go for a walk."

"I'd like some fresh air," Crisp said eagerly. "I'll just ring the operator and let her know I'll be in the grounds: the professor doesn't like us to get out of touch. Shall you wait here, sir? The phone's in the corridor, and there's nowhere to sit."

Left to his own devices, Honeychurch examined the refectory minutely, found nothing to give pleasure to the eye, and suspected that in due course there would be nothing to gratify the palate. From this sombre consideration he turned to a notice board suspended at a height that suggested that the residents as well as the patients of this hospital were well below the usual stature. Somewhere about the level of his waist terse typewritten directives over the initials "C.S.P." demanded the immediate attention of all medical staff. A few more prolix documents recommended lecture courses, journals, clinics of various sorts, to the fortunate few who were left with any time on their hands after attending to the professorial imperatives. But it was a larger notice in a familiar hand that caught Honeychurch's itinerant gaze.

> Analgesics other than aspirin and phenacetin are no longer to be given on the authority of house physicians and surgeons. Any case in which a more potent drug is required is to be referred at once to myself or Dr. Rutherford for inclusion in the Pethidine Investigation.
>
> M. SANDEMAN.

It was at this moment that Honeychurch first clearly realised the significance of Sandeman's death. Somebody must have disliked him even more than I did, Honeychurch reflected, to feel that he was worth hanging for. To have inspired a distaste in many people is after all a common enough attribute of men of his type, pushing, egoistic, cold: but to have roused some one person to the act of murder—I wouldn't have thought Sandeman had it in him.

Crisp's return broke off his reverie; exercise, he felt, had much to recommend it. They left the Residents' House by the front door, walked down the road, and were at the gates of the drive up which a travel-stained Honeychurch had made his way the evening before: a policeman summoned up by processes of subterranean intricacy stood guard at the entrance. Crisp approached the constable with a nod, opened the gates, and led the way up the drive. A few yards further on he turned sharply to the right and disappeared between the trees. Honeychurch had some difficulty in following him.

The body of Martin Sandeman had been dragged, apparently by the heels, through the cypresses and on to a handkerchief-sized lawn beyond. No real attempt at concealment had been made: Honeychurch had the impression that the murderer had been concerned merely to get his victim clear of the gravelled drive. The dead man lay in a heap, face upwards, looking shorter and more slightly built than in life. There was very little blood: a few dried smears on the jacket were hardly to be discerned in the flecked tweed. Sandeman's face, scratched only superficially by his journey through the undergrowth, was singularly devoid of expression.

Crisp said quietly, "We haven't moved the body, but when you get closer you can see he's been bashed on the back of the head. Hobbs is guarding the weapon."

Honeychurch's gaze travelled absently to Hobbs, evidently a porter, and the weapon at his feet, evidently a short, thick bar of scrap iron, about the same size as the cranking handle of a car: a piece of rusty junk, he immediately thought, that any disused cellar or dumping yard would yield by the dozen, the sort of thing one tripped over on dark nights in country lanes or saw lovingly preserved in any city backyard where children play. An undistinguished weapon, mercifully undecorated by its brief and final contact with the back of Sandeman's head.

Crisp was talking, but Honeychurch had lost the thread. It was a moment or two before he realised that he was being given a first-hand account of the finding of the body. It had not occurred to him before that someone must have found it, and now it struck him that a tour of the grounds in the early hours is no part of a resident's daily duties: the explanation forestalled enquiry.

"She got in a flap and told the nurse he was probably in the lavatory or under the bed—"

"Sandeman in the lavatory or under the bed?" said Honeychurch, bewildered.

Crisp looked at him in some surprise.

"No; the Bryant child, of course. I was just telling you."

"I'm sorry," said Honeychurch humbly. "I seem to have difficulty in concentrating this morning. You must put it down to an exceptionally uncomfortable night. And of course"—he added tardily, and with a guilty motion towards the body—"the great shock of hearing about this."

"Well," Crisp said, in the patient tones he was probably cultivating for interviews with the more obtuse type of parent, "it started when Taylor, the junior night nurse on Bannister, was doing the morning temperature round. She always ends up on the balcony, and when she went out she found Teddy Bannister, still asleep as usual, but no Tom Bryant. So she told the senior nurse—that's Reeves, she's wonderful—and they both had a quick look round. Reeves looked in the locker where they keep their outdoor things. And his clothes were there, shoes and everything, so it didn't look as if he'd gone far. Then she got hold of Night Sister, the one you met last night"—he turned on Honeychurch a look of genuine admiration—"and she made a terrific shindy and told them to look again. Then she got me up. I thought I'd better make sure he wasn't just having a game with us, so I got Hobbs along with the keys of the outbuildings and we searched all round the back first. Then Hobbs reminded me of this little lawn; and when we got here we found Sandeman. It was rather surprising," he said with praiseworthy restraint. "I forgot all about Tom, I'm afraid, till Hobbs reminded me and suggested I might tell the prof about both things at once."

"Could Tom have gone off directly I left him?" said Honeychurch.

"The earliest he could have gone is half past ten; that's when Sister Starke finished her round on the balcony. And as for Sandeman—"

"I saw him at his window in the Department of Child Health at about half past ten, too," Honeychurch said, thinking aloud, "but probably many other people saw him later than that. I suppose he must have been going home?"

"It looks like it."

"Would his car have been left at this entrance, then?" Honeychurch asked; a sudden picture had come into his head, and a moment's concentration established its validity. A car of doubtful age and yet more doubtful pedigree had been parked by the gates when he came through them the night before.

"No. Sandeman didn't run a car," Crisp said. "He only lived just up the road."

There was a pause, which Honeychurch brought to an end by describing the car he had seen.

"That's Rutherford's," Crisp said immediately. "Everyone else uses the car park behind Outpatients."

"I suppose," Honeychurch said slowly, "Dr. Rutherford left the hospital after he took me to Pemberton's house?"

"I wish I knew. I do know Sandeman didn't go before eleven, because I rang him over in his room to tell him that the child in the oxygen tent had died. But I don't know when Rutherford left. He didn't come back to the ward, anyway."

Honeychurch said, "I wouldn't worry if I were you. You cannot seriously imagine Dr. Rutherford doing *that*—"

"I can't," said Crisp. He looked distraught. "But perhaps the police could. And I suppose all that wretched row will come out, and heaven only knows what they'll make of it."

"But a mere difference of opinion over a professional matter—"

But there had been, Honeychurch recalled, no difference of opinion: only a curious remark from Rutherford that in the presence of witnesses Sandeman had committed himself to a certain course of action and would have to take responsibility for it. Even at the time this had seemed peculiar.

34

Honeychurch said, "You are talking about some other 'row,' I take it, and not the very minor affair that took place last night?"

Crisp looked wary.

"Why should you think I meant anything else?"

Honeychurch gave it up. He said pointedly, "I think it's time for breakfast. And here come the police. We had better leave the field clear—unless they wish to question you."

But the police, it appeared, had no urgent wish to question anyone. Three men, armed with the impedimenta proper to their crafts, one clearly a doctor, approached the two objects in view and began diligently to examine them. Photographs were taken, features of the surroundings were noted with reverent care. Before Honeychurch could think of a polite formula to cover their withdrawal, one of the men who had been bending over the remains of Sandeman straightened up and addressed them, consulting a scrap of paper in his hand.

"Is one of you gentlemen Dr. Crisp?" he asked.

Crisp acknowledged his identity.

"You found the body, I understand, sir? Would you be so good as to come along with me? Inspector Grimshaw would like a word with you."

Crisp looked apologetically at Honeychurch, who smiled, and assured him that he could find his own way back to the refectory.

"Just one moment, if you please, sir," the policeman said. He poised his pencil hopefully above his list of names. "You are—?"

"Fabian Honeychurch."

The policeman frowned.

"I am not on the staff of this hospital," Honeychurch said. "I am Sydenham Professor of Child Health in the University of London. But I was here last night, and at one time I knew the dead man well. By the way," he added, "I suppose Inspector Grimshaw has been told that the loss of Dr. Sandeman is not the only untoward happening that demands his attention? A certain Master Bryant has also left us, and a lost child in the hand may be worth any number of conjectures in the bush. It has just occurred to me that Tom's bed on the balcony must have commanded a remarkably good view of the drive."

T W O

There are people to whom lists, timetables, and the methodical classification of facts are the banal necessities of existence; others to whom they are the very breath of life. Inspector Grimshaw belonged to the latter and perhaps more exclusive class. Amid a stack of flyblown files in the small and exceedingly dusty office that was all the hospital saw fit to offer him by way of accommodation he pored over a typewritten list of the medical staff, handed to him by Professor Pemberton, and decorated by that meticulous person with appendices and asterisks in red ink to indicate those persons who had to the professor's certain knowledge been in the hospital in the course of the previous evening.

Grimshaw allowed his hand to hover over the page for a moment before his own pen added a discreet tick to the names of Crisp and Pemberton himself. Performing this simple action mildly comforted him and gave him the feeling that he had an essential contribution to make to the conduct of this case. A very young detective-inspector investigating homicide for the first time on his own account might be forgiven a measure of timidity: Grimshaw, a diffident soul on even the simplest occasions, had hastily telephoned the Chief Constable for instructions and accepted the demand for a prompt application to the Yard for experienced aid with mingled regret and relief. Experienced aid could not arrive, however, till round about eleven, and would presumably expect the routine stuff to be well under way by then. And so it was, Grimshaw assured himself, glancing at his notes. The mode of death had been established; the weapon had been examined and had yielded no fingerprints; the body and its surroundings had been photographed; footprints had been looked for and not found. The time of death had been roughly fixed at between ten and two, according to the police surgeon, but the interview with Crisp had put the earlier limit forward to eleven, since Crisp had spoken to the deceased on the internal telephone at that time. And now the police surgeon had carried off the body to the post-mortem room, promising to let him know the details as soon as possible.

Grimshaw returned to the list. At the top was Pemberton, followed by a galaxy of letters; at the bottom Crisp, conspicuously humble. Below Crisp's name two more had been added: one in Pemberton's hand, PHILIP AINSWORTH, M.D. (CORNELL), the other in the writing of one of his own men, PROFESSOR HONEYCHURCH. It was tempting to dwell on these two evident interlopers. A rigid ascetic, Grimshaw eschewed temptation and went back to Pemberton.

It was difficult, he realised, to separate his own immediate smallboy's reaction of bashfulness in the face of the professor's overwhelming efficiency from the more objective conclusions arrived at by reading his statement. The dead man, on Pemberton's showing, emerged as a tenuous but admirable figure; "a conscientious and thorough worker" was one of his phrases, and this was precisely the sort of moderate praise Grimshaw himself craved. But there ended any resemblance between himself and Martin Sandeman: Pemberton had also brought with him a photograph of his staff taken some months back on the steps of the hospital. And there was Sandeman, a man of middle height with smooth fair hair and an expression at once ingratiating and peculiarly repellent. Young Dr. Crisp's description of him as all sorts of a sarcastic blighter had the correct ring to Grimshaw's ear; correct, that is, in point of psychological acuity if not of conventional politeness. Dr. Crisp's account of his own movements before and after eleven was vague, but seemed likely enough; a lengthy talk with a nurse, followed by a bath, followed by bed—all innocent activities, Grimshaw hoped, and the first easy enough to check. He himself favoured fixing the hour of Sandeman's death as early as possible: it was difficult to see why the man should have hung around the hospital so late, though Pemberton had said that he frequently worked at night in the Department of Child Health and to leave at two in the morning would not be particularly unusual for him. It was after this remark that Grimshaw had put his brief enquiry as to whether the dead man was known to have had any enemies.

"A man as outstanding as Martin Sandeman," Pemberton had said, "is bound to provoke a certain amount of jealousy in his less able colleagues. Dr. Rutherford comes to my mind."

Grimshaw looked down his list and traced a faint circle round one of the names. William Raines Rutherford, M.R.C.P., D.C.H. He wondered whether the dislike had after all been so unreasonable. According to Crisp, there had been other grounds for it than jealousy: there had been, apparently, a difference of opinion between the two men late the previous evening in the ward.

"Nothing very much," Crisp had hastened to assure him. "Sandeman was always a bit overbearing, and it's natural enough that Rutherford shouldn't like being ordered about as if he were doing his first job, like me."

William Raines Rutherford. Grimshaw looked at the photograph. There was nothing to suggest a propensity to violence in Rutherford's face; nor was there in any of the other faces. He saw that physiognomy might be misleading and wondered what Rutherford was doing at this moment: Crisp had spoken to him on the telephone and given him the news—if it was news—of Sandeman's death and told him he was expected at the hospital. If he came, would that suggest innocence? Clearly not. A doctor—at certain times Grimshaw's mind moved in primitive paths—was of necessity a subtle creature: to bolt would not be subtle.

Rutherford trudged down the lane, thanking heaven it was a warm morning and the sky was clear; though since this was April a clear sky meant little enough. In this mild light the bleak stone hedges acquired an indefinable charm; he could have found it in his heart to be unreasonably happy. But between his heart and the external world was a barrier of social convention which demanded at least the appearance of solemnity the morning after Sandeman had died.

Far along the Pitts Leighton road he could see the bus approaching. He broke into a run and solemnity instantly deserted him. Instead, he swore at the futile errand that necessitated his leaving the car behind today of all days, at the delay over clearing up last night's fire because the charwoman refused to work on Saturdays, at the altogether unpredictable punctuality of the public services. But he beat the bus to the stop, clambered aboard into the unfamiliar discomfort of proximity to many unwashed bodies, and was borne at no very great speed towards Bantwich, towards interrogation, towards the first intimations of his own disastrous insecurity.

There was nothing to be done about it, Grimshaw decided, but to sit tight and wait, and in the meantime there were others on the list. There was Julian George Evelyn Garside, against whose sufficiently villainous name Pemberton had inserted a different and more flamboyant asterisk. At the bottom of the page he had written by its twin, "At present absent on study leave in the U.S.A." That would seem to preclude Garside's being of any marked interest, but Grimshaw paused over him all the same. The name was strangely familiar: within recent months he was convinced he had heard it in connection with something sinister, or at least unpleasant. His memory refused to offer any more definite information, but his pen drew a little question mark on the paper. It might be as well to make sure of the dates of Dr. Garside's study leave.

Garside turned over in bed and saved himself from a painful tumble by sheer presence of mind: such are the penalties of changing one's sleeping accommodation many times in a few weeks. The luxuriant buoyancy of the bed he had last occupied had lingered in his mind and erroneously informed his body that space abounded for stretching and rolling in the delicious twilight state between waking and sleeping. But this bed offered no such delights to the voluptuary; was narrow in fact, short in relation to his own excessive height, and presented him, when he finally opened his eyes, with a view of Bantwich that made him close them again promptly. There was, after all, no reason to hurry. He was free to go to hospital or not as he chose; he could even go home if he wanted to. But on the whole he didn't want to. He preferred to lie warmly in bed: and after the rush, the hectic efforts of the night before, he deserved a little peace. He pulled up the blankets and shut out Bantwich for another hour.

Peebles, Porter, two names unmarked in any way: Grimshaw skipped them. Whoever they were, they would probably have to be questioned later, but for the present the few people who were known to have been on the spot promised to yield greater dividends for the time spent on them. A girl's name came next, and she was also out of the running on this count. Below her was Crisp: below Crisp the added names. Philip Ainsworth, he read again and wondered where Cornell was. He picked up the telephone; a helpful operator gave him the number he required, and in a few moments he was speaking to Ainsworth's landlady.

No, she didn't know what time Mr. Ainsworth got in last night: she hadn't waited up for him. And she was used to Mr. Ainsworth's queer ways, but this morning, she protested, he had gone too far. The telephone had rung for him at half past seven, which was better than it might have been, for she was used to having to call him up at all hours; and when he had finished answering the phone his behaviour had been altogether too much for her. Bounding up the stairs without a word of thanks and making enough noise in his room to waken the dead— then down the stairs again, knocking over a plaster Psyche on the way, and it was all very well his saying he'd replace it, but they'd bought it in Skegness on her honeymoon and it wouldn't ever be the same again even if he stuck it together piece by piece which he promised to do when he realised it had sentimental value. All of which proved that Mr. Ainsworth's heart was in the right place, though his feet and hands never were, and how anyone so clumsy about the house could be trusted to do an operation, she couldn't think. Then he'd hardly touched his breakfast and left the house without telling her whether he'd be in to lunch. Not for the first time she had decided to give him notice, and not for the first time she would change her mind when it came to the point. There was no denying it, she would have found life dull without him, and what she would do when he went back to the States in August, she simply didn't know.

He put down the receiver, then picked it up again to ask the operator if Professor Honeychurch could be found. Then he turned the list over. On the other side Pemberton had written an account of the boy who was missing from Bannister Ward. Tom Bryant was nine years old, the note informed him. He had been admitted on February 27 with a diagnosis of acute nephritis. To this the professor had considerably attached a definition: acute nephritis was an inflammation of the kidneys. Whatever it was, the child had never been more than mildly ill, and after the first three weeks was well enough to resume treatment with a local psychiatrist. The child was not, in Pemberton's opinion, in need of any such treatment; but he was an illegitimate child abandoned by his mother and living in an institution, and had upset the authorities by persistent fabrications and inventions. Of all this Grimshaw made heavy weather. The boy told fibs, he gathered. Was it possible, he wondered, that this child—a queer child, evidently—might have attacked Dr. Sandeman? He dismissed the idea. Unless the boy were abnormally tall for his age, he could hardly have managed a blow that would fell a grown man.

There was a knock on the door. Grimshaw relinquished his flight of recondite fancy and braced himself to meet Fabian Honeychurch. Could this professor, he asked himself, be as authoritative as the other? He devoutly hoped not. Set as he was on performing his duty, he had no great wish to be told for the second time within an hour the best way to perform it. He said, "Come in!" very sternly, and felt himself to be formidable.

Honeychurch opened the door: the formidable Grimshaw revealed himself as a man in the middle thirties of quiet and pleasing manner at present overlaid with a rather touching anxiety. Honeychurch guessed that this was his

41

first major assignment and foresaw that his opening gambit would take the form of an apology.

"I'm sorry to disturb you, sir. We are trying to get the preliminaries of the case in order before Inspector Burnivel gets down from London. If you wouldn't mind answering a few questions—"

"Burnivel?" said Honeychurch, and frowned. "An unusual name: I once treated—But no matter. Perhaps you would be good enough to ask Inspector Burnivel if his daughter was recently a patient of mine at the Hospital for Sick Children? I should be pleased to renew our acquaintance."

Inspector Grimshaw looked, not unnaturally, a little put out by this excursion into the social round and recalled the interview to safer ground by embarking on a number of straightforward questions. In less than ten minutes the inspector knew all about Honeychurch's adventures on the previous evening. If Honeychurch was conscious of some minor reticences in his description of the fracas around the oxygen tent, he trusted Grimshaw was not. After all, Honeychurch told his conscience, since it seems to me quite improbable that this man Rutherford had any part in Sandeman's murder, there is no point whatever in my confusing the issue. . . .

A telephone on the table rang. The inspector made an excuse and answered it. Honeychurch rose to go. It was nearly nine, and the desire to be present at Pemberton's council of war was strong within him. But Grimshaw replaced the receiver and detained him as he approached the door.

"You've known the late Dr. Sandeman some time, Professor Honeychurch. Do you happen to know if he was a diabetic?"

Honeychurch, arrested in Gargantuan flight, looked all astonishment.

"It's possible," he said promptly, "but most unlikely. The only time I ever remember his being a patient in hospital was when he broke a leg in an accident: that must be six or seven years ago. I should ask Professor Pemberton if I were you. He would know if Sandeman developed diabetes more recently. May I ask what gave you the idea?"

Grimshaw seemed not at all put out by this reversal of

the roles of questioned and questioner. He became confiding.

"Because of the pricks," he said with charming simplicity. "He had pricks all over his upper arms and thighs. The police surgeon just rang up to tell me in case it was important. I wondered—if he wasn't a diabetic—perhaps he'd been having some other sort of injections, and not insulin. Some kind of drug, perhaps. I wondered if he might have been an addict. Lots of doctors are, aren't they? Thank you for your assistance, Professor Honeychurch. Good morning."

THREE

The room Professor Pemberton had selected for himself at the removal of the Department of Child Health from its home in a cupboard under the stairs of the Bantwich Medical School into more spacious premises lately vacated by the Faculty of Fine Arts (always ailing and at this time moribund) was chiefly remarkable for the memories it evoked of all the headmasters' studies ever entered by erring and equivocally repentant youth. Pemberton's windows, alone in the building, were curtained: with, as befitted them, a sepulchral material exhaling an odour of incipient decay. Painted an austere cream from ceiling to shoulder level, the walls plunged ultimately into a hinterland of mephitic puce; bookcases, packed though they were with paper-jacketed volumes fresh from the printers, signally failed to dissipate the prevailing gloom. Pemberton's desk, the high altar of his own beloved cult of the severe but tolerant administrator, the teacher feared yet loved, was tidy with the extreme tidiness of the incurable reformer. Such oddments as human weakness permitted to clutter the polished infinities bespoke a purpose unchallengeably sound: never, if Cyril Pemberton had his way, would a moment of that precious commodity time be allowed to slip away unused. To this end he had assembled a calendar, a clock, a pad for memoranda, an engagement book, a diary; and these propitiatory offerings to the twin gods of record and foresight were interspersed with the instruments proper to one dedicated to filling the unforgiving minute with—if he could only make it—sixty-five seconds' worth of distance won: to wit, a telephone, a dish of compressed milk tablets, and a bottle of vitamin capsules.

Behind the desk was a fireplace. On the mantelshelf, as a concession to the warmth of sentiment that might reasonably be expected to throb in the breast of a husband and father, stood a sickening little group in gesso depicting the Pied Piper of Hamelin playing away for dear life to six infants all wearing expressions of broadly moronic rapture. Two feet higher the shields of Bantwich City and the University of Bantwich were mounted in regrettable juxtaposition; for while the city beneath a hart sable on a field gules demanded with honest Midland bluntness "*Quo vadis?*" the University, under a lion couchant but not yet dormant, murmured "*Cui bono?*" thereby putting the dilemma of thinking man into an heraldic nutshell. The furnishings of the room were completed by an examination couch, a single large and superlatively shabby rug, and a number of chairs of notable discomfort, designed to prevent any hedonistic urge to indolence on the part of the professional staff.

At the door of this holy of holies Honeychurch presented himself at two minutes past nine. Pemberton was, inevitably, delivering a lecture on punctuality.

"I can't have you people turning up late and wasting my time. When I call a meeting for nine, I intend it to begin at nine."

Honeychurch smiled amiably, chose a chair, and sat down without waiting for an invitation he judged unlikely ever to be given. He was aware that the reprimand was not primarily intended for him; nevertheless, he felt himself to be included in it. He surveyed his companions. It was easy enough to separate the sheep from the goats. Of the former he recognised only Rutherford, who was sitting by the window and looking out on the Gothic glories of the Bantwich City Baths. The other innocents included a young woman of blameless insipidity and two men sitting side by side on the examination couch. Both were older than Crisp and younger than the late Sandeman; otherwise they had little in common, one being stout, plethoric, and prematurely bald, the other slender, pale, and tall enough to sit with his back against the wall and his feet on the floor—a power clearly envied by his neighbour, who alternated between perching in discomfort on the extreme edge or sitting well back with his feet in the air like a baby in a bus. The guilty were given away by the ostentatious disinterest they took in what was passing. Ainsworth was engrossed in his cigarette lighter; Crisp, full of righteous indignation, studied the rug with an attention its design scarcely merited. Honeychurch, considering that he might well deflect a fraction of Pemberton's wrath from those less constitutionally well adapted to lodge pointed shafts in unimportant places, waited only for a moment's pause in the monologue to ask Pemberton whether he had yet been questioned by the police.

Once fully launched upon a tide of rhetoric, Pemberton obviously disapproved of interruptions calculated to make him pull in his sails and tack in another direction. He nodded a terse affirmative, glanced at the clock, and prepared to embark again while the tide still flowed. Honeychurch hove into view, a reef of irreverence and impiety.

"This man Grimshaw," he informed the assembled company, "is an extraordinarily nice fellow. I'm sure you'll all like him. It's a memorable experience, being interviewed by a detective: something quite out of the usual run. I wasn't frankly, expecting much satisfaction from this weekend: conferences of this sort lose their attraction as one grows older; one merely attends from a sense of duty and a desire to encourage younger folk. No"—he folded his hands comfortably over a generous abdomen— "I can't say I was looking forward to it particularly. I suppose one should be grateful to poor Sandeman for relieving the drab with a little lurid colour. I'm sure you'll agree, Pemberton, that you couldn't have wished for anyone less obtrusive than Grimshaw. He will do everything that is required him without making us feel that anything the least untoward has occurred."

The effect of this speech exceeded his modest intentions. Pemberton's face was suffused with an unaccustomed dusky scarlet; Ainsworth had forgotten to light his cigarette, and the unknown pair on the couch looked demurely aghast. The young woman's mouth had fallen open, giving her much the look of a rabbit confronted by a stoat. Only Rutherford turned on him a glance of unmixed amusement. Honeychurch observed with pleasure that this particular suspect did not look as if he had spent the night tossing upon a bed of guilt; nor indeed had he the physical configuration that Honeychurch in the innocence of his heart believed proper to a murderer; Honeychurch's first impression of a cheerful sturdiness of contour had been correct. Between thirty and forty, Rutherford already gave some promise of attaining in time to his own epicurean bulk, only without perhaps the height to carry it off.

Thus thought Honeychurch, sustained by a little harmless vanity; and how prejudiced I am, he thought, against tubular people; men as trees, walking. He looked with disfavour at Pemberton, who was still engaged in stirring the sloth of his subordinates into some assumption of antlike activity. Honeychurch merely smiled and closed his eyes: he knew this manoeuvre to be unnerving even to the very self-possessed, and to this fortunate category Pemberton had never belonged. When silence finally came, he followed up his advantage with a request to be introduced to the gathering. Subliminal murmurs of protest came from Tweedledum and Tweedledee on the couch, who evidently shared a pressing engagement: Pemberton muttered something under his breath and revealed that these two had been christened by their parents George Peebles and John Porter. Peebles was a medical registrar; Porter aspired to the high function of university lecturer in child health. Both were young men preternaturally aware of the dismal necessities imposed upon them by working within the range of Pemberton's demanding eye. It was evidenced by the uneasy grace with which they submitted to being called George and John by their overlord. Abominable affectation, Honeychurch thought sourly. How would he like it if these poor devils started calling him Cyril?

"But, my dear Cyril," he said, since neither Peebles nor Porter seemed likely ever to achieve this acme of spurious intimacy, "to revert to a former topic—I'm sure these gentlemen will forgive me if I take up a little more of their time?"

These gentlemen would all too evidently forgive him anything by now. Honeychurch continued:

"Do you really intend to proceed with the meeting? I

only ask because it seems to me that our admirable inspector will have quite enough people to keep an eye on without having a number of strangers cluttering up the place. Besides, you can hardly expect your guests not to evince a little curiosity about Sandeman's violent demise. I can imagine the afternoon session deteriorating into an unseemly scramble to get to the scene of the crime."

"You seem to me," Pemberton said, "to have a very low opinion of your colleagues. I find it hard to believe any reputable paediatrician would indulge in the sort of vulgar sensation hunting you describe. They are here for a weekend of instruction; they will naturally see things in their correct proportions."

"Oh, come," said Honeychurch. "Surely that's just a little unfair to, eh—Martin? Wouldn't he have expected some small acknowledgment of his departure from the scene? After all, the most esoteric diseases of childhood could scarcely hold a candle to the extreme rarity of an outbreak of crime in a children's hospital."

"May I ask what you mean by an outbreak of crime?" said Pemberton. "One criminal offence can hardly be regarded as an outbreak, except by the gutter press."

"I have a lot in common with the gutter press," said Honeychurch ruefully. "I think the murder of one of my fellow men an event of rather staggering importance. Sufficient importance, indeed, to think it an adequate reason for altering—though with regret—certain plans that seem now perhaps a little out of place."

Pemberton consulted his agenda with a tightening of the lips that indicated how little appeal this viewpoint had for him.

"I had intended," he said pointedly, "to cover a good deal of ground this morning. But we've been here long enough. You've got your work to do and so have I. Before you go, Rutherford, I'd like to have a word with you. You'll be reading Martin's paper tonight of course. It's a pity that that should have been the main item on today's programme."

"I am sure Martin would have postponed being murdered if he had only realised how greatly he was inconveniencing you," said Honeychurch gently and decided from the look on Pemberton's face that silence would henceforth become him best.

"I take it you can lay hands on Martin's notes, Ruth-erford?"

"Yes; they're in his desk upstairs. You wouldn't like to read it yourself, sir?"

"I make a point," Pemberton announced severely, fix-ing Honeychurch with a cold eye, "of giving the younger men working in my department every chance of putting their own work forward. After all, you made some con-tribution to this particular piece of research."

"All the same, I'd rather not," Rutherford said. "Per-haps Peebles would like to do it."

Ainsworth uncurled himself to remark: "What Ruth-erford is trying to say, Prof, is that he and Sandeman didn't see eye to eye about the results of this work, and he'd prefer not to look as if he agreed with all Sandeman's conclusions. Only Rutherford is much too sweet a char-acter to speak ill of the dead, even if the dead cooked the figures a bit here and there to make the paper look nice and tidy."

"Cooked the results? In this department? Under my supervision? I never heard anything so absurd," Pem-berton snapped. "I can't see any need for you to butt in, Ainsworth, and if that was what Rutherford was getting at, he could have said to himself. And"—he rose to a magnificent crescendo of righteous rage—"even to sug-gest such a thing the morning after his death! It reflects no credit on either of you. It's the sort of thing you'd do very much better to keep to yourselves in the presence of people who appreciated Sandeman—Martin, I mean—at his true worth."

Ainsworth and Rutherford looked at each other and rose to go as if by mutual consent.

"Sit down, sit down," said Honeychurch kindly. "Everyone's nerves are a little strained this morning, and everyone is saying a little more than they should, myself included. I'm sure Professor Pemberton has only been led away by the warmth of his attachment to poor Martin; you intended no sort of deliberate hint, Cyril, we know. Do return to your agenda, my dear fellow. I'm sure we're all dying to get away and find out what's going on."

Pemberton breathed hard.

"There's nothing more of immediate importance," he

said, "but I'd like to get this paper of Sandeman's cleared up. Well, Rutherford?"

"All right, I'll read it," Rutherford said with some impatience. "It's not as if it's of any world-shaking significance. We knew when we started that the pethidine experiment wouldn't be worth the effort."

Honeychurch said, struck by a sudden thought, "Surely pethidine is a drug of addiction?"

Pemberton's eyes became sharp.

"Of course. It's on the dangerous drugs list."

"I suppose you didn't know," Honeychurch said, forgetting that he did not *know* himself, "that Sandeman was an addict?"

To his considerable surprise, Pemberton looked confused. He had so seldom looked confused before that the expression took on a curiously extreme quality, as if some major convulsion were taking place behind the narrow forehead.

"I did know it," he said defensively. "It didn't detract from the value of his work, and it wasn't my business. I believe he started taking morphine after his leg was crushed in an accident."

"And yet," Honeychurch said, picking up his seniority as rapidly as he had discarded it, "you let him arrange an experiment that would give him access to a supply of pethidine without anyone's being the wiser? Plenty of addicts have changed over from morphine to pethidine in the last few years—surely you realised that?"

"Yes, I did." Pemberton looked round his wondering juniors. His voice rose to a higher pitch. "And it still wasn't any of my business. If a man needs a drug to keep on working, I believe he has a right to it. If it were merely alcohol or tobacco he wanted, no one would think any the worse of him. Why should he be condemned to a hole-and-corner existence and forced to spend so much money that he's bound to deteriorate through sheer anxiety? I wanted Martin to keep his energies free for his work. He suggested doing this experiment himself, mind you, and I only guessed he was an addict from one or two things he let slip: but if it all comes out later when they catch his murderer, I'll stick to my guns."

"Dear me," said Honeychurch. "How unexpectedly well you come out of this, Cyril! I don't agree with a word you've said, but I must admit I think highly of you for saying it. Is that a policeman I see coming up the path? How thoughtful; we are no doubt to be told of the latest developments."

The policeman's mission was devoid of drama. Grimshaw had sent him over merely to pave the way for a search of Sandeman's room. The assembly broke up, bereft of the force that had held it together—for Pemberton went off with the policeman—and for a moment the air was rich with astonishment at his unorthodox sentiments and guesswork about his relationship with the dead man. Honeychurch stood aloof and felt uncomfortable; but then Peebles and Porter remembered their baby clinics, Ainsworth vanished with startling rapidity, Crisp and the young woman went off in the direction of the wards, and he was left alone with Rutherford.

"I suppose Sandeman had been pinching the pethidine?" he asked.

"I don't know. There was something wrong with the experiment," Rutherford said. "Rightly or wrongly, I thought it was something to do with me."

"Why should it have been?"

"Anything I did for Sandeman was bound to be wrong. You remember you asked me last night if he had anything to do with my losing my job, and I rudely changed the subject?"

Honeychurch remembered asking the question and denied noticing any rudeness.

"There was more to it than that. One might almost say he got me fired. I suppose that ought to constitute a motive for murder. Pemberton thinks so, anyway."

"Does he?" said Honeychurch. "You had better tell me what happened; it will give you a chance to get your facts in order before you see the police. And it will satisfy my curiosity, which is beginning to get a little out of hand. Shall we go to your room?"

FOUR

"There's only one chair," said Rutherford. "That's the official allowance—if you like to sit on it, sir, I'll borrow one from Garside's room. Can I get you a cigarette? I don't smoke myself, but there's a packet of Ainsworth's in the A-to-G drawer of the filing cabinet."

"Thank you, not before luncheon."

Honeychurch settled himself with a distant approximation to comfort on a chair uncompromisingly wooden and armless: Rutherford had already disappeared, and he was able to subject this monastic little apartment to a rapid and intensive scrutiny. The windows were bare, the walls plain. There was a laboratory bench of teak and a writing table both collapsible and collapsing; there was no shade over the light and no rug on the floor. Even the most pious monk may yearn on occasion to scribble on his celibate walls, and to this temptation Rutherford had in a sense succumbed. Thus the shelves over the bench, designed for a worthier burden of books or chemicals, carried an eclectic array of potted plants. Magazines emphatically not journals and photographs patently not clinical were strewn on the table or stuck on the walls. There was no power switch in the room and no official source of heat, but the single lamp socket had been harnessed to a fire, a small wireless set, and an electric fan. All these devices and the lamp itself could be operated from the solitary chair merely by reaching up and forward

52

and selecting one of four little egg-shaped switches painted blue, white, red, and yellow. Irresistibly, Honeychurch was drawn to experiment; his first effort set the fan in motion.

"I can quite see why the switch for the fan had to be blue and the fire switch red," he said to Rutherford, returning with a chair and—not altogether surprisingly—a tin of biscuits, "but why is the wireless yellow and the light white?"

"Because I like the colours."

"I see inconsistency is to be numbered among your virtues; I am no longer surprised at your dismissal—only that you should ever have got here in the first place. Did Pemberton appoint you himself?"

Rutherford had his back turned and was doing something with a Bunsen burner.

He said over his shoulder: "This sort of extramural talent doesn't get into one's references, you know. As a matter of fact, I look quite sound on paper. Besides, you're bound to look at the thing a little one-sidedly, being a professor yourself. The mistake was at least as much mine as Pemberton's: I must have been out of my mind to come here."

Honeychurch nodded.

"I admire your fine impartiality," he said gravely, "almost as much as your gift for electrical engineering."

"It's not a patch on what I rigged up at St. Barnaby's," said Rutherford with some modesty. "I left my toaster behind, and I've not yet solved the problem of making decent toast on a Bunsen burner. You'll have some coffee, won't you, sir?"

"Thank you: my breakfast was deplorable. I shall welcome a hot beverage."

"And some biscuits?"

"And some biscuits. An excellent idea." Complacently he selected a *café noir*, eschewing the more cloying delights of Lincoln cream.

Rutherford said suddenly: "It hadn't struck me before Pemberton said what he did just now that anyone might think I'd been—well, involved in Sandeman's death. But I suppose it looks rather bad, having a public row with a man a few hours before he comes to a violent end."

"On the contrary, I think it looks rather well. One can

hardly see a murderer picking a public quarrel with his victim just before he commits the crime. The whole notion is preposterous."

"Murder is preposterous," said Rutherford soberly. "In the face of a fact like Sandeman's death, mere likelihoods and probabilities come to seem a bit shadowy, don't you think? Yesterday anyone's murdering Sandeman and anyone's suspecting me of committing murder would have seemed about equally fantastic. But once allow that the first has happened and the second no longer looks so farfetched. I began to see that about ten minutes ago, and now I find it rather difficult to see anything else."

"No one," Honeychurch said, "has yet accused you of having any part in Sandeman's killing. Wait until they do, my dear fellow, and don't waste time and energy in worrying about it. Now, if the coffee is ready, let us drink it, and you can tell me what is at the back of all this."

Rutherford poured coffee into two beakers and sat down on the bench. A clock somewhere in the building struck ten.

"You remember the child who died last night? Did you know she died, by the way?"

"Crisp told me."

"Well, the great row was about a very similar case—a baby with pneumonia who wasn't getting any better. We started the Terramycin survey in January and this baby came in in March. Up to then most of the severe cases had come into the group we were treating with Terramycin, and none of the others had died without it. Then this baby turned up; she should have been treated only with sulphonamides and penicillin, according to the rules. She was obviously going to die; not being of the stuff of which great scientists are made, I felt rather badly about it. Crisp called me in late one evening. Of course, I wouldn't have given her Terramycin simply on my own authority; the survey is pretty important, and the Medical Research Council is only releasing small quantities to approved centres like this hospital. Pemberton had gone to a conference at Leeds, so I rang Sandeman." Rutherford sipped his coffee in a momentary abstraction: then went on. "He was at his oily best: 'Of course, Rutherford. Oh yes, I do agree.' So we started treatment at once, and the next day there was the baby very much alive and Prof

54

saying what a good thing it is not to jettison all the established remedies as soon as some new wonder drug comes along. So stepping in where any intelligent angel would fear to tread, I told him we'd given the baby Terramycin. He nearly exploded."

"I can imagine," said Honeychurch. "And then you waited for Sandeman to come forward and say he'd given his permission. But—"

"But the late lamented insisted that he'd expressly forbidden me to alter treatment in any way."

"Even for Sandeman," Honeychurch said thoughtfully, "that must have established a new low level of behaviour. What did you say?"

"I called him a bloody liar. And it was only my word against his."

"I see. And Pemberton dismissed you for that?"

"To do him justice," Rutherford admitted, "I've no right to be annoyed with Pemberton. Given that Sandeman was his blue-eyed boy who could do no wrong, the rest followed. If Sandeman was telling the truth, then I'd deliberately mucked up a piece of essential research and tried to shift the blame. He stormed at me for about half an hour for the benefit of anyone who liked to cock an ear in the right direction—I was a ham-handed, bumble-headed nincompoop not fit to be trusted near a drug cupboard; and if medical science had depended for its progress upon people like me, we should still be applying leeches to the affected part. Which is probably true," he added with disarming candour, "but I didn't greatly relish being told so in public. He ended with an invitation to the sepulchre at nine the next morning."

"Had he thought of anything finally annihilating by then?"

"Yes. He gave me the choice between making Sandeman a full apology in writing or leaving at the end of my first year. Hobson's choice. I said I'd rather go."

Honeychurch nodded thoughtfully.

"That is precisely what I should have done in your place. By the way, I trust I'm not keeping you from your work?"

"It's my weekend off. I wouldn't be here today at all if it weren't for the meeting—and Sandeman, of course. I couldn't very well stay away. And then there's this queer

55

business of the Bryant child. I suppose he's just taken it into his head to run off."

"Could there be any connection between Sandeman and the child?" Honeychurch asked.

"No; I don't think so. Tom was in one of my beds, and Sandeman never took much notice of him."

"I don't understand the mechanism of your bed system at all."

"It's quite simple really. There are thirty beds on the Paediatric Unit—Peebles and Porter and I have ten each: the prof and Sandeman and Garside exercise a sort of general supervision over all of us, and we share the two house physicians, Crisp and Miss Hatherly."

"Who is Garside?" Honeychurch asked.

"He's the second assistant. He's in America on study leave." Struck by a sudden thought, Rutherford added: "And he'll be back on Monday; I've got to fetch his car from the garage this morning. I wonder if I'll have time."

"Sandeman was in the States in forty-four, if my memory serves me correctly," Honeychurch mused.

"And last year too," Rutherford told him. "He went off with the prof to a medical congress. That shows you how high his stock stood with Pemberton."

A peremptory knock on the door preceded Ainsworth by so short an interval that any denial of the right to enter could never have been anticipated.

"Say, Bill, you know that cop's tearing the paper off the wall in Sandeman's room looking for the vital clue. If you wait much longer, they'll impound his precious lifework and you won't have to read it after all. Or maybe I'm just putting my hoof in it again, am I?"

Rutherford sighed.

"Don't apologise for your impulsive nature, Philip. I suppose you're right. Will you excuse me, sir? Make some more coffee for yourself, Philip, and finish up the biscuits. I won't be long."

He had gone. Ainsworth explored his pockets with hands which to Honeychurch's fastidious eye were coarse, stubby, and without delicacy of touch. There was, all the same, plenty of power in the short, splayed fingers, and each ended incongruously beneath a nail of superb shape, well-manicured and almost femininely pink. It occurred to Honeychurch that here was a dichotomy conspicuously echoed in other facets of Ainsworth's character. How, for instance, could one reconcile the caustic tongue and the brusque manner with the again almost feminine protectiveness that Rutherford seemed to arouse in him? Undeniably, his first essay in chivalry in Pemberton's study had been worse than useless; his second, a few moments ago, seemed to be prompted by the suspicion that Rutherford would rather not present himself to the police any earlier than need be. The question rose to Honeychurch's mind whether this disastrous brand of goodwill did not constitute in fact a most effective method of concealing an actual hostility: but it was hard to believe that this young man could be anything else than what he seemed—sincere, outspoken, and of an embarrassingly loyal disposition.

"You wouldn't happen to know where Rutherford put my smokes?"

"They are classified as cigarettes and filed under A-to-G," Honeychurch said. "Matches or a lighter would presumably be two drawers further down."

Ainsworth looked at him suspiciously.

"What makes you think so?"

"One fact supplied by your friend and a knowledge of the alphabet; also my enviable capacity for estimating possibilities."

"Well, I reckon you're right at that," Ainsworth admitted, taking what he wanted from the drawer Honeychurch had suggested. "Thanks a lot. What about you?"

"Not before luncheon," Honeychurch repeated absently. After a moment during which Ainsworth swung himself up on the bench and began to inhale, he said, "Shouldn't Dr. Rutherford be back? It wouldn't have taken him long to find the paper, would it?"

Ainsworth took the cigarette out of his mouth.

"See here, if you think Bill's made a bolt for it, you're backing the wrong horse. That guy's as white as they come."

"Oh dear," Honeychurch said. "It had never entered my head that he would either wish or try to 'make a bolt,' as you put it. But now that you have mentioned it, I have at least to convince myself that it is unlikely to be so. Fortunately, I find myself open to conviction; but to another and less well-affected mind than my own, your remark might well start a whole train of speculation, not

57

at all calculated to increase Dr. Rutherford's chances of ultimate safety. Curb your tongue, Mr. Ainsworth, in the interests of justice: you only harm your cause by a too blatant championship."

Ainsworth was staring at him.

"You mean I ought to keep my mouth shut? Hell, that's a tall order. Has Rutherford told you what Sandeman did to him over the Terramycin racket?"

"Yes; he told me. How generally known was his side of the story?"

"No one *knew* it," Ainsworth said, "but we all guessed what had happened. There wasn't anyone on that round who wouldn't have taken an oath that Sandeman was lying."

"If you all suspected it," Honeychurch demanded, "why didn't you tell Professor Pemberton? He'd have had to take notice of his staff's opinion if it were expressed strongly enough."

Ainsworth gave him a look tinged with contempt.

"And you've known Prof for years? Don't you know he's stubborn like a mule? You couldn't make him change his mind about a thing like that if you kept at it till the Day of Judgement. Mind you, I thought of it: but it wouldn't have been any use, since I'm no part of the Paediatric Unit anyway."

"Didn't Sandeman ever exercise his peculiar talents on any of the others?" Honeychurch said. "Would you mind opening the window a little wider?"

Ainsworth contemplated his cigarette affectionately.

"Nothing like these for fumigating a room. John"—this to Crisp, who had come in close on the heels of his testimonial—"switch the fan on. The professor here doesn't care for my cigarette."

Crisp switched on the fan and opened the window, revealing an anxiety to please that endeared him at once to Honeychurch.

"What was that about Sandeman and the others?" Ainsworth picked up the thread again. "You mean, was he just out to get Rutherford or was it all of us? It's not so easy to say . . . there's not much you could actually lay a finger on—"

"It was just little pricks here and there for most people," Crisp said.

"And what he did to Rutherford wasn't unique of its kind," Ainsworth said. "It was only his biggest effort in that line. Have a biscuit, John."

Crisp helped himself. "The best example of the sort of beastly tomfoolery he seemed to enjoy is what he did to Peebles."

"To Peebles!" Honeychurch echoed. "I can hardly imagine anyone so inoffensive tempting even Sandeman to do him any harm."

"You'd be surprised," said Ainsworth bitterly. "He was pretty catholic in dispensing his little prize packets."

"Peebles," Crisp went on firmly, "was going to give a talk one evening, and he brought along a set of slides to use on the projector."

"You don't know Peebles," Ainsworth interpolated, "but he's every kind of a careful Johnny who sweats blood making sure everything's just so."

"But when he started putting the pictures up, they were all in the wrong order. There was one of a blotchy-looking infant with its eyes streaming which came on when he said he'd show us a chart of the age-distribution of pink disease. Then he got worried and said the next picture would be a close-up of the same baby's face—and so it was, only it was upside down. And so it went on."

"And when he was almost in tears," Ainsworth supplied, "and everyone else was tying themselves in knots trying not to die laughing, Prof insisted on having the lights turned up. 'Peebles,' he says, and we could see he was hopping mad, 'would it have been too much trouble for you to have prepared your slides beforehand?' Of course Peebles said he had, and naturally *we* believed him because, as I say, Peebles just would have."

"We never knew for sure," Crisp said, "but Kate Hatherly remembered later she'd seen Sandeman come out of the lecture theatre about an hour before the show started."

Honeychurch looked from one to the other in sheer bewilderment.

"It seems almost impossible that any grown man—any sane grown man!—Still, people are always odder than one would think."

All three were momentarily silent. In the silence the clock struck again.

"Was that half past ten?" Ainsworth said. "I'll have to

leave you. Lisle Sunderland's repairing a tracheal fistula in a few moments' time."

"Before you go," Honeychurch said heavily, "you couldn't tell me, I suppose, why Rutherford didn't want to read Sandeman's paper?"

"Well, it so happens that I can. I was in on that stunt myself. Look, John, do me a favour. Go over to the theatre and give me a ring when Lisle's ready to start, will you?"

Crisp obligingly went off.

"A nice boy," Honeychurch said.

"One of the best. Let's himself be imposed on, though. What were we talking about? Oh, the pethidine racket. That's recent history—a week ago today, to be precise. You know about the scheme of investigation?"

Honeychurch shook his head.

"It's just the sort of goddam useless effort you'd expect from paediatricians, saving your presence. Believe it or not, Cyril Stagforth doesn't like to see kids in pain. So he ups and tells Sandeman to find some sort of analgesic that really works. Morphia and heroin are out, we know, for anything under ten, because they depress respiration too much; aspirin and phenacetin and codeine are also-rans when you're dealing with anything more than a face ache. Don't get the idea that I think I'm telling you anything you don't know; I'm just describing the way Prof puts over this proposition to the late Sandeman."

"And the late Sandeman decided to use pethidine: not a choice to arouse suspicion. In fact, the work may well have been very valuable."

Ainsworth looked at him pityingly.

"It might have been, but it wasn't. Roughly, it worked out like this. Pethidine comes in ampoules for adult use, which means it had to be diluted to reasonable strength for the brats. When any kid came in with a pain or came round after an operation, the houseman sent for Sande- man or Bill, and the child had a dose either out of the pethidine bottle or an inert solution. No one was supposed to know which was which, and according to Bill it never made any difference anyway. That's what I meant when I said he wouldn't want to seem to be agreeing with Sande- man's conclusions: Sandeman insisted that the kids he watched—they used to watch them for an hour after they had the injections—all settled off to sleep, or even if they didn't, their pulse rates slowed, which was the sort of objective evidence he was looking for. And Bill used to get mad and tell Sandeman the whole thing was a washout. Then a week ago—Do you really want to hear all this?"

"Yes, indeed. I believe I'm beginning to see daylight."

"Maybe you can guess what happened. Last Saturday Bill was on call, and a boy came in with a really nasty fracture. I was standing in for the orthopaedic house surgeon, so I did the reduction. When the kid came round he began to scream the place down; I got hold of Bill and he came along with one of the bottles and nurse gave the injection. As usual, it didn't do any good. After half an hour listening to the kid yelling, we'd had enough. Bill went and got an unopened ampoule of pethidine in case the bottle had been made up from a dud batch or was only the control solution: ten minutes after the boy had the second injection he was fast asleep. On Monday Bill told Sandeman what he'd done and said he'd better throw away all the old set of dilutions. Sandeman flew into a rage and told Bill he'd finish the work off by himself because their results never seemed to tally."

"I suppose," Honeychurch said, "we must assume that the dilute pethidine failed of its effect because Sandeman had been helping himself out of the ampoules and making up weaker solutions than he actually claimed. Had this experiment been in progress for long?"

"Eight months," Ainsworth told him.

"Then he may have intended to lay up a stock sufficient to last him through the lean period ahead when the source dried up. It will be interesting to hear whether the police find it."

"Right now," Ainsworth said, "the only thing that interests me is what's happened to Bill. You don't think they've arrested him, do you?"

"Why?" said Honeychurch. "I repeat, Mr. Ainsworth, occasional differences of opinion, even violent ones, are not universally accepted as likely to lead to murder. And there's your call."

Ainsworth briefly answered the phone and made for the door.

"Lisle's just beginning—shall you wait here?"

Honeychurch shook his head.

"No; I have a little work to do. It has struck me that a few words with Master Bannister on the balcony might not be out of place."

He switched off the electric fan, turned off the Bunsen burner, and left the room.

FIVE

It was not daybreak; it was not even the climbing sun coming over the brow of the hill and peering narrowly through the small window that woke Tom, but the loud, hard splutter of rain on the roof. For a moment he confused the steady drumming with the throb of an engine, the beat of his heart, his feet running in a flare of panic across a cold pavement. Then he relinquished sleep abruptly with a sudden acute perception of where he was and what had happened to him.

He was still alive. So probably his first guess was right and Rutherford, who had brought him here, was to be trusted. Then he had only to wait until he came along and opened the door and they could go back to the hospital together. Or better still, Tom suddenly thought, he could call out and see if help didn't come a bit earlier that way. He went to the doors, put his lip to the crack between them, and shouted with all his might. When he stopped for breath the silence was ominous. Gradually sounds began to creep back into it, the daily sounds that had been there all the time: birds singing aimlessly in the rain, the dazed murmur of bees under the garage eaves, the continuous, low-pitched tapping of the rain itself. Tom stood quite still with one foot on the instep of the other; there was no point in them both being uncomfortable at the same time. He peered through the crack. The view was restricted, but the little he saw was enough to make his heart sink.

He was looking down a very short drive in very bad repair towards a pair of spidery iron gates interrupting a high, ill-kempt privet hedge. On the left he could see a lawn with a border of flowers and the corner of a house. The corner went up a long way, and it was covered with some sort of sparse climbing plant. It was a big house, and just beyond the corner he could see a step jutting out and a porch of white stone. On the step were two milk bottles. Something about them worried Tom, but he couldn't make out what. He tried looking to the right, but there was nothing on that side but another line of privet hedge with some trees in front of it and more flowers.

He padded round the garage to the window and saw that what he had fallen over the night before was a big zinc bath. Bath suggested water, and sure enough there was a tap on the wall. Tom made for it, turned it on, cupped his hands and drank. The water was very cold and tasted strongly of mould. Tom spat it out and wished he had something to take away the taste. However, life itself might depend on the presence of this water supply.

If he had been locked up here on purpose to keep him from telling all he knew, there ought to be bread as well as water. But perhaps they meant to starve him into submission. Well, he wouldn't submit—never! They could do their worst, but he'd never swear to keep their guilty secret. He visualised himself emaciated to vanishing point, croaking defiance while they threatened him with unspeakable tortures. He felt momentarily disappointed that he was in so mundane a prison as a garage. Stone walls and chains would have been more in character. Then, lying huddled and bleeding on a filthy bed of straw, he would have looked up at the inhuman faces of his gaolers and whispered hoarsely but bravely, "I will never tell!" And, thinking himself unseen, one of the gaolers would have wiped away a tear of admiring compassion on his sleeve.

"I will never tell!" Tom said aloud and thrillingly to a zinc bath, a battered car, and sundry empty pots of paint. But the words, like the milk bottles a few minutes earlier, seemed somehow wrong: and he knew why. The whole point was that he wasn't going to keep silent—but who was he going to talk to? There was no one within hearing distance unless they had deliberately ignored his cries. And the point about the milk bottles was that they were full. The milkman had been and gone and no one had taken the milk bottles in. So it was probably late and the house was probably empty.

He climbed back into the car and looked at the clock on the dashboard; it said ten to eleven. Then why hadn't the car gone? He remembered suddenly that it was Saturday; but then if it wasn't Dr. Rutherford's weekend on, why hadn't he heard Tom, why didn't he come and let him out? Surely it could only mean that he was the murderer and Tom's first startled certainty had been quite wrong. But how could he be? It was very difficult to imagine Dr. Rutherford doing anything but sitting on the end of the bed with a jigsaw puzzle or coming up with a syringe to take blood when Crisp couldn't get into his veins: it was impossible to think of him passing stale hunks of bread through the gap in the door with a malevolent glare on his face.

Tom shook his head as if trying to shake it free of fantasy. If he wasn't in danger from Rutherford himself, then he was probably safe. This seemed so obvious, he wondered why he hadn't thought of it before. All he had to do was to wait until he heard someone approach the house or come away from it, and then shout again. There was only one person he needed to be afraid of, and how could that one guess where he was?

He felt about in the leather pockets on the car doors and found a pocket diary, a paper-backed novel called, rather promisingly, *A Passage to India*, and, best of all, an untouched bar of chocolate. Tom had no moral qualms about demolishing it: he had a sixpence in his locker at hospital which ought to pay for another bar this size. He broke it into three pieces; one for breakfast, one for lunch, one for tea—and ate two out of the three immediately because it was too late for breakfast and too early for lunch and he was extremely hungry. The chocolate did something towards quieting the pangs, but not much. He turned to the novel, but after the first paragraph his attention wandered.

He got out of the car again and went to the window. It was above his head, but by turning the bath upside down and standing on it he could see the hill behind the house, with a long, straggly garden where sporadic fruit trees encircled a plot of tall grass and dandelions. That meant no gardener: and if the neglected milk bottles meant no servants and the silence no Rutherford, it looked as if he would be here all day. Tom's heart sank as he felt infinities of boredom closing in on him. Thinking himself in deadly danger had been better than this by a long way. He explored the possibilities. Perhaps the murderer would remember there had been another car beside his own at the gates and guess that Tom had got in the wrong one. He might even know that it was Rutherford's car. If he did, he would try to track down his prey; and if he came across Tom helplessly imprisoned in the garage, what would he do? Pitch a grenade through the window? Puff poison gas at him through a rubber tube? Set the roof alight? Worst of all, release a venomous snake under the door? Tom trembled, and not with cold. He was, despite the forebodings of the matron of the Laurel Homes, in no daily danger of confusing fact with fantasy, but now his most lurid imaginings took on an aura of plausibility from the gross unlikelihood of what had already in sober truth befallen him.

He got back into the car and curled himself up on the floor: he wasn't going to be surprised by the enemy: here at least he had a chance of keeping hidden for a few minutes if the garage door were broken in. He took up the diary, ate the piece of chocolate reserved for tea without thinking about it, and began slowly to turn over the thin, small pages. He read it from beginning to end with a queer feeling compounded of guilt and disappointment. It was the page-a-day kind with lines printed very lightly and close together. Where Rutherford had written anything at all he had ignored the lines; the very blue ink sprawled haphazardly in oblique pennants across the prim print. There were some figures, which seemed to be doses of drugs: a name from time to time, with sometimes an explanatory note and sometimes not. On March 18 Tom found his own name; he tried to remember what could have happened that day and decided it must have been the first time he went to Dr. Henchard's clinic after he got to hospital. He flipped over the pages till he got to April 22, which was yesterday by now: it was blank. But on today's page there were two entries. One was "Breth-erton's—Garside's car," and under that was "R.S.M. Pae-diatric Meeting 2:30."

Tom closed the diary and put it away. Now things began to fall into place. For if Dr. Rutherford had gone off to attend the meeting that everyone had been fussing over for weeks he might be very late indeed. Tom wished that he had not finished the chocolate.

The shower was over; a faint, silvery brilliance stole into the square of sky beyond the window and was chased away by scurrying puffs of cloud and a clear, rich blue like the ink in the diary. The window gave Tom an idea: he was standing beneath it again in a moment, looking for something to smash it with and taking off his jacket at the same time. The window was too small for him to get through, but he could signal from it, waving his pyjamas till someone climbing up the bare grey hill beyond noticed him; if anyone were to climb up the bare grey hill, which seemed improbable.

Then he had a better idea: he picked up a paintpot. He had thought it was empty, but there was a little puddle of vivid grass-green at the bottom and the familiar smell made his head swim. He stirred it about with a little stick; it was a glorious consistency like melted toffee, like golden syrup, like thick chocolate sauce poured over pudding. He licked his lips and searched for a brush; there were three or four in a jam jar full of turpentine. He looked lovingly at the car, imagining Rutherford's delight if he came back to find its rusty black carriage-work a radiant green. But there was only a very little paint left, and the other tins had only dry cracked flakes of colour on the sides. Tom climbed up on the bath with the pot in his hand and the brush in the pot. With his tongue flickering slightly between his lips, he began to paint HELP on the window backwards like a mirror image. It took a lot of concentration to get it right.

When it was done he put the paint away, wiped the brush clean on his jacket, and returned it to its jar of turps. Then he got into the car. The clock said twenty past twelve. A second dial on the dashboard said that the car had travelled 7,463 miles. It was a long way.

He picked up *A Passage to India* and began to read.

SIX

The promising day had clouded over: crossing the space between the Department of Child Health and the hospital itself, Honeychurch saw with regret that a few drops of rain had already fallen. He had some difficulty in finding his way into the main building, and more still in retrieving Bannister Ward; so far in his excursions about the place he had always had a guide, and he half regretted not having gone with Ainsworth on this occasion. But a certain barely recognised purpose had driven him to venture out alone. He wanted to talk to Teddy Bannister; he also wanted a few moments by himself. He had heard and seen enough during the morning to require a little peace for assimilation. He was not seriously perturbed, therefore, when he realised he had mistaken some turning or other and was in a small library instead of the ward. Two or three students were sitting round a table, their eyes glued tenaciously to the books in front of them. An elderly man stood by the window: on Honeychurch's arrival he hurried across the room.

"Do please excuse my bothering you. My name is Henchard. Could you tell me where I might find Dr. Crisp? I was told he would be coming here to fetch me, but that was half an hour ago; and I'm most anxious to get to Bannister Ward."

Honeychurch said resignedly, "I am on my way there

now. Perhaps you would like to come with me? You must be Dr. Henchard, the psychiatrist."

"Yes." Henchard looked somewhat taken aback at this prompt recognition. "I came up here to talk to Professor Pemberton about a patient of mine who seems to have run away. I thought it might perhaps be helpful if I talked to some of the children in the ward. One of them might have noticed something. But I beg your pardon, I don't think I caught—"

"My name is Honeychurch. I am here to attend the clinical meeting."

"Fabian Honeychurch?" Henchard asked.

"The same. Shall we leave these young people to the pursuit of knowledge? I fear we are disturbing them."

Three pairs of lifted eyes plunged immediately back towards the printed page. Honeychurch ushered Henchard through the door, inspecting the back of the psychiatrist's head on the way. A smooth pink dome emerged above a short fuzz of grizzled hair; the neck was thin, the ears small, flat, and nicely suited to their secondary task of carrying a pair of gold-rimmed spectacles. As if aware of this minute and—to do Honeychurch justice —altogether unconscious inspection, Henchard turned round suddenly and made an odd little grimace.

"I must say I've had a most unusual morning," he said. "Pemberton rang me up at seven—psychiatrists rarely get called out at odd hours, you know, it's one of the great attractions of our calling to the habitually indolent like myself—and that was strange enough to begin with. Then he told me about the missing child and asked me if I'd got him. Of course I hadn't; the last time I saw him was in my clinic yesterday afternoon."

"I suppose it wasn't unreasonable of Pemberton to think the child might make his way to you."

"Well, no. But he wouldn't have known my private address. Is this the way?"

"I hope so." Honeychurch negotiated a number of angled passages with some misgivings.

"And then"—Henchard, though perturbed, was obviously anxious to talk—"to crown everything, when I arrived here they told me that Martin Sandeman had been murdered! I was even asked to talk to a policeman; he wanted to know if Tom Bryant—that's the name of my patient—might have bashed Sandeman on the head. Fortunately, I was able to assure him that poor Tom was not at all given to violent attacks on adults. Ah, here is the ward."

"Now, Dr. Henchard, I'm nearly as much a stranger here as you are yourself: we shall have to throw ourselves on Sister's mercy. Here she comes. She seems to have plenty of mercy for us to throw ourselves on."

By day the ghosts of Bannister Ward were laid; high drama was exchanged for low comedy, shadowed beds and muffled breathing gave way to playpens and the shouts of furious infants. That the cheerfulness and friendly bustle was the doing of the ward sister admitted of no question as soon as she came towards them. She was middle-aged, broad, and plain, but her face and figure were motherly and full of an enviable good temper. Much more than a runaway patient, more even than a violent death, would be needed to shatter her warm serenity. She turned upon her visitors a smile that partly welcomed, partly questioned.

"Good morning. Are you the gentlemen from the police? You will hurry up and find Tom, won't you? He's a bad boy, running away like that with only his pyjamas on; and now it's coming on to rain and that won't do him any good when he's only just over his nephritis."

"We are not the police," Honeychurch said apologetically. "Nothing so exciting, I'm afraid, Sister. This is Dr. Henchard, who used to see Tom at his clinic, and I am Professor Honeychurch. Night Sister may have told you that I broke into the ward through the balcony last night."

"Oh, it was you, was it," she said, beaming, "leaving your finger marks all over the parapet, as if it didn't look bad enough already? Now, don't think I'm telling you off, sir, but are you sure Tom didn't let on he was going to give us all a scare?"

"Do I look as if I would be the repository of guilty secrets?"

"I don't know about that," Sister said, "but Dr. Crisp was saying you seemed to have had quite a chat with the child."

"I'll admit," said Honeychurch slowly, "that he struck me as a little overexcited when I first spoke to him, but he was asleep before I came into the ward, and he didn't tell me anything, I assure you, Sister."

"Of course," said Sister, leading the way to her desk, "we've had children run away before. It happens everywhere, doesn't it, no matter how well they're treated? But then they usually run home. I don't see why Tom should feel homesick for that horrid place he lived in."

"Oh, come, Sister," Henchard mildly remonstrated, "it's quite a satisfactory institution, as these places go. The matron's a remarkably enlightened woman. We really shouldn't put any blame on the Laurel Homes. It's his feeling of having been deserted by his parents that's at the root of all Tom's troubles."

"That's just what I've always told them," said Sister with sturdy inconsequence. "There's no substitute for a mother's love, is there? Yes, nurse, what is it?"

A small nurse muttered something in a small voice, was thanked, dismissed, and scurried away behind a pair of screens.

"Yes. Well now," said Sister, "I said I'd show that poor, harmless girl how to clean a really nasty dirty head. If you gentlemen want to see Tom's things, his locker is still out on the balcony. We brought Teddy's bed into the ward; it was lonely for him out there without Tom. That's him down at the end with red hair."

She whisked—if so much embonpoint could be said to do anything as capricious as whisking—behind the screens, whence her voice, rich with an infinitely kind contempt, could be heard raised in protest: "No, nurse; nits won't bite you. Whoever heard of an egg biting? Search as if you meant it, my dear, or the beasties will get away. Here, I'll show you." Then, with positively plummy satisfaction: "That's the way to do it; crush him between your fingernails. You'll learn in time, nurse."

Henchard shuddered, and moved away in the direction of the red-haired boy. Edward Michael Wesley Bannister, whose nine or ten years had been spent in the delicious, downy caress of the Bannister millions, was at first sight something of a disappointment. A prolonged period of semistarvation in the most destitute of hovels could scarcely have made this rich child's jutting wrists and obtrusive neck more slender than they were. But the bony face, the thick tufts of coppery hair, the whole gawky,

71

graceless shape, was not without interest. In his own and quite different way, this child, Honeychurch surmised, would probably be as intelligent as the other; there was a highly developed wariness, for instance, in the fixed determination Teddy showed not to notice his visitors: the boy was burying his face in one of those appalling publications so misleadingly described as comics. Professionally, Honeychurch observed that he was holding the pages with a steady hand and sitting extremely still —perhaps abnormally so, considering his recent history of St. Vitus's dance. Either Pemberton's favoured treatment or the course of nature—more probably the latter in his own cynical estimate—had reversed the accepted ritual and exorcised the saint at the cost of reinstating any number of little devils. Henchard was evidently thinking along the same lines; he remarked that the boy really seemed well enough to be going home.

"I am going home," the boy said, studiously evasive, "when the professor's been in to see me. He said I could go this weekend if I was all right. Look—"

He put down the comic and held his hands out in front of him, perfectly still. It was obvious that he had demonstrated this action over and over again to relays of devout students. Honeychurch held out his own hands and looked at both pairs critically.

"Nothing to choose between us," he said finally.

"They didn't give me any tablets this morning either," said the boy.

"Why was that?"

Teddy shrugged his thin shoulders and slid down under the bedclothes, letting the comic slip to the floor.

"They forgot," he said indistinctly.

"Because they were looking for Tom Bryant?" Honeychurch suggested.

Teddy looked away.

"I don't know."

Henchard glanced at Honeychurch with raised eyebrows.

Honeychurch said, "You were awake when I came over the balcony last night, weren't you? Tom was too."

Teddy turned over.

"Did you come over the balcony?" he said. His tone was politely incredulous. "I had the tablets last night."

72

Honeychurch sat down on the edge of the bed and picked up the comic. He turned over the pages, contemplating with distaste the aggressive nubility of various underdressed ladies bound to trees.

"How did Dick Dauntless come to be trapped like that?" he said at last, pointing to a square-jawed, broad-shouldered and probably anencephalic oaf sharing a small cage with two tigers—labelled MAN-EATING by a considerate caption. Teddy sat up.

"That's a lot of tripe," he said disgustedly. "He's going to quell them by the power of the human eye, I bet. I tried it once with a rabbit I had."

"What happened?"

"It bit me." Teddy thrust his left arm even further out of his sleeve and displayed a small irregular scar. "Well, if a rabbit did that when I was looking it straight in the face, what would two man-eating tigers do? He couldn't even look at them both at once, stands to reason." An idea struck him. "Mavis could do it," he said with admiration.

In the next bed a small girl with an engaging squint drooled gratitude for this unsolicited testimony to her natural powers.

"Why didn't you go with Tom?" Honeychurch said. "It would have been much better if you'd gone together. I should think Tom would get a bit fed up with no one to talk to."

Teddy stared at him.

"I couldn't have gone," he said patiently. "I'm going home today or tomorrow. Besides—" He stopped.

Honeychurch looked a query.

"I didn't know he was going. Perhaps he walked in his sleep."

"That's a good idea," Honeychurch said. "That would explain a great deal. Why he only wore pyjamas, for instance. But when people walk in their sleep they don't usually get far before someone stops them."

Teddy's attention seemed to have wandered.

"Why doesn't the professor come and tell me if I can go home?" he demanded. "He said he'd come early, and it's nearly time for lunch. Why doesn't he hurry up and come?"

The child's face was suddenly contorted with misery.

His angular body snapped too like a jackknife and disappeared under the blankets again. This time Honeychurch knew the gesture was final. He walked slowly down the ward, pushed open the swing doors, and was out on the balcony with Henchard on his heels. The psychiatrist looked bewildered.

"Professor Honeychurch, do you think that boy was telling the truth?"

Honeychurch sat down on one of the six empty beds.

"From you to me," he said, "that question seems strange."

Henchard said humbly, "I think you may have been misled: I have had very little to do with children in my work. I am not a child psychiatrist, you see. Tom Bryant is the first child I have had under my care for many years, and that was only because the matron of the Laurel Homes is a friend of mine. I must admit I found him puzzling in some ways. And the Bannister child is even more beyond me; at first I thought he was prevaricating, but now I'm not so sure. Perhaps he genuinely had no notion that Tom meant to run away."

"Could Tom have kept a secret like that? Could any boy?"

"Not perhaps any boy," Henchard said, and added with growing confidence, "but Tom might be better able to do it than most other children. He was reticent with me; I found it difficult to establish any sort of rapport. I haven't the knack of getting on with boys, I fear, and I never felt I was anywhere near the heart of the matter. He was very polite and rather distant with me as if I were a not very amusing uncle who'd come to his birthday party without a present. Yes; I should say Tom could probably keep a secret if he had one."

"Of course, it's quite likely that he might have run away on the spur of the moment," Honeychurch said. "But it does seem an odd chance that it should happen on the night that Sandeman was murdered not twenty yards away. Suppose the child saw something and rushed off in a panic?"

Henchard looked horrified.

"You mean to say that Dr. Sandeman was murdered only twenty yards away from here? In full view of the hospital?"

74

"It depends," Honeychurch said cautiously, "what one means by full view. The other balcony is empty; you can see that from here. On this one there were only Tom and Teddy, both of whom should have been asleep. It must have been very late, because I gather Sandeman spoke to Dr. Crisp on the phone at about eleven. All things considered, the murderer stood very little risk of being seen. On the other hand, if Tom were awake—"

He did not finish. Henchard looked over the flower beds to the cypresses, inexpressibly mournful under the driving rain. He said, "If anything should have happened to the child—if, to take your theory a stage further, the boy in fact saw something and the murderer knew himself to have been seen, might he not have decided to silence so dangerous a witness?"

Honeychurch shook his head.

"There's one absolute objection to that. Since no second body has been found—thank God!—one would have to suppose the murderer to have carried it away with him. But why should he have encumbered his flight with such a burden? A man cannot be any more decisively hanged for two murders than for one. No; I think we can safely assume that Tom left the hospital alive."

He got up and opened the locker by the bed Tom had occupied the night before. An avalanche of toys, comics, scraps of paper scribbled over with drawings of aeroplanes and ships, and finally an assortment of clothing tumbled to the floor. Honeychurch sank to his knees and began to replace the clothes and the toys. The drawings and scrawls he handed to Henchard. The psychiatrist looked them over in increasing dejection.

"Nothing interesting?" Honeychurch asked. "Nothing to suggest he wanted to run away to sea or climb a mountain or find his parents? Not that one would have expected it."

"The drawings are rather unexpectedly neat," Henchard said, "but quite impersonal. And I can't read his awful handwriting. No; I don't think we shall find anything helpful here. Still, one never knows. I sometimes wonder if the psychiatrist shouldn't be regarded merely as a rather highly trained snapper-up of unconsidered trifles."

"The most private of all private eyes, as Philip Ainsworth would put it."

Henchard looked rather at a loss.

"I don't quite follow you."

"Ainsworth is a young American surgeon who's working here at the moment. 'Private eye' is a private detective in his language."

Henchard said apologetically, "I'm sorry. I didn't understand your allusion to Ainsworth. The expression itself is quite familiar to me. I am really rather a voracious reader of crime fiction. I find the psychological explanations altogether absorbing. But I mustn't keep you any longer, Professor Honeychurch. Shall we go? I fear I shall never be able to find my way out without your assistance."

SEVEN

The front hall when they reached it was not empty. Among those present were Inspector Grimshaw and the two tired, conscientious plainclothesmen Honeychurch had seen by Sandeman's body; a policeman, by way of contrast, in the full glory of his uniform; and a strange person—strange in the double sense of being at first sight unknown to Honeychurch and eccentric to a degree in his behaviour. A short and undistinguished figure topped by a small and undistinguished head was engaged in executing a complicated dance ritual with a fine disregard for the surroundings. He was clothed inadequately for the changeable weather; a thin dark suit, selected as being cool and comfortable for a warm spring day, had proved a very traitor in the event: enormous patches of a greater darkness with an ominous dullness to them showed where rain had soaked unkindly into the cloth; there was a small puddle medial to each discreetly padded shoulder. His trousers were splashed with mud as well as being soaked through, and at the opposite extremity his black hair was flattened to his scalp, while tiny droplets of water plopped from the lobes of his ears. Comprehension dawned with a closer inspection, and recognition followed. This was the awaited Burnivel, the bringer of light, truth, and justice; and his elaborate *pas de chat* was no more than an endeavour to shake the water out of his turn-ups while still carrying on a staccato conversation with the natives. The natives, in the muted tones of Inspector Grimshaw, tried to pour oil on troubled waters by assuring their London colleague that they could not be held personally responsible for the vagaries of the weather or the layout of the hospital, which made it virtually impossible for a car to be parked within thirty yards of the main building. Unappeased, Burnivel demanded what the hell he was going to do, sitting around all day in wet clothes, and him so subject to catarrh at the best of times? Honeychurch felt warmed towards him, catching the cadence of South London, the speech that lapses imperceptibly into a snivel or a whine whenever the circumstances warrant it. Not for the first time that day he hurried to the rescue.

"It *is* Inspector Burnivel, isn't it?" he said, crossing the hall and extending a colossal hand to the unfortunate traveller.

"That's right," said Burnivel. Then, with a quick frown, "Who are you? Who's this, Grimshaw? Anyone I ought to know about?"

"You do know about me," Honeychurch said gently.

"I've got no memory for faces," said Burnivel. "What's your name? I don't forget names."

"Honeychurch," said Honeychurch.

Amazement, followed by real pleasure, took from Burnivel's small predatory features their accustomed expression of shrewd mistrust.

"Why, Professor Honeychurch! Whatever are you doing here, sir?" He rounded like lightning on the helpless Grimshaw. "Why didn't you tell me he was here?"

"I was going to," Grimshaw said, "but it didn't seem important."

"Didn't seem important," said Burnivel witheringly. "Who are you to decide what's important and what's not? This is Professor Honeychurch, and he's more important than ever you'll be, my lad. Now get a move on and find me something dry. I can't hang about all day dripping like a blooming sponge."

Grimshaw opened his mouth to vindicate himself, thought better of it, and said something to one of the plainclothesmen, who disappeared forthwith.

"How did you come to be mixed up in this?" said Burnivel, turning back to Honeychurch with a look of some wonder.

"There's a meeting of the Paediatric Section of the Royal Society of Medicine here today and tomorrow," Honeychurch explained, "and I arrived last night."

"That's a bit of luck," said Burnivel. "I suppose you didn't come up to bash the bloke, did you?" He laughed incontinently. "Because if not, you can tell me what happened, when you've got the time. Grimshaw, where've you been working?"

"Professor Pemberton has given us a room just round the corner here, sir, if you'd like to follow me."

"You come too," Burnivel said to Honeychurch in the tones of one accustomed to prompt obedience. "And who's that hanging around the door and trying to get away when no one's looking?"

"That's Dr. Henchard," said Honeychurch, feeling a little embarrassed. "You've heard about the boy who's missing? Dr. Henchard was looking after him. He's a psychiatrist."

"Pity he didn't look after him a bit better," said Burnivel shortly. "He can come along too, if he likes. The more brains the better. I suppose psychiatrists do have brains, though you mightn't think so to hear some of the tommyrot they talk."

Henchard cast at Honeychurch a look of wild alarm.

"I'm sure you'll find Dr. Henchard's knowledge of Tom Bryant very helpful," said Honeychurch. "How is Electra?"

Burnivel looked pleased.

"Fancy your remembering her name! Oh, she's doing quite nicely now, thanks to you. Still wets the bed, but my wife says she'll get over that when she's forgotten about being in hospital."

"I should think your wife is absolutely right," said Honeychurch and added, "Inspector Grimshaw's man seems to have been lucky in his search."

Inspector Grimshaw's man carried over one arm a dressing gown of thick blanketlike material boldly striped in red and white.

"Lucky!" Burnivel exploded. He advanced menacingly towards the luckless messenger. "What d'you think I am? A football coach? Am I supposed to sit down and take statements from people in that—that bath towel? What sort of respect do you think that'd inculcate in the criminal

79

if he saw it? You jump to it, my lad, and find me something I needn't be afraid to put on. Where's this room we've been given?"

Shown it, he shook his head.

"Not big enough. Ring up this Pemberton chap and tell him I can't work in a rabbit hole." He wrinkled his nose in anger. "Disrespect for the police, that's what it is, giving us a room like this."

In Burnivel, thought Honeychurch sacrilegiously, I think Pemberton may have met his match.

Five minutes' telephoning ensued, during which Henchard made a variety of little impatient movements as if he were longing to be off, but didn't quite like to risk exposing himself to Burnivel's wrath; then a maid appeared and led them by labyrinthine ways to a large bare lecture theatre, which wouldn't be wanted before Monday, she told them. Burnivel surveyed it morosely.

"Not homely," he said, "but at least there's room to swing a cat. Now if you gents will look the other way, I'll change my clothes."

From somewhere or other the attendant spirit had conjured up a pair of old grey flannels and a blazer. These garments, unlike the dressing gown, Burnivel evidently considered not altogether derogatory to the dignity of the force. Once decently covered, he sat down at a bench liberally carved with the names of several generations of students and began to read a sheaf of papers handed to him by Grimshaw at incredible speed, strewing the pages as he finished with them in several little heaps along the bench. When he had done, he got up, filled a pipe, lit it, and began to walk up and down a central aisle; he went from the door at the back to the lecturer's dais in the front, turned, and retraced his course, all with a jerky rapidity extremely trying to the nerves of the onlookers. At last he stopped walking and pounced upon the litter of papers: these he shook threateningly at the cowed and miserable Grimshaw.

"What d'you make of all this twaddle?" he demanded.

Grimshaw had sense enough not to make anything of it.

"I'll tell you what," Burnivel said, abruptly lowering himself into his former place. "Something sticks out a mile. There isn't one of these people who stood to gain a brass farthing by bashing this chap's head in."

Grimshaw said rashly, "Dr. Rutherford—"

"Rutherford!" Burnivel rounded on him. "Least of all him, I should say. Now, here's ten pages of what you got out of Dr. Rutherford, who doesn't seem to have kept much back, and how much the wiser is anyone? He hasn't got much of an alibi, I'll grant you: he took Professor Honeychurch here over to Professor Pemberton's house at twenty past ten, and then he says he went to the library to look up some work for the meeting today. But there wasn't anyone else there and no one saw him leave the place. Well, it's just the sort of story anyone might tell, and he'd probably have done better than that if he'd planned to cosh this Sandeman."

"He'd had a row with Sandeman just before," Grimshaw pointed out, "and he told me it was Sandeman who got him fired."

"I can read!" Burnivel bawled. "I can think too, which is more than you can. So Rutherford picks a quarrel with Sandeman and then goes right out and cracks his head open with a bit of iron that he's been carrying around just in case he feels like murdering anyone, and then he comes out with the story of an *extra* row that he didn't have to tell you about, and an alibi that proves nothing. Looks as if he can't wait to get his head in a noose, doesn't it?"

"There's such a thing as bluff," Grimshaw said, stung to resentment at last. "He might have counted on everyone thinking as you do."

"What did he stand to gain by it?" Burnivel demanded. "You tell me that. Would killing Sandeman get him his job back? No. Would Sandeman have left him a fortune in his will? Not likely. Was there a woman in the case? We shall see, but everyone you've talked to so far seems to think the deceased wasn't much of a one for the girls. So why did he do it?"

Grimshaw said guardedly, "Revenge, perhaps."

"Not on your life. That's a chap coming home and finding another chap in bed with his wife, that's the lad who finds his dad beating up his mum once too often. *News of the World* stuff, not the sort of thing that goes on in a high-class dump like this. Now, if this Rutherford had picked up a medicine bottle and hurled it at the chap in the ward in the heat of the moment, that'd make sense. But lurking around in the bushes waiting for his victim doesn't sound like what this man's statement sounds like."

Honeychurch was quite unconsciously beaming his approval of this workmanlike analysis. Burnivel's quick eye caught the movement.

"You've met Rutherford, Professor? What do you make of him?"

Honeychurch said, "Sandeman seems to have treated him abominably, but I wouldn't say he was unduly bitter about it."

"He could afford not to be bitter if he'd put Sandeman out of the way of doing him any more harm," Grimshaw suggested.

Honeychurch nodded. "That point must be conceded. But it's still true that he stands to gain no material advantage from Sandeman's death."

"Would anyone?" Henchard asked.

They had almost forgotten his presence; he had been standing in silence by the window, warming his hands absently over a cold radiator.

He went on, evidently gathering courage: "I didn't know Sandeman very well, but he was quite a young man, not more than forty, and I don't think he had any private means. It's most unlikely that anyone could have achieved any material profit by killing him; in fact, it's doubtful if a man of his age would even have made a will. But no doubt you would know about that?"

He looked enquiringly at Burnivel, who looked at Grimshaw.

"I've rung up his bank manager—he had his cheque-book in his pocket, sir—and he doesn't know of any will. I thought we might have a look at his flat after lunch when we've decided which people need keeping an eye on."

Burnivel nodded approvingly, and Grimshaw blushed with relief.

"Did _you_ know Sandeman?" Honeychurch asked Henchard, unable to conceal his surprise.

"Oh, yes. Not intimately, of course. He came to see me on the suggestion of an old patient of mine: he wanted, or professed to want, advice about a personal problem."

"His addiction?"

It was Henchard's turn to look surprised. "I'd no idea it was a matter of general knowledge—"

"It wasn't," Honeychurch said. "Inspector Grimshaw thought of it when he heard there were puncture marks on the body."

Henchard seemed relieved.

"I had wondered whether it was my duty to inform the Home Office of his aberration; but he only came to me about three times in all: he'd already been tackled by two specialists in the treatment of addiction, and neither of them was able to do him any good. It was always so easy for him to get what he required, working in hospitals. And then he had no positive wish to be cured, which made it even more difficult. He used to say he had very little in life apart from his work: he found it hard to make friends, and he had no sort of overt interest in women. A most sadly inhibited person. He dreaded his spare time."

From this account Honeychurch watched emerge a more complex Sandeman than the one he had known, a figure that might have been almost pitiful in its talented isolation: one driven perhaps to extremes of unpleasantness in order to make any contact at all with the ordinary run of his fellows. But *tout comprendre, c'est tout pardonner*, was a point of view that had never commended itself to Honeychurch.

Henchard was going on: "But it seems to me that if nobody profits by his death in any obvious way, you should look for someone rather different from the usual type of murderer—someone neither obviously brutal, nor obviously concupiscent. Sandeman seems to have grated on the nerves of his colleagues to a remarkable extent—could it be that a series of small and unimportant displays of his malice towards a particular individual might constitute a motive? You are no doubt cognisant of the system of dialectic?" He turned to Burnivel, who looked carefully noncommittal. Henchard hurried on: "The dialectician argues that we are constantly observing as independent and inexplicable phenomena the end points of continuous and comprehensible processes."

"Is that so?" said Burnivel grimly and stood up. "What you're trying to say is that just being rubbed up the wrong way once too often might make even a straightforward chap like this Rutherford commit a premeditated murder?"

"Oh, good gracious, no!" Henchard threw up his hands in a touchingly outmoded gesture of horror. "I have never spoken to Dr. Rutherford: I am not in a position to say what would be his reaction to a series of petty persecution. No, I merely intended to shake your disbelief in murder committed for any other than a very dramatic reason."

"Well, there may be something in what you say," Burnivel said grudgingly. "That line would apply quite well to some of the other people you've questioned, Grimshaw. There's this American fellow you were packing off when I arrived; he doesn't seem to have made any bones about hating Sandeman's guts. And there's Professor Honeychurch here."

Honeychurch felt rather indignant, but had the sense not to show it. He thought of Ainsworth's unavailing efforts to get to Lisle Sunderland's display of surgical fireworks. Presumably he had been hauled in for questioning as soon as Rutherford had been dismissed.

"Another thing that strikes me about all this," Burnivel went on. "Nobody seems to have made much effort to hide their feelings. These days nobody seems to think twice about speaking ill of the dead, but all the same . . . the only one who seems to have a good word to say for him is Professor Pemberton, and that's hardly what you'd call a glowing tribute." He dived furiously into the papers and surfaced with the sheet he wanted. "'A conscientious and thorough worker . . . a credit to the department . . . an original thinker . . .'" Burnivel blew his nose thunderously on a handkerchief that must have been in the pocket of the blazer when the henchman brought it. "Nothing there to suggest the professor's nursing a broken heart."

"To be quite fair," Honeychurch interjected, "Professor Pemberton would never describe anyone in more personal terms. I think you should take that as uncommonly warm feeling on Pemberton's part."

"All right. I believe you," said Burnivel. "You know him and I don't, so you're probably right. It doesn't make any difference to what I said about the others. Seems they've all gone out of their way to let us know they didn't like the man."

"There's an obvious reason for that," Honeychurch said apologetically. "Any of them might have told you about the rest. That includes myself, of course. It would be merely stupid to pretend to an affection for the late Sandeman that anyone else could disprove offhand."

Grimshaw said unexpectedly, "Could the others have been exaggerating their own dislikes to cover up for Dr. Rutherford? Crisp fairly hero-worships him—and the American seemed to think we'd been putting the chap through some sort of third degree. When he came along, Rutherford was just leaving: Ainsworth rushed up and told him he should have refused to make a statement without having a lawyer present."

Honeychurch said sorrowfully, "Mr. Ainsworth is an impulsive young man much given to tilting at windmills. At present he cannot see how much embarrassment he is likely to cause by his effusions. At least," he added, "I don't think he can." He spared himself the necessity of explaining this ambiguous statement by rushing on to say, "What do you make of the boy's disappearance?"

"Boy? What boy?" Burnivel leapt up again, quivering all over like a terrier who scents a rat fields away.

"I mentioned him on the first page of my report," said Grimshaw resignedly, "but perhaps you overlooked it."

"I never overlook anything." Burnivel bristled and grabbed at the nearest pile of notes, picked out a page, read it at top speed, and apologised—handsomely, for him.

"Can't read your writing. Thought it was 'a toy is missing from one of the wards'—naturally I didn't attach much importance to that." Comprehension suddenly dawned. "Oh, the *boy*! The one the psychiatrist lost—what boy? Where is he?"

Honeychurch, Henchard, and Grimshaw gave a simultaneous and detailed answer to the first part of the question, and protested their entire ignorance of Tom Bryant's present whereabouts. Burnivel held up a hand.

"I get it. The boy's walked out—either on his own two feet or slung over somebody's shoulder." He rounded on Grimshaw. "What the hell are we wasting time for? Put every man you've got on to tracing that boy. If he saw anything last night, we've got to get hold of him before the murderer does."

"You are already too late," said Professor Pemberton from the door.

Who would have dreamt, thought Honeychurch, that the old man had so much blood and thunder in him?

"I have just had a telephone call which seems to throw a little light on Sandeman's death and what has happened to the Bryant boy. Sir George Bannister has received a letter from a gang of criminals who claim to have kidnapped his son from this hospital."

EIGHT

Honeychurch at any time in his later years might have attended a fancy-dress ball as stout Cortes and won a substantial prize: for a brief moment Henchard, Burnivel, and Grimshaw gazed at each other with a surmise correctly wild, while Honeychurch himself stared at Pemberton: silence upon Darien may well have lasted no longer than it lasted now. The large indifferent spaces of the lecture theatre were suddenly full of raised voices, each endeavouring to persuade itself and its hearers that it had seen the point first. At last, by dint of standing on a bench and waving his arms, Burnivel succeeded in restoring order; yet the first remark to be fully audible in the sudden hush was a peevish and irrelevant one.

"What is this man doing in my blazer?" Pemberton demanded.

"Yours, is it?" said Burnivel, unabashed. "Didn't know whose it was. Doesn't look the sort of thing anyone would wear in a hospital. Who are you? Who's this, Grimshaw?"

"I am Professor Pemberton," said Pemberton. *Medea superest*, thought Honeychurch irreverently.

"Yes, I see," said Burnivel. "If I were you, I should stop wearing things like this at your age: it won't do you any good with your students."

"I wear this blazer when I have been playing squash," Pemberton said. "I do not find it necessary to maintain my authority by a rigorous attention to dress."

"Gentlemen, gentlemen," Honeychurch pleaded. "Enthralling as we all find these sartorial exchanges, I am sure I speak for everyone when I say we are all agog to hear more of Sir George Bannister and his letter."

"Positively agog," said Grimshaw with that total lack of irony that seemed the hallmark of his patient, anonymous labour.

"He's driving into town directly to show you the letter," Pemberton said. "All I had time for over the phone was just to assure him that his boy was safe in the ward and another boy had disappeared."

"Do I understand," Henchard said, passing a hand over his brow, "that an attempt was made to kidnap the Bannister child from this hospital—and that Tom was somehow taken instead?"

"Of course that's what happened," Pemberton snapped. "The fools must have been in such a hurry that they just snatched up the first child they came to and ran." An idea came to him. "Good heavens! Sandeman must have tried to stop them and the scoundrels bludgeoned him. I felt there must be some connection—"

"So Dr. Sandeman died a hero," said Burnivel.

"An appalling sacrifice," said Henchard, shaking his head. "And Tom, poor child! What will they do with him?"

HIs thin hands were trembling with alarm. He removed his spectacles and began to polish the lenses with slight nervous movements.

Honeychurch said comfortingly: "If these people were scared into committing murder last night, they are hardly likely to repeat it today, do you think, Burnivel?"

"I don't know," said Burnivel glumly. "I've no experience of kidnappers. Not my line of country at all. All I can say is I wouldn't like my child to be in this boy's shoes."

"He wasn't wearing any shoes," said Grimshaw with a resolute determination to stick to the facts. "That was one of the things I chalked up against his having run away. He only had pyjamas on."

"It all fits in," Pemberton said. "To think that Sandeman should have met his death by such a mischance! Yet, in a way, I must admit I'm relieved. It has really been most distracting this morning, knowing that someone on my staff might actually have killed a colleague. I found it almost impossible to concentrate on my work."

"Maybe your staff is clear of murder," Burnivel said. "It looks like it. But how did these kidnappers know they'd find the child on the balcony? How did they know when it would be safe to have a shot at it? How did they even find out the child was in the hospital? It strikes me you're not out of the wood yet, Professor. Someone who knows this place has been talking."

Pemberton sat down, resting his head on his hand. After a moment he said, "The implication had escaped me, Inspector."

"Well, now you know. Can you think of anyone round here who'd go a long way for a little money? Anyone who might be in debt, for instance?"

Pemberton shook his head.

"I find it impossible to believe any of the medical staff would be capable of doing such a thing." He looked at Honeychurch. "I don't know how to put it into words."

"What Pemberton means," Honeychurch said helpfully, "is that a gross breach of trust such as you suggest is quite unthinkable—"

"Someone thought of it," Burnivel said. "But you needn't be so outraged. There's no reason to pin it on your precious medical staff. A nurse, a porter, a ward maid—I imagine any of them could have got the necessary gen and handed it on. Who's this?"

The same maid who had conducted them to the lecture theatre was ushering in a very tall, very lean, very upstanding gentleman waving a letter in the air by way of passport. Burnivel's question had been merely rhetorical. To him, as to them all, Sir George Bannister's decisive features and aristocratic bearing were familiar from their regular appearance on packets of the small essential domestic article that had made the Bannister millions.

"Pemberton!" said the industrialist. "What a deplorable business this is! You can really assure me that Edward is safe and sound?"

"I told you so over the phone," Pemberton said irritably; evidently he did not like to have his word doubted even by the chairman of the Regional Hospital Board. Honeychurch was disposed to admire him for it. "Nobody's touched Edward; they've got away with another child—and the wretches killed my first assistant in the process."

Sir George looked all genteel horror.

"You don't say so! Did he try to rescue the child? Jove, what a hero! We must do something for his widow."

"He hasn't got a widow," Pemberton said brusquely, "and we don't know exactly how it happened."

"How could we?" Burnivel said. "He's dead and we haven't caught the blokes that killed him. And we shan't find out by sitting around pinning medals on Dr. Sandeman's body."

That this was in shocking bad taste was shown by Sir George's cool stare and the offhand way in which he permitted himself to have the pleasure of meeting Inspector Burnivel, Inspector Grimshaw, Professor Honeychurch, and Dr. Henchard. He turned back to Pemberton with a simple, peremptory gesture indicating that he required attention: just so he might have summoned a shop assistant—his own butler would have expected a more delicate touch.

"The oxygen tents arrived safely?" he demanded. "You received the incubators by the date the manufacturers promised? No, my dear chap, there is no need to thank me all over again: the letter you wrote was quite sufficient. I think you will find us"—he turned to Honeychurch—"by no means tardy in introducing every reasonable innovation to this hospital. Pemberton's premature baby unit, which I had the happiness to endow personally this year, is said to be in advance of anything of its kind in the country."

Honeychurch murmured a few words, conveying to a fine shade the precise mixture of surprise and gratification that was expected of him. More, looking at Pemberton, he could not do. Burnivel meanwhile was simmering with impatience and only waited for this useless ceremony of introduction and polite exchange to end before he burst out with a request to see the kidnapping letter. Sir George relinquished it: five heads bent over it, but Henchard's was soon withdrawn; he had noticed the time and remembered an appointment. Honeychurch was hardly aware that he was going until Pemberton pressed upon the psychiatrist an invitation to return and attend as much of the meeting as interested him. Then the note again compelled his attention.

It was not exactly a letter. A piece of white card had been cut to fit the envelope: the message had been concocted of individual words and sometimes complete phrases cut out of various sorts of print. Some had come from newspapers, others from magazines printed in darker ink on thicker and glossier paper. The message itself was admirably concise:

YOUR SON EDWARD HAS BEEN KIDNAPPED FROM THE CHILDREN'S HOSPITAL. DO NOT TRY TO GET IN TOUCH WITH THE POLICE. YOU WILL HEAR FROM US AGAIN. HE WILL NOT BE HURT IF YOU OBEY ORDERS.

The envelope was of a familiar and inexpensive brand. The address was made up of scraps like the enclosure, but the senders had been hard put to it for the proper names and had actually made up "Bannister" of individual letters. "Sir" and "George" they found entire. "Forest Court," though both words began with small letters, were complete words cut out in one piece.

"Easy money," said Burnivel happily. "Any postman would have noticed where he picked up that one. Get on to it quick, Grimshaw." He snatched the note up again as Grimshaw left them, looked at it with minute attention, and whistled under his breath.

"Look at that," he said, pointing to the word "kidnapped." It was printed in block capitals, and the paper around it had been trimmed off very close to the first and last letters.

"Go on, Professor, tell me what you make of that."

Pemberton and Honeychurch both craned forward and began to speak. Both stopped, looked at each other, and began again. Then they gave up.

"Supposing," Burnivel said triumphantly, "you wanted the single word 'kidnapped' for a job like this, where'd you look?"

"Any children's comic," said Pemberton.

"Robert Louis Stevenson," said Honeychurch.

"In this case, I think Professor Honeychurch wins," said Burnivel with undisguised delight. "Wouldn't a page heading out of any old copy of *Kidnapped* be just the job?

An enterprising cove could just hop into the nearest public library and lift it. It's the only word in the whole thing, if you use your eyes, that the writer couldn't bank on getting out of a newspaper any day of the week. 'Bannister' was the only other word he got stuck on, and you see what he had to do to get over that. But 'kidnapped' —what are you shaking your head for?" He turned angrily to Honeychurch.

"Are you not crediting your criminal with a certain amount of erudition, if you're going to send him to literature to fill up his handiwork?"

"What with elementary education," said Sir George, "and school broadcasting, both of which are paid for, I might add, out of the taxpayer's pocket, there seems no reason why any bumpkin shouldn't have concocted this tomfoolery."

"The rest of the note's good English, isn't it?" said Burnivel wrathfully, "and the letters have been gummed on the card very nice and tidy."

Honeychurch sighed. "I'm still unconvinced. How about you, Pemberton?"

Pemberton said slowly, "I think there's something in what you say, Inspector. The note does seem all of a piece. One can't help noticing," he went on, with clear approval, "that the whole thing is the work of someone with an orderly and well-regulated mind."

"I cannot conceive how anyone with an orderly and well-regulated mind could carry off the wrong child in a venture of this sort," Honeychurch retorted. "That seems to me to be most remarkably slipshod."

"But the writer and the actual kidnapper may not have been the same person," Pemberton suggested.

Burnivel nodded.

"In fact, the writer might be the inside man—the accomplice in the hospital. Someone with a bit of background. I suppose you don't happen to know if there was a copy of *Kidnapped* hanging around the wards anywhere? It's the sort of thing someone might bring a child to read."

"I haven't the time to check up on everything the children stow away in their lockers," Pemberton said. "The ward sisters would be able to tell you. A small collection of books is kept in Outpatients too, for children attending clinics. I have frequently suggested that some control should be kept over them: they disappear at an alarming rate."

"Very orderly and well-regulated mind you've got," said Burnivel, and grinned sardonically.

Pemberton essayed a smile also; the product lacked conviction. Sir George seized the opportunity to remark that some determined effort should surely be made to bring the criminals to justice or at least to get on their trail. Burnivel scowled at him.

"What trail? There isn't any. I can't send police cars all over England looking for I-don't-know-who I-don't-know-where. I can find out where this letter was posted, which might give us a lead; and I can go and have a look at the place where they killed Sandeman. Then I'll see what's what."

"Of course, I'm not presuming to advise you on your course of action, officer." Sir George spoke as from a great height, yet one could feel the Chief Constable's presence peering over his shoulder. "In the meantime, Pemberton, I take it you'll have no objection to my removing Edward from the ward at once? I understand he was to come home this weekend in any case."

"Hold on—not so fast. There were just the two children on the balcony, were there?" said Burnivel. "Didn't Edward hear anything?"

"He has had chorea," said Pemberton. "St. Vitus's dance," he explained. "He was being heavily sedated. It is quite likely he would have slept through his own abduction if the scoundrels hadn't made a mistake."

"I must say it's odd that no one should have noticed anything in the ward," said Honeychurch thoughtfully. "Tom was a big boy; one would have expected him to put up quite a struggle."

"Here comes Grimshaw," Burnivel said. Honeychurch suspected him of deliberately shying off the subject. "Any luck?"

Grimshaw shook his head.

"It depends on what you call luck. They found the postman who collected it all right. Seems he'd had the whole sorting office gathered around thinking it was some kid or other having a joke."

He paused; even Grimshaw had a rudimentary feeling for the value of suspense.

"It was posted in the box at the gates of this hospital," he said.

NINE

Burnivel and Honeychurch walked together between the dripping cypresses. The rain had stopped: from time to time a large drop splashed on to the gravel; less frequently but more devastatingly such a drop insinuated itself between Burnivel's neck and the collar of his borrowed blazer or bounced with vehemence off Honeychurch's shining sinciput.

"What are you doing for lunch?" Burnivel asked, shaking himself out for the third time with a muffled expletive.

"I expect I shall have it in the hospital refectory," Honeychurch said without enthusiasm. "There will be a vile mess of undercooked cheese and a healthy dish of stewed prunes. There always is."

Burnivel was not listening. He had seen where the comings and goings of a variety of policemen had produced a recognisable track through the trees on to the handkerchief-sized lawn beyond. Sandeman's body had been taken away; all trace of its short, involuntary tenancy had gone with it. From his pocket Burnivel produced some photographs and compared them with the actual scene. Honeychurch looked over his shoulder and saw that these were the pictures of the body that he had himself seen taken: Burnivel explained that they had been developed and printed in the hospital's own darkroom and even gave Grimshaw credit for some initiative in getting the job done so quickly. Then he examined the ground with closer attention, squelching through the churned-up conglomerate of mud and grass in shoes selected like his original dress in the certainty of fine spring weather. He looked down at his splattered toecaps with disgust.

"Gawd, how I hate the blooming country!" he said, in the tones of one offered a personal insult by the vagaries of landscape and climate. Honeychurch felt some mild astonishment at hearing Bantwich condemned as rural; yet country, in the sense of not being London, it most surely was, and to Burnivel all other distinctions were without importance. He stood in the middle of the lawn, the perennial, anguished town mouse brought face to face with the intransigeance of wet vegetation on a clay soil, and glanced about him with a practised eye.

"Pity it didn't rain yesterday," he said finally, "then we'd have got some footprints. Just my perishing luck. Ground must have been like iron last night."

Picking up his feet daintily, he negotiated a visible puddle, only to land dismally in a miniature bog hidden in the lee of a rhododendron bush. Honeychurch averted his ears and mind from the audible outcome of this catastrophe and paid heed again only when Burnivel abandoned obscenity for the moment in favour of demanding the whereabouts of the pillar-box.

"It's let into the wall on the right-hand side of the gate as one comes in," Honeychurch said. "I noticed it last night."

Burnivel nodded, then frowned and said, "Observant chap, aren't you?" And then, swiftly, "I came out here for a reason, but I'm blowed if I can think what. Just had a hunch that looking at the place might give me an idea."

"What I cannot understand is how—"

"I can't understand anything," Burnivel said ferociously. "I can't make head or tail of it. Still, it suits me for the moment to have everyone else thinking there's nothing to make head or tail of. Gives me time to think."

Honeychurch said, after a brief hesitation: "Just now I started to say something about how unlikely it was that a nine-year-old boy shouldn't put up a fight when he was being abducted. From the peremptory way you changed the subject I gathered you wanted me to hold my tongue."

"Doesn't do to talk too much at this stage. There's nothing to talk about yet."

96

He stood still, as if expecting inspiration to descend from the heavens, preferably not in the form of rain. Bounteous if watery nature must have attended to his needs, for Honeychurch, feeling a vague urge to go through the motions appropriate to one searching after truth, had hardly begun to peer at the earth for some vital if unlikely clue when Burnivel yelped with correctly terrierlike triumph.

"Got it!" he exclaimed. "Use your eyes and you'll get it too."

Honeychurch used his eyes to no effect.

"Which way was Sandeman going?" Burnivel said. "Which way were the kidnappers going?"

"Down the drive, of course," Honeychurch said blankly.

"And which was in front?"

"I suppose Sandeman must have been, since he was struck from behind. But then—Oh. Oh, yes, I see."

"What crook in his right senses would have rushed ahead to commit murder if he could avoid being seen altogether by hanging about for a few seconds?" Burnivel demanded.

"Then," said Honeychurch reluctantly, "I gather Sandeman must have been behind the kidnappers."

"Imagine yourself coming out of that door. It's late at night. You're alone. Ahead of you, you see two or even three men carrying off a child. What do you do?"

"I shout for help," Honeychurch said promptly, "and I run after them, and then one of them turns round and bludgeons me."

"On the back of the head?" Burnivel asked.

"They might have stationed someone in the trees to keep a lookout," Honeychurch suggested. "But I can't believe anyone would give chase like that without calling for help. It doesn't sound right to me. And there's something I'd like to add, though you'll dismiss it as mere theorising."

Burnivel victorious was Burnivel generous.

"Any theory of yours would be worth listening to," he said handsomely.

"I knew Sandeman rather well, and I find it impossible to believe that in those circumstances he would have given chase at all. I fear he would remember some urgent engagement elsewhere."

Burnivel looked sceptical.

"You mean he'd have thought it was none of his business? Don't you think anyone would have gone after them, just by instinct?"

"Sandeman," Honeychurch said with authority, "was the last man in the world to be led away by an altruistic impulse. He would have weighed up his chances of survival and acted accordingly."

"Let's keep to the facts," Burnivel said. "Two things we can be sure of. Somebody killed Sandeman and somebody went off with the Bryant child. It may be they aren't even the same person."

"You don't really believe that, do you?" Honeychurch said. "Surely this preposterous abduction must have been staged to give Sandeman's death the appearance of a purely chance encounter? I'm blest, frankly, if I can see why. It seems to me a ridiculously complicated way to set about confusing the issue."

"Look," said Burnivel and paused. "Do me a favour, will you? Keep this to yourself. I think you're right: someone's trying to pull a red herring under our noses. I'm going to take a long loud sniff at it. It'll do no harm to let the someone think we like the smell."

"Very well," Honeychurch agreed. "I'll preserve a discreet silence on the subject."

"Thanks. I've just had an idea."

"Dear me," said Honeychurch, "there seems to be no limit to the profit derived from the contemplation of Mother Earth."

"Suppose Sandeman had been going the other way —the right way from the point of view of this kidnapping yarn?"

Honeychurch said wearily, "I have never been capable of concentrated thought on an empty stomach."

"Somebody might have called Sandeman into the hospital, meaning to kill him on the way in—he comes up the drive, you see, while the kidnappers are on the balcony, that's what it's meant to look like. And before he can see what's going on, their lookout comes out of the trees and bashes him. Now that would have looked convincing enough. But if anything prevented its being done then, somebody would have had to wait until he left."

"I can answer your question," Honeychurch said, feeling suddenly that he did not after all much want his luncheon. "Rutherford called him in, but he had a perfectly good reason for doing so."

"I bet he had," Burnivel said.

"You've left your facts a long way behind," Honeychurch reminded him. "How did your murderer arrange the kidnapping if he had to hang about the place waiting for Sandeman to go home? What's he done with the child?"

Burnivel looked at him in sudden pity.

"If I knew that I wouldn't be standing here talking to you," he said. "Now, let's go and eat. Me, I'm starving."

The refectory provided, it seemed, a better meal than one might have expected. It was already crowded when Honeychurch and Burnivel arrived, but at the end of one long table two places had been left. They sat down, Honeychurch next to Ainsworth, Burnivel facing Rutherford across the table. Honeychurch introduced them, feeling the situation to be awkward in the extreme. Ainsworth's impetuosity was useful for once; it ended a pause that could not help but be strained.

"This surely is an unique occasion. Did ever a hound sit down to lunch with a couple of hares before?"

"You gents can leave off thinking of yourselves as hares," Burnivel said. "Something new's turned up. You've not heard anything?"

"No-o?" Ainsworth said on a note of enquiry.

"Sir George Bannister had a note from someone this morning who claimed to have kidnapped his boy. We think now that the late Dr. Sandeman must have been killed in an attempt to stop the blighters getting away—and they took the Bryant child in error."

Ainsworth whistled on an indrawn breath. Then he leaned over the table and seized Rutherford's hand.

"Well, thank God that's over. Didn't I tell you everything would be all right?"

Rutherford could hardly feel so sanguine. To eye the world—and to be eyed by the world—through a haze of mistrust and suspicion was a new experience for him: Porter had been distant, Peebles shy, the Common Room had emptied five minutes after he wandered in to look at a newspaper. He had been amused at first and later angered; gradually he had begun to read doubt into every face, sometimes with an admixture of sympathy, and the combination was unbearable. He told himself that to see in Honeychurch's apparent friendliness towards Burnivel the evidence of a change of attitude was as absurd as it was disgusting—yet here he sat, avoiding Honeychurch's eye, refusing to look at Burnivel, behaving in short as murderers behave confronted with kindness on the one hand and condemnation on the other. Desperate conversational efforts might be better than a studied silence; silence could hardly avoid the impression of sullen reserve: but he could not talk, could not even think of anything to talk about. However Burnivel had got here, whether by way of Honeychurch's general benevolence or on some solid pretext of verifying his junior's impressions, he would be less than human if he did not follow up his advantage.

Without Ainsworth conversation would certainly have lagged. Burnivel said little, as becomes the hunter, dealing faithfully with his soup while his sharp eyes shifted from face to face. He knows it's a lie, Rutherford thought: he knows it doesn't even begin to explain the facts, that Sandeman would never in his life have taken such a risk—otherwise he wouldn't be wasting his time over mere food and drink if there were kidnappers to follow and a child to rescue. He still thinks somebody killed Sandeman with—what's the phrase?—malice aforethought, and of course he's right. Now, where is he likely to go from there? Will he jump on the obvious person—myself presumably—or is he too subtle for that? If I could talk to him freely, he reflected, I might be able to get some notion of how bright he is: as things stand now, it's only guesswork for both of us. He doesn't know whether he is or isn't sitting across the table from a murderer. I don't know if I'm passing the salt to a man who'll spend the rest of his day sniffing around for a chance to put me behind bars. And why should I try to clear the air? he asked himself. Why make myself ridiculous by uncalled-for protestations of innocence? Who knows if a little reserve about the place won't be of use to us all in the long run?

Superbly tender sirloin, well-cooked potatoes, and early peas of faultless flavour claimed his attention, but hardly got as much of it as they deserved. Ainsworth heaped horseradish in a terrifying little mound at the side of this delectable offering and began to divide his beef into small neat squares. Then he laid down his knife, transferred his fork to his right hand, picked up a bit of bread in his left and began swiftly and appreciatively to steer his food to its destination. To Burnivel this accepted transatlantic mode was a new and infamous phenomenon. He looked, looked again, and finally forgot to eat himself in intent and disapproving observation. Ainsworth's nerves were not made of steel: he stood the incredulous scrutiny for some time, but at last his resistance broke.

"What's biting you?" he demanded. "Didn't you ever see a guy eat this way before?"

"When I was a child, I used to mop up the gravy with a bit of bread," Burnivel said, "but I never heard of a grown-up doing it, not in public."

Ainsworth sighed and picked up his knife again.

"Is that better? I hate to see your food getting cold while you shake your head over my low habits."

Burnivel must have suspected that he was being laughed at: at any rate, he immediately began to bristle. That Ainsworth failed to see the bristling could not with fairness be blamed on Honeychurch, yet Rutherford momentarily did blame him. The professor had put himself in the position of the small boy who brings his father along to a gang meeting: and like the small boy he was now obviously suffering an agony of regret, or at least of acute social embarrassment. But he was also fascinated, and his fascination was peculiarly infectious. Even Rutherford had to concede Burnivel a certain finesse in his approach.

"It's just as well," he was saying, "that this case looks like being cleared up without our dragging any of you medical chaps through the mud. Otherwise you'd have to accuse Professor Honeychurch here of hunting with the hounds and running with the hares."

Which would be no more than the truth, Rutherford thought, with unaccustomed bitterness.

"After all," Burnivel went on, spreading a thin layer of mustard tidily on his meat, "none of you gave very satisfactory accounts of yourselves. Look at Professor Honeychurch here, climbing over a balcony at his time of life! Illegal entry wouldn't look too good in a court of law, would it? As for you, Mr. Ainsworth, I'm surprised you couldn't produce anything a bit more colourful with your background."

101

"What d'you mean, my background?" Ainsworth said, holding his fork poised in midair. Rutherford had an acute moment of apprehension.

"Coming from the States, crimes of violence ought to be nothing out of the way to you."

The fork continued its journey: Rutherford relaxed, Ainsworth chewed for a moment, then said lightly:

"Aw, you don't have to believe everything you hear. I've spent most of my time in university towns, and even in the States they're homely sort of dumps. Believe it or not, this is the first time I've ever talked to a cop—except for Grimshaw this morning, that is. You know, I've often wondered just how much weight you people attach to an alibi. Think how many hours a day a guy spends all by himself or with people who wouldn't know him from Adam if they ever saw him again."

Burnivel nodded agreement.

"Now, take me. Last night I went to the movies; it just so happens I've never been to that particular theatre before, and I guess I'm not the sort anyone would sit up and take notice of." (Burnivel cast one brief look at his tie, his alpaca jacket, his enormously thick-rimmed glasses.) "I was there well over an hour at the end of the show, but I might just as well have been anywhere else. Apart from ten minutes odd when the prof here can vouch for me, the rest of the night was a dead loss. I didn't even see my landlady when I got in. Now just suppose that I had any reason for wishing the late Sandeman out of the way—any more reason, I mean, than any right-minded fellow would have—I'd find it mighty difficult to convince you I wasn't the murderer."

"You would indeed," Burnivel said gravely, "though outside thrillers, perfect cast-iron alibis are pretty rare—and in thrillers you'll usually find it's the murderer who's got the best one of the lot. Either they turn back the hands of the town clock or they happen to have twin brothers. That sort of thing doesn't ever happen. Frankly, I'd be surprised if anyone could give me an account of their movements between ten at night and two in the morning that didn't leave a good deal to depend on their own word."

"That's what I'm getting at," Ainsworth persisted, "the whole thing seems so chancy."

"That struck me when I was reading Dr. Rutherford's statement," Burnivel said. "I suppose normally there'd be quite a few people reading in the library between ten and eleven?"

"No, sir." Ainsworth shook his head. "I never yet heard of anyone using it out of hours. What's got into you, Bill?"

Rutherford said slowly, "I was miles away; I'm sorry. I was thinking about circumstantial evidence and how dangerously misleading it could be."

"So were we," Ainsworth said, with no very great attention to accuracy. "I was just asking why the heck you took it into your head to hang around the library last night?"

"Is this another interrogation? I told Inspector Grimshaw I waited an hour in case Crisp wanted me to see that child again."

"You didn't attempt to find Dr. Crisp before you left?" Burnivel said.

Here it is, Rutherford thought, and put down his fork with a gesture he knew at once to be too emphatic, too nearly savage.

"I thought we were supposed to be congratulating ourselves on being rid of the whole bloody business! No; I didn't see Crisp. I went along to the ward, but I could hear him billing and cooing in the kitchen, and I didn't want to interrupt. Then I looked through the door and saw the oxygen tent had gone—which meant the baby must have died. So I came away."

He stood up.

"I'm going to collect Garside's car from the garage, Philip. Are you coming?"

"What's bitten you?" Ainsworth demanded. "Sit down and finish your lunch. The Inspector and I were only having a little talk on the subject of alibis in general. Didn't you hear us?"

Rutherford shook his head.

"*You* were having a little talk, but he wasn't. Look," he said to Burnivel with a sudden access of courage, "I shouldn't have lost my temper, but you were trying to trip me up, and I've already told Grimshaw all I know. Can I go now?"

* * *

Watching their retreating backs, Burnivel said grimly, "Rutherford isn't taken in one little bit. Either he knows or he guesses that there's something wrong with the kidnapping yarn. About Ainsworth I'm not so sure. That chap strikes me as too good to be true. I'd say he had brains, but he thinks it's safer to keep them under lock and key for the moment."

Honeychurch sighed.

"You may be right, but I deplore your methods."

"All's fair in love and war," said Burnivel, who believed it.

Unwillingly Honeychurch asked, "What happened to Rutherford after he left the hospital? Didn't he see anyone on the way home?"

Burnivel drained a minute cup of coffee at a single gulp.

"Not a soul. He shares a house up on the moors with this bloke Garside, who's in America." He looked at Honeychurch narrowly. "It's that hour he spent in the library that interests me. In a case like this, what I look out for isn't what people say they do, but whether they do the same thing when their friends aren't being murdered. If I were you, I wouldn't put too much faith in Dr. Rutherford's nice open nature."

He got up and waited while Honeychurch dealt with the waitress.

"Haven't enjoyed a meal so much in years," he said with a certain wistfulness. "Let's go and have a look at Sandeman's flat."

TEN

Disposed round three sides of a square of well-cut grass, three small blocks of flats that would have been called luxurious and exclusive in advertisements were collectively described on a stone slab facing the road as Cedar Court. In the middle of the grass a bedraggled monkey puzzle tree threw a crisscross pattern of shade over a circular seat. An army of daffodils was drawn up in perfect order in flower beds on each side. Burnivel stopped his car by a no-parking sign and sat for a moment looking round. When he finally made a comment his tone was aggrieved.

"That's no cedar," he said, pointing to the monkey puzzle tree.

"It certainly is not," Honeychurch agreed.

Burnivel's mouth tightened as if he discerned hitherto unguessed-at depths of Midland duplicity in this harmless botanical misrepresentation. He stepped out on to the pavement, leaving Honeychurch to squeeze painfully past the steering wheel, and looked at a scrap of paper with Sandeman's address on it.

"Doesn't do the springs any good," he said morosely, as Honeychurch with a final heave and lurch achieved his freedom. Then, as if to assure his passenger that this was merely a general reflection and not to be taken too personally, he added, "Driving over these flaming tramlines, I mean."

"My dear fellow," Honeychurch said pacifically, "there is no need to temper the wind to this particular shorn lamb. I apologise deeply for any damage I have done your little car, and if it will help the springs to recover, I will walk back to the hospital when we've finished here."

"No, no, no!" Burnivel almost jumped up and down in his distress. "I never meant—well, anyway, let's get a move on. It's Number Eighteen. Where's that? Yes, I see—the block on the right."

There were six flats to each block, and the common front doors were fitted with locks. Five small electric bell-pushes were identified by tiny cards. One placed rather lower than the others was labelled "Housekeeper."

"Won't get an answer there," Burnivel said, jerking a thumb at Sandeman's card, "so let's try this."

He rang the housekeeper's bell three times in rapid succession.

"That ought to fetch her," he said.

There were the soft intimate sounds of slippered feet on uncarpeted floors. Then the handle turned and, surprisingly, a heavily built, middle-aged Jewess confronted them. She looked at Honeychurch in some wonder and then at Burnivel with alarm and closed the door until they could only detect her continued presence by a single suspicious eye beyond it; it was evident that she regarded her visitors as perfectly capable of inserting a foot in the door and knocking her down in order to abscond with the movables. Nor did she seem to find Burnivel's statement that he was Inspector Burnivel of the Criminal Investigation Department especially reassuring.

"You ain't a plainclothesman," she stated with conviction.

Right was on her side. Burnivel in zebra stripes and baggy flannels merited no such description.

"When I'm on a job in the country," Burnivel said disingenuously, "I wear informal clothes. Makes me feel less conspicuous."

She hooted derisive mirth.

"You'd better go away or I'll call the police, young man."

Honeychurch said, "I was a friend of the late Dr. Sandeman, ma'am. This gentleman really is Inspector

Burnivel of the CID. He is wearing these clothes because his own were soaked in the shower this morning."

"That's different," she said at once. Then, severely, to Burnivel, "Why didn't you say so? If you'd told me you'd got wet, I'd have said, come in, take your things off, have some coffee—What was that you said about Dr. Sandeman?" She turned back to Honeychurch. "He hasn't been back here since yesterday evening. He's all right, isn't he?"

Honeychurch said quietly, "Dr. Sandeman is dead, ma'am. There are one or two things about his death that are worrying the police. Inspector Burnivel needs your help."

The housekeeper raised a hand to her throat and began to fidget with a lace collar. She said something they did not catch, opened the door, and motioned them to follow. They mounted two flights of stairs, went through a door on the left, and found themselves in a sizeable sitting room.

"This was his flat," the housekeeper said. She sat down on an armchair upholstered in an exquisite pale silk and wailed suddenly, "Dear God! Whatever happened to him?"

"He was killed by a blow on the back of the head," said Burnivel concisely, "a little before midnight last night, we think. Now, if you'd like to help us catch his murderer, you can tell us something about him."

"Is he a detective, too?" she asked, looking at Honeychurch.

Honeychurch said, "No, ma'am. I'm a doctor. I knew Sandeman very well some years ago."

She took out a handkerchief, dabbed her eyes, and patted the arm of her chair as if she were offering it comfort.

"Anything I can tell you, I'll tell you," she said. "Isn't anybody safe these days? Terrible times we live in when people go about killing doctors."

Burnivel asked for and noted down her name, which was Rachel Michaelson, while Honeychurch stood at the window and looked at the room. He came to the conclusion that Sandeman's personality had left no trace whatever here. The lush, mistaken carpet, the long, screen-printed curtains, the pottery, the little Dufy over the book-shelf, these things were anonymous in their comfortable, polished charm. And also, Honeychurch realised, suggestive of an income spent with abandon as well as taste. The same thought had apparently struck Burnivel.

"These flats aren't let furnished?" he asked.

Mrs. Michaelson shook a dejected head. Burnivel gave vent to a low and horrible whistle.

"Must have spent a fortune on this."

"Dr. Sandeman always liked everything of the best," Mrs. Michaelson said: a faint maternal pride printed the ghost of a smile on her face. "Only last month he bought this armchair; if he'd only known he wouldn't have the use of it!"

"Well, someone can have it," Burnivel said practically. "That's the first thing I want you to tell me, Mrs. Michaelson. Do you know if he had any relations?"

"None at all," she answered immediately. "Poor boy, he lost his mother when he was nothing but a baby. No brother, no sister, no father, one cousin only in America."

"Or any friends?" Burnivel suggested.

"He was a very quiet gentleman. He had visitors sometimes, not often. He never went out in the evenings hardly except to hospital."

"Did you know he went to hospital last night?"

"Oh, yes. He always told me when he was going to be out late so I could get a hot drink ready for him in the thermos. They sent for him at half past nine yesterday; thank God he had a good meal before he left."

"I'm sure it must have been a great comfort to him. Weren't you worried when he didn't come back?"

"It wasn't so unusual. Sometimes when he got there, he used to go and do some work in his little room, and then he might be very late. Once or twice he's slept at the hospital when he's been very busy. But he always let me know before—"

"Now, Mrs. Michaelson, can you tell us something about his visitors? Was there anyone who came specially often?"

She shook her head.

"Perhaps once in a month he told me he was having a visitor. 'Mrs. Michaelson,' he'd say, 'you buy me a nice little chicken and do it real nice with sauté potatoes and green peas.' His professor fellow came sometimes with his wife."

Burnivel was exploring his pockets and nodding his head understandingly at the same time. "Here we are," he said at last and handed the housekeeper a sheet of stiff card on which, Honeychurch could see by dint of craning his neck, a photograph had been stuck. "Now, can you tell me if any of these gentlemen ever came here? Take your time about it, Mrs. Michaelson."

The tip of the housekeeper's tongue protruded between her lips: she moved a shapely fingernail over the surface of the picture. Burnivel waited a minute or two, and then his impatience got the better of his caution.

"Him, for instance. Did he ever come here?"

"I never saw him in my life," she said decidedly. "Now, him"—she jabbed a finger forward—"he's been here; and that's the professor, isn't it?"

"Yes, that's right," Burnivel said, and then, with an obvious effort not to sound too eager, "When did you say that one came?"

Honeychurch crossed the room and saw her touch Ainsworth's face, broadly grinning in sepia over a hilarious sports jacket.

"Only this week," she said, "only this Wednesday, he came to supper. I made bortsch and a chicken and a soufflé, all very nice."

Burnivel was nearly, but not quite, rubbing his hands.

"Has he been here often before?"

"Just the once," she said. "Never before. And now never again, I suppose." She sighed. "He was American, wasn't he? Ainsworth, his name was."

"And you don't ever remember seeing Dr. Rutherford?" Burnivel said and pointed.

She shook her head. "I don't forget; he's never been up here, officer."

Honeychurch wished that this proved something, but knew that it didn't. He looked with some curiosity at the photograph, which was of a group taken in front of the hospital in weather discernibly cold; the medical staff were in their white coats with their collars turned up round their ears. Crisp stood between Rutherford and Ainsworth: Sandeman was on one side of Pemberton with an unknown face separating him from Peebles and Porter. The girl house physician stood in the place of honour on Pemberton's right and seemed transfixed with horror at her unaccustomed glory. The bottom of the card was irregularly torn, as if it had borne a list of names and these were undesirable for Burnivel's purposes. Honeychurch heard Mrs. Michaelson disowning Crisp and was stimulated to ask Burnivel how he had come into possession of this medical rogues' gallery.

"Grimshaw," Burnivel said shortly. "Pemberton gave it to him, as you might expect. Now, Mrs. Michaelson, you're sure there were no other visitors? Didn't Dr. Sandeman know any ladies?"

She hesitated a moment. "There was a lady used to come here sometimes."

Burnivel pricked up his ears.

"A lady?" he echoed, carefully expressionless.

"She used to come nearly every week," she said, "but of course she's not been here for a long time now."

"Was she"—Burnivel essayed an unaccustomed delicacy without success—"was she Dr. Sandeman's fiancée, would you say?"

"No, she wasn't," Mrs. Michaelson said with assurance. "She was a married lady."

"And did Dr. Sandeman ask you to cook a chicken on the nights she was coming?" Burnivel asked, making heavy weather of what was intended to be mere whimsical suggestiveness.

She drew herself up.

"This isn't that sort of flats. The lady only came afternoons. Not more than half an hour ever."

Honeychurch noted with regret that Burnivel considered half an hour's dalliance with another man's wife (even in the afternoons) sufficient evidence of depravity to account for any number of violent crimes. He felt impelled to remark that the acquaintance sounded innocent enough. Burnivel snorted an outraged South London snort and plunged further into these Paphian revels.

"What sort of a lady was she?"

"A real lady. Nicely dressed," Mrs. Michaelson said decidedly. "I wish I could remember her name."

"Do you *know* her name?"

"I'm telling you," she said, "I know it but I can't remember. It'll come back. Shall I make you some coffee? There's plenty of everything in the kitchen and Dr. Sandeman won't be wanting it now."

Before Burnivel could get a word in, Honeychurch said, "That would be very pleasant. Perhaps the name will occur to you while you're in the kitchen."

To an accompaniment of clinking cups and saucers and the hiss of a tap running, Burnivel started to go through the drawers of a Hepplewhite bureau while Honeychurch wandered desultorily along a row of books chiefly conspicuous for their unvarying medical format. It occurred to him that the rigidly austere lines of Sandeman's professional life would hardly have been expected to include a taste for contemporary French painting, curly eighteenth-century furniture, and the enervating caress of this white carpet. A prodigious amount of money must have been spent on furnishing this flat. Had Sandeman enjoyed a private income? Honeychurch mused. As if in answer to the unspoken question a telephone rang on the broad window ledge. Burnivel answered it at once.

"Dr. Sandeman's flat," he said. "Who's speaking? Oh, Grimshaw!" He sounded disappointed. "What d'you want?"

The pause that followed was ended abruptly by Burnivel giving tongue in evident astonishment.

"How?" he said. "I mean, cheques or notes or what?"

The answer was short: he put the receiver down without another word. "That was Grimshaw," he explained unnecessarily. "He just heard from Sandeman's bank manager. All strictly confidential. Seems he had eight thousand quid in his account. That's a lot of money for a man of his age these days. How much would he be earning?"

"Something well under two thousand a year."

"It would have taken him a long time to save all that," Burnivel said, making a swift calculation. "What with income tax and superannuation and so on, he'd only be netting a clear twelve hundred, let's say. I wouldn't be surprised if he paid ten guineas a week for this flat, you know. And the furniture"—he turned an appraising eye on the bureau—"wasn't bought on the never-never. So either he had some money of his own or he was making a bit on the side. It sounds like the second: he used to pay in fifty or a hundred quid at a time in notes, the bank chap says."

"A little judicious gambling, do you mean?" Honeychurch said. "I shouldn't have thought so. Sandeman was not the type to attempt a flutter."

Burnivel was looking at him almost affectionately.

"I wasn't thinking of a flutter. I wondered—" He broke off and frowned. "It's too soon to start wondering. I'm going to have a proper look round while that woman's making coffee. Coming?"

Honeychurch answered in the negative. He stood by the window and looked down on the monkey puzzle tree; on how many spring Saturdays had Sandeman, that lonely and unrevealing soul, stood in this precise corner of the room and watched small moving figures on the pavement below obeying calls to meetings, achieving rendezvous, pursuing invitations, negotiating purposes trivial and tremendous—believing himself to have, perhaps, some unknown power over these scurrying lives performing their infinitely varied and infinitely monotonous rituals? For this insidious suggestion of wealth, plopped into the mind by a bank manager's bald statement of his client's circumstances, was causing small eddies of distasteful suggestion in Honeychurch, a man habitually disposed to think well of his fellow men. For if neither gambling nor the monthly crumb returned undigested from the maw of the Inland Revenue had provided these surroundings— then what had? A nasty word came into Honeychurch's mind: could Sandeman have been a blackmailer?

If the idea lacked the final impact of conviction, it was not, Honeychurch admitted with infinite regret, from any incompatibility between the man and the crime: what made him doubt his intuition was a settled belief that the society encompassed by a provincial university, even a whole provincial town, was unlikely to afford much in the way of pabulum for the appetites of the professional Peeping Tom. Lost in thought, Honeychurch was hardly aware of Burnivel's return. Indeed, the man's first remark seemed to him of an inconsequentiality ill adapted to the time and place.

"There's nothing much in the bathroom," Burnivel said.

"What exactly were you expecting to find there?" Honeychurch asked. "In my experience there has seldom been anything much in bathrooms. Apart from essentials, of course."

"For Sandeman," Burnivel said, "what I was looking for *was* essential. But look here—"

He held out a small rectangular tin. It contained only a small syringe in a tube of spirit with half a dozen hypodermic needles and four ampoules labelled PETHIDINE HYDROCHLORIDE.

Honeychurch said, "I don't quite understand—"

Burnivel was scornful. "I don't know much about pethidine addiction, but there's only four hundred milligrams there; barely enough to keep an established addict going for a day: and if what Rutherford suggested is true, I'd have expected him to have laid in a pretty big stock from this experiment of theirs. Of course, Rutherford may have been lying; or he might have been taking the stuff himself, which opens up a lot of interesting possibilities."

Honeychurch could see that it did, and for him they included one that Burnivel could hardly have guessed— for this was a suggestion that would account for Rutherford's unwillingness to read Sandeman's paper and have the work discussed in public. Then, if Sandeman *knew*, and had been blackmailing his junior—Honeychurch stopped thinking altogether. In what had once been Sandeman's vicinity the air was poisonous.

He said: "Rutherford would hardly have gone out of his way to put the idea into our heads if he'd done such a thing. And it would be easy enough to check the quantity that's actually missing, if you want to. All that would be necessary would be to analyse the stock solutions Sandeman made up: if they're weaker than they're supposed to be, that would be strong presumptive evidence."

"How long would that take?" Burnivel demanded: he had once again his air of being a small dog worrying a bone.

Honeychurch admitted that the processes involved might require an experienced analyst and that, given such an analyst conveniently cloistered in the university's Faculty of Science on a Saturday afternoon, these same processes would probably take some little time.

"But since I can't claim to be anything of a pharmacological chemist myself," he finished modestly, "I can't be sure that there *is* any simple quantitative mode of assay available for pethidine in any case. There's a crude biological method, of course; rats' tails are exposed to radiant heat—"

Burnivel's expression, having ranged from intent purpose through scepticism to limitless despair, now became frankly annoyed.

"Well, just remember that we're after a murderer; I don't know if we've got the time to tinker about with any other sort of rat."

Honeychurch said mildly, "I understood you wanted to verify Rutherford's statement."

"Humph." Burnivel was unappeased. "Fat lot of use it's been coming here." He brightened. "Still, we have got three things out of it. There's a woman in the case, to start with."

"Mrs. Michaelson?"

"I'm coming," said that lady, emerging from the kitchen with a tray.

"The other one," Burnivel said tersely.

"I've remembered that name." She deposited the tray. "It was Garside. And she don't come here any more because she can't."

"You mean her husband found out?" Burnivel asked hopefully.

Mrs. Michaelson looked bewildered.

"They must have told him, mustn't they," she said, "when they took her to the infirmary?"

"What infirmary?"

"Where she died, of course," said Mrs. Michaelson, "after she threw herself under the train."

"Mrs. Garside's suicide: Ainsworth's visit," Honeychurch said. "What was the third thing?"

Burnivel took his eyes off the road for just long enough to raise a brow.

"You said you'd got three things out of your visit to the flat. I can only think of two."

Burnivel frowned: then he dug his hand into his pocket and tossed the group photograph into Honeychurch's lap. A moment later another photograph followed it. Honeychurch looked from one to the other disbelievingly.

"It was hidden in his top drawer under a pile of collars. Makes you think, doesn't it?"

"It does indeed." Honeychurch plumbed immense

depths of improbability, staring at Rutherford's face enlarged two or three times from the now familiar group.

"Now why," said Burnivel, "should Sandeman have a picture of Rutherford hidden under his collars?"

"Perhaps he used it to take it out and stick pins in it when he felt more than usually ill-disposed."

"There aren't any pinpricks in it," Burnivel said. Honeychurch glanced at him quickly. There was no mistaking his seriousness. The preposterous notion had already entered that seemingly prosaic mind; had been subjected to simple objective scrutiny; had been dismissed.

"Or perhaps," Honeychurch heard himself say, "Sandeman may have entertained some sort of perverted liking for Rutherford. It's far-fetched, of course, but it might be so. One would have to ask Dr. Henchard."

"What's it got to do with him?"

"It would be rather in his line of country: psychiatrists make a lot of mingled attraction and repulsion."

"Oh, *ambivalence*, you mean." The car jerked forward. Honeychurch was shaken, as much by Burnivel himself as by his driving; and behind his wonder at the man's unsuspected knowledge was an annoying little worry at the back of his own mind. Somewhere or other this curious anomaly of Sandeman's concealing the likeness of his enemy struck a chord in his memory: surely it fitted in with something he had heard or seen in the course of the morning—something else that had seemed to him incongruous, out of place?

ELEVEN

Grimshaw, the true sick-hearted slave, lunched meagrely off half a dozen corned beef sandwiches, a slice of Swiss roll, and a cup of tea wheedled out of a reluctant maid. He ate at the lecturer's desk, eyeing with mounting concern the little pile of crumbs around his paper bag. When he finished, he glanced towards the doors and windows, opened a drawer in the desk and swept the evidences of his epicurean debauch into its remoter depths: then he completed the covering of his traces by carefully wiping off his own fingerprints with the corner of a pocket hand-kerchief. Fortified by much carbohydrate and a pleasing sense of his own guile, he determined to use the hour or so of Burnivel's absence to put in a little more of the dull but necessary spadework that was, he repeated to himself with a confused reaching after the right metaphor, the backbone of all criminal investigation. If there was one thing that Grimshaw saw more clearly than another it was this: that no murderer was ever yet brought to book without evidence. And even if it only led to the humblest cog in the wheel, he knew it was his duty to follow up the one real clue he had been given. He took the card out of his pocket and looked at it.

Somewhere or other must be the book from which the word "kidnapped" had been cut: and if Burnivel had guessed correctly, the book would be Robert Louis Stevenson's classic, which he'd read himself years back. The chances that the book had come from the hospital itself were at least good enough to warrant a search.

He wondered if to wash up his own cup and saucer in the sink on the lecturer's bench would be derogatory to the dignity of the force and was saved the necessity of making any decision on this knotty point of etiquette by realising that even if he washed them, there was only a chalky duster available for drying up. The need for action stirred him out of hesitation. He saw that he had at least thirty minutes to go before Sandeman's bank manager would be calling him, and he was as determined as Cyril Pemberton might have wished that these thirty minutes should be well spent.

By now he had the hospital layout by heart: the four wards radiating from the main building and an Outpatient Department in the grounds. On the first floor of the central administrative block was something dubiously described as a "Prem. Unit." Since getting there only involved climbing a flight of stairs, it was in the Prem. Unit that he decided to begin his search.

The door when he reached it stated uncompromisingly that there was no admittance. Grimshaw had been ignoring such notices in the name of the law for upwards of ten years. He knocked and opened the door. It was as if he had been transported to the tropics by that simple action, so hot, so humid was the atmosphere that enveloped him.

He had never seen so much plate glass in his life, not even in a department store. The room was very large and divided by glass into cubicles from floor to ceiling. At a table between the cubicles a tall figure in blue, identifiable as female only by the starched contrivance on its head, was making little dots in red ink on a number of charts. Grimshaw looked nervously from left to right and saw that this was no place for him. Each cubicle housed a box of chromium plating with windows at the sides and in the top: each box was hitched up to an oxygen cylinder and each was occupied by a tiny red rag of a baby smaller than he had ever guessed a baby could be. As one in the presence of a mystery, he stood rooted to the ground. Before he recovered his power of movement the woman at the table looked up and saw him.

Grimshaw braced himself to meet the expected rebuke,

but none came. The sister rose, took a small linen object out of a glass jar on the table, and advanced towards him, holding this in her outstretched hand. The apology he had been framing died on his lips as it became evident that a miniature white nosebag with tapes attached was being offered to him. A similar contraption already hid with almost Oriental evasiveness the lower part of Sister's face; he accepted the thing without enthusiasm.

"You're a little early, Doctor," she said. "We weren't expecting you till after three. Are there many more of you coming?"

Grimshaw tried to extricate himself from a tangle of tapes to explain that he was not a doctor and had mistaken his way: but for a fatal moment his courage deserted him, and in that moment she bore down, seized the mask from his unnerved fingers and tied it uncomfortably tight under his chin and across his nose. He caught sight of his reflection in one of the partitions; an abashed and deplorably furtive figure with a white bow nestling ludicrously on top of its head. The mask aroused in him an overpowering desire to dribble, and this infantile urge had to be combated before he could essay any such mature activity as coherent speech. In the meantime he followed miserably in the wake of the formidable Eurycleia. They stopped outside a cubicle: gowns of thin white cotton were suspended on hangers on the inner side. Sister opened the door and motioned to him to take one; such was the force of her personality that Grimshaw, as one in a trance, took down the hanger and pulled the garment off. It fell to the floor. Grimshaw followed it, picked it up, shook it out, and turned it round to survey the damage. He was immediately conscious of a chill in the atmosphere. He glanced at Sister; above her yashmak her eyes were terrible.

"Shall we go outside? Bring that gown with you, please." Grimshaw obeyed.

"I think I ought to explain," he said miserably as she snatched the offending article from his hand and stuffed it angrily into a laundry bag; "I'm not a doctor."

"That much is clear," she said, "and to think I was just going to show you little Gregory."

"Little Gregory?" Grimshaw looked round. In the cubicle lay an inscrutable human fragment some twelve inches from head to foot; that such an object should possess a name seemed improbable beyond the wildest myth.

"He only weighs two pounds," Sister said proudly and added with dire emphasis, "If he dies of gastroenteritis tomorrow, I shall know who's to blame. What are you doing here? Didn't you see the notice on the door?"

Grimshaw evaded the direct question with practised diplomacy.

"My name is Inspector Grimshaw. I'm from the Bantwich City Police, investigating Dr. Sandeman's death and the kidnapping of the Bryant child."

Heavily sarcastic, she waved a hand towards Gregory.

"I suppose you suspect that innocent babe of murder—"

"Not exactly." Aware that this was an absurd remark, Grimshaw hurried on, "I'm searching for a particular piece of evidence. Perhaps you can help me."

"Well?"

"Have you a copy of Robert Louis Stevenson's *Kidnapped* up here?"

The eyes lately flinty and sardonic became amused.

"My dear young man—Anna, Margaret, and Anthony are less than a month old, Sylvia and Paul have no right to a separate existence for some time yet, and Gregory has many weeks owing to him. You'll understand that I don't encourage them to read adventure stories in bed. It would be far too exciting."

Grimshaw knew when he was beaten. He allowed himself to be ushered rapidly down the glass passage and through the door; a disturbing sense of repetition assailed him—surely, many years previously, something rather like this had happened to him?

The door shut behind him. The giant mechanical womb had cast him forth into a hostile and peculiarly chilly world.

He ran his quarry to earth in the Burns Unit, a small appendage tacked on to the end of a large surgical ward. The staff nurse in charge assured him that a copy of *Kidnapped* had figured largely in the library kept for the older children.

"When did you last see it?" Grimshaw demanded with excusable eagerness.

She chewed the end of her pencil: a pretty girl, and fully aware of it.

"Well, it was there at the end of March. I remember taking it away from one of the kids before he tore it to ribbons."

"Nobody would have borrowed it and not returned it?"

"Somebody must have, mustn't they?" She turned a pair of blue eyes on him; they were not devoid of intelligence.

"Do many of the medical staff come in this ward?"

"Not if they can help it." She sighed. "I haven't seen an adult male in here for heaven knows how long."

Grimshaw thumbed over one or two books on the windowsill and said over his shoulder:

"Would Dr. Rutherford be likely to come?"

"They're all saying he did it, aren't they?" she said. "You can take it from me it's rubbish. He wouldn't hurt a fly."

"You'd be surprised," Grimshaw said, "how many criminals that has been said of. I mean, of how many criminals that has been said. Especially," he added darkly, "poisoners."

"Sandeman wasn't poisoned as well as coshed, was he?"

"No, of course not." Grimshaw waded through much deep water. "Now, look here, Dr. Sandeman was killed in an attempt to stop kidnappers carrying off Sir George Bannister's child."

She wrinkled her nose in contempt. "Some story. Sandeman would never have stuck his neck out like that."

"I'm just trying to point out that there needn't be any discussion of Dr. Rutherford's being involved in this affair."

"I didn't start discussing him," she said. "You asked if he ever came in here. Yes, he did—over the pethidine experiment. Most of the kids in this unit were in on that, poor little beasts."

"Would he have been here in the last three weeks?"

She flicked over the pages of an impressive record book.

"Yes, he was here on the eleventh. So was the great Sandeman, in the evening. We did well that week. Phil Ainsworth came in three times." She yawned, showing nice teeth. "I can't imagine why."

"Professor Pemberton wouldn't have dropped in?" Grimshaw stuck to his brief manfully.

120

She stared.

"Oh, no! Good gracious! He never comes in here. He ignores the surgical side. We're the absolute dirt in his eyes."

Not for the first time Grimshaw felt that life in hospital was too complicated for him. Why should Pemberton ignore the surgical side? Why should it be the absolute dirt in his eyes? How could this young woman be dirt in anyone's eyes?

"Thank you very much for your assistance," he said politely and left.

Back in the lecture theatre Grimshaw found a note waiting for him. The telephonist who had been on duty the night before had made a statement: there had been two telephone calls for Sandeman at eleven—one from Crisp on the inside phone, one from the outside in a voice the girl did not recognise. There had been only a short conversation, and she had heard none of it. Grimshaw sat a moment with his notebook poised before him. Finally, he committed himself to a comment after the bald transcript of the girl's information. This may not mean anything at all, he wrote: anybody may have rung Sandeman up for any reason on earth. And he added: the voice may have been disguised—if it *was* the murderer's. Appropriately enough, the telephone by the window rang while he was writing. He answered it, relayed the bank manager's message to Burnivel, allowed himself a moment to feel proud of having thought of asking how the money had been paid into Sandeman's account, and then settled down to sifting through the odd scraps of evidence that he had picked up so far. Nearly half an hour passed before he put down his notebook, and at the same moment a shadow fell across its pages. He raised his head. A very tall man was standing over him. Grimshaw frowned.

"How did you get past the constable on duty, sir? I haven't told him to let anyone in."

"Such a nice fellow," said the tall man kindly. "I once awarded his baby first prize in a show. I've just come back from America, and they tell me Sandeman's dead. I thought it would be just as well to come to you and get it straight from the horse's mouth—if you'll forgive the expression."

Grimshaw was affronted; he had better things to do with his time.

"No doubt you'll hear the whole story in due course, sir. I have rather too much on my hands—"

"—To concern yourself with an intruder like me." The tall man having taken the words out of his mouth offered to replace them with a cigarette which Grimshaw refused with some acerbity. He lit one himself and said thoughtfully: "If Sandeman is dead, sooner or later I suppose someone will want to ask me some questions. I put myself at your disposal: I merely require a little information in exchange. I should have thought my terms quite reasonable."

What Grimshaw would have replied to this unparalleled effrontery must remain for ever unrecorded. For Burnivel, full of lunch and hopeful of adultery, stood in the doorway and answered for him.

"Quite reasonable, Dr. Garside. It is Dr. Garside, isn't it?"

TWELVE

Burnivel was a joyous, a jocund, a jubilant man. Sex had at last reared its by no means ugly head; he greeted it as a friend long lost and expanded the welcome to include Julian Garside. Since luck or intention had brought this protagonist into the arena most aptly upon his cue, Burnivel could do no less than offer him a round of applause.

"It's very good of you to come and look us up at once, Dr. Garside. Only wish everyone had as much sense."

Garside looked as impressed as Burnivel had intended that he should; to be taken on the instant for a man of unusual mother wit is always a heartening experience. He glanced at Honeychurch and recognised him at once. Compliments and reminiscences followed; to the waiting Burnivel it seemed for a few maddening moments as if the vast presence of his protégé was becoming an encumbrance altogether too weighty to be borne. But he was by no means inclined to dispense forthwith with Honeychurch's unwitting services, for Honeychurch clearly knew the ropes. Thus Burnivel to himself, meaning that there were questions the professor might ask that he could not, and answers Honeychurch might obtain that mistrust and discretion would keep from an interloper like himself.

The social consciences of everyone appeased, the investigation could once more take its course. Garside, likely cuckold, possible murderer, sat down, crossing long legs with a lithe movement that attracted Burnivel's attention. The man was most remarkably all of a piece, from the grey hair cropped short above the ears to the slender, handmade shoes; from the fanatically trim moustache to the no less trim creases in his trousers. Hence no doubt the house "miles outside the town"—so finished a portrait required a frame made to specification. Less immediately clear was the relationship between the man and his profession. Burnivel saw that there was a riddle here, wondered for a moment if it were germane to the central problem, and opened battle with a side step into pure metaphysics.

"Where would you say Dr. Sandeman is now?"

"Roasting in the embers, I should think. Or did you want a literal answer? In that case, on a cold slab in the mortuary—a more Scandinavian concept of Hell, but quite as valid as the other."

"Yes," said Burnivel. "You didn't like him?"

"My feelings are surely irrelevant: otherwise I would have gone to some pains to hide them."

"You know best about that," Burnivel said shortly. "Now, sir, one or two personal particulars if you don't mind."

His full name was Julian George Evelyn Garside. His residence, The Hall, Pitts Leighton. His age, forty-seven years. His condition widower. He had no children. He was clinical assistant to Professor Pemberton and senior lecturer in child health to the University of Bantwich. He had, as his appearance abundantly confirmed, private means.

"Hang on a minute." Burnivel broke into his own progress as a thought came to him. "You're older than Professor Pemberton, but he's your boss—how's that?"

"I had the misfortune to begin my sojourn on this blighted planet some three years earlier." Garside was elaborately grave.

Burnivel was grave also, preferring—as do most people—to be accorded some measure of serious attention.

"Don't trifle with me, Dr. Garside."

"I apologise." Garside inclined his handsome head, smiling ruefully. "This is no time to be facetious. You must forgive me. I'm a very tired man."

Burnivel pounced on this. "You've had a long journey?"

"My plane got into London Airport at seven o'clock last night."

"Your friends weren't expecting you back till Monday."

"My leave of absence expires on Monday," Garside ever so gently corrected him. "Normally I would have spent Saturday to Monday in Town, but I happened to remember the meeting and changed my plans."

It sounded plausible, even to Burnivel.

"And when exactly did you arrive in Bantwich?"

"At about two this morning."

"Can you tell me what you've been doing since then?"

"I had a cup of coffee in the station buffet. Then I went to the Railway Hotel—frightful!—and took a room. This morning I didn't get up till about eleven."

Burnivel interrupted.

"Didn't you go home? Why didn't you go home?"

Garside raised tailored eyebrows.

"My dear chap, you obviously don't know the district. Now any local man would tell you my place is about ten miles out. There's no earthly way of getting there at night without a car, and mine's been laid up in dry dock while I've been away."

At this moment an idea of beautiful simplicity sprang full-blown into Burnivel's mind; he postulated a more sinister and complex association between Garside and Rutherford than that which normally obtains between a host and a presumably paying guest. For, given that Garside had the motive, most certainly Rutherford had had the opportunity. For some time Burnivel had been reluctantly admitting to himself the need to assume a conspiracy of sorts behind this murder. On the simplest physical computation, a would-be murderer would find it embarrassing to tuck a vigorous child under one arm while he achieved his primary aim with the other: on a more subtle point, there was the apparent schism between the methodical accuracy of the kidnapping note and the impulsive high-handedness that bore off the wrong boy at a moment of high tension. Allow two men to have designed and worked this creaking machinery, and its imperfections might yet be explained.

Burnivel recalled himself firmly to the task in hand and listened to Garside's account of the way he had spent the morning. A prolonged breakfast, a slow stroll round the city centre, a phone call to The Hall, unanswered, from which he gathered that Rutherford had already left for the hospital, luncheon and a drink, a yet slower stroll up the hill to the university—and once there he had been thunderstruck at the news that greeted him. For, whatever one personally felt about Sandeman, dammit, one could hardly help being put out by the discovery that someone had at last thought fit to put the miserable blighter in his place. If this was acting, it was skilled and purposeful. Burnivel watched every movement of the long fingers, every twist of the mouth, and unwillingly admired. Then, with deliberate coolness, Garside turned away from him towards Honeychurch.

"And then there's all this extraordinary story of the kidnapping. Peculiarly rum, that. I mean to go to so much trouble to cover up a murder almost anyone might have done after a long day's work with the brute."

"Story?" Burnivel caught him up at once. "What d'you mean, story?"

"But you don't seriously mean to say . . . my dear chap! how can you? Surely it must have occurred to you that Sandeman was leaving the hospital? And naturally that implies—"

Burnivel was speechless.

"But of course, you don't believe it, do you? Otherwise you wouldn't be questioning me. After all, I'd hardly be likely to act as inside man for a gang of thugs."

This was undeniable. Burnivel let it pass, and before he could return to the offensive he heard Honeychurch's gentle boom from the lecturer's desk.

"Did you work that out for yourself, Dr. Garside? Inspector Burnivel here pointed out the incongruity to me."

"I should be ashamed of myself," Garside said. "As a matter of fact, Bill Rutherford told me."

"Told you what?" Burnivel snapped.

"That the kidnapping yarn simply wouldn't hold water."

Burnivel sat back, clasping and unclasping his fingers. Well, at least Garside had talked things over with Rutherford: that was a tiny point in favour of their being in collusion.

"When did you talk to Dr. Rutherford?" He was a little taken aback at the harshness of his own voice.

"About half an hour ago. I found him getting out of my car."

"Then he was the first person to tell you Dr. Sandeman was dead?" Burnivel leapt on this superficially harmless statement.

"How you do jump to conclusions!" said Garside with some amusement. "No. As a matter of fact, it was Dr. Peebles or Dr. Porter who told me. I don't remember which."

Burnivel sensed that he had let an advantage slip. Firmly he took the reins of this most unsatisfactory interview back into his own hands.

"Perhaps we'd better go back to the beginning. Some time ago I asked you how you came to be acting as assistant to Professor Pemberton, who's younger than you."

"Is this a veiled invitation for me to tell the story of my life?" Garside rose, stubbed out his cigarette, walked across the room to the nearest window, and stood for a moment looking out. Then he faced them again.

"Gentlemen," he said, "my story is not very entertaining. Regard me if you will as one of the freak survivals of an extinct species—a medical dilettante who ought to have become an object of only the slightest archaeological significance at least a generation ago. Paediatrics is my hobby rather than my profession. My family has lived at Pitts Leighton for three centuries, and I found the prospect of removal thoroughly distasteful. Otherwise I should certainly have left Bantwich when Pemberton came. Especially"—he smiled an intimate smile that included them in his personal dilemma—"as I naturally anticipated being awarded the chair of child health myself after fifteen years' work in the university. However, they wanted someone with more—how can I put it charitably?—more drive than I was considered to possess."

He toyed with a convenient blind-cord, twisting his mouth into a wry smile.

"It was rather a bitter pill to swallow at the time. I thought of handing in my resignation, but habit was too much for me; besides, I dislike dramatic gestures."

Surely his glance was openly laughing? Burnivel was

mentally afire at this flippancy. He did not trust himself to do more than nod.

"So here I still am." Garside relinquished the blind-cord and stuck his hands deeply in his pockets with the alarming unconcern of the man who knows his wardrobe to be infinitely well stocked.

"Of course," he added, looking over Burnivel's head to the patient Grimshaw, making notes as if his life depended on it, "there were other reasons for my staying in Bantwich. My wife, for example. You probably know that my wife is dead? Yes, I thought you would have heard. She is popularly and correctly supposed to have done away with herself. The coroner was at school with me, so the verdict at the inquest was death by misadventure: the local press was singularly unconvinced. One must allow a certain measure of implausibility in a young woman losing her physical balance and falling under an oncoming train—but presumably it was the balance of her mind that was disturbed."

"You had been estranged for a long time, Dr. Garside?" Honeychurch's tone was apologetic.

Garside looked at him with unaffected gratitude.

"For years Helena and I only tolerated each other. Lately even tolerance seemed to be wearing a little thin. I won't say that her suicide left me quite unmoved; of course not. It's hardly gratifying to one's ego to know that one's wife would rather die than continue to accept one's presence around the house."

"Did you know that she was going to do it?" Burnivel said bluntly.

"She seldom bothered to announce her plans. To put it another way, I was not at that time in a mood to take much notice of her state of mind. I had this American scheme on hand, you see, and there were naturally last-minute preparations to be made. However," he added thoughtfully, "I must admit I found her even more irritating than usual in the last two weeks. Come, my dear Inspector"—he looked at Burnivel, who was drumming menacingly on the bench before him with one indignant index finger—"you surely don't subscribe to the notion that death ought to act as a sort of whitewash for any little moral imperfections in the departed? My wife was always a shrill sort of woman; at thirty-five she was fast evolving into a prolonged piercing note of complaint. I am sufficiently candid to admit that I find silence less exhausting."

Burnivel said abruptly: "Did you know that your wife had been visiting Dr. Sandeman's flat clandestinely?"

Garside sat down and lit another cigarette, taking his time over the operation. When he finally spoke, it was to Honeychurch: "Do you think he really wants me to tell him what he asked? For of course I knew that Helena was in the habit of dropping in on Sandeman. . . . No, I rather think he'd like me to tell him if Helena and Sandeman were—in the police court sense—intimate." He shuddered. "Vile expression! Yes, I had known about it for some time—about six months, in fact."

"And you can't think," Burnivel went doggedly on, "of any reason why your wife should have killed herself? You've given us plenty of reasons why you didn't grieve over it."

As if it had suddenly dawned on him just how severe a provocation he had been offering to a potential enemy, Garside's brittle manner snapped. He said soberly, "I don't know why she did it. We'd had no particular scenes, she hadn't asked me for a divorce. As far as I know, she was still seeing Sandeman right up to the last few days."

"And how did Dr. Sandeman take the news of her death?"

"I never discussed the subject with him. As far as I could see, he felt no especial grief."

"Just one more thing," Burnivel said, "how did you know they were lovers?"

"Helena told me," Garside said simply. One side of his face twitched for a moment. "She said he gave her everything in life that she wanted, which was high praise, coming from Helena."

"And incredibly high praise, applied to Sandeman," said Honeychurch, but he said it under his breath.

THIRTEEN

Burnivel sucked his knuckles: this was not the undiscarded, comfortable habit of his nursery days, but an action dictated by sheer necessity as a consequence of premeditated violence. Convention and law alike having denied him the chance of relieving his feelings by punching Garside's shapely jaw, he had waited only till the doors of the lecture theatre closed behind the erect, fastidious figure to punish the bench before him with a mighty blow from his clenched fist.

"Cold-blooded swine!" The imprecation was hissed through his teeth in the most approved manner of the barn-door theatre. Honeychurch was alarmed. This childish display of temper augured no great reserves of self-command. Then he observed with relief that the outburst had magically cleared the air. In great good humour, Burnivel had tilted back his chair, thrust his thumbs under the lapels of his blazer, and was by now smiling as broad a smile as there was room for on his thin face. This sunny mood was as transient as his anger: a moment later he was leaning forward tapping with a forefinger while he questioned Grimshaw closely on the use he had made of his lunch hour. He reserved judgment over the telephone call, but his eyes narrowed over Grimshaw's account of the tracking down of *Kidnapped* to its source.

"Rutherford, Ainsworth, Sandeman himself," he

130

repeated. "Pemberton's not likely, and Garside's out of the running for that part of the job at least."

"What I should like to know," Honeychurch said firmly, "is, what do you think has become of Tom Bryant? It has just occurred to me that there mightn't after all have been any mistake about the boy. I mean that Tom was taken by design and not by accident."

"What's that?" Burnivel leant forward. "What d'you mean?"

Honeychurch chose his words carefully: "Suppose that a person or persons unknown wished to rid themselves of Sandeman and suppose them to have hit upon this overelaborate scheme for accomplishing their ends. Now, if someone had abducted the Bannister child, there might have been considerable difficulty in getting rid of him again: abandoning him without waiting for the payment of a ransom would have looked extremely odd. Now if"— he paused to take breath, observed that Burnivel's eyes were fixed on him with a look of some wonder—"this hypothetical murderer kidnapped the wrong child— apparently in error—you see how the situation changes. They—he—need only leave the boy in a suitably lonely spot—"

"As if," Burnivel supplied, "they just dumped him as soon as they realised their mistake."

"—and provided the child was prevented from recognising his abductors, the whole thing would appear reasonably plausible. If one assumes that such was the murderer's intention, a search of all the empty buildings, sheds, and so forth in the vicinity, ought to yield the most gratifying results."

Burnivel said, "How did you think of that?" His tone was faintly peevish.

"It seemed so unlikely. There was the right child drugged to a state of virtual insensibility, but instead of him a lively, healthy boy gets carried off."

Burnivel nodded. He got up and began his catlike walk up and down the hall. When he passed Grimshaw for the third time, he stopped with alarming abruptness.

"Now, quick, Grimshaw, my lad! When did those two boys come into hospital?"

"Edward Bannister had been in the ward ten weeks, and Tom Bryant only seven."

131

"And Garside went off to the States two months ago," Burnivel said with grim satisfaction. "Now, let's have a shot at working out how it might have been done. Impromptu, this is, so there'll be a lot of mistakes. For what it's worth, I think you'll agree we have to make out there were two people in on this business. Agreed?"

The question, impartially addressed to both his listeners, drew a ready affirmative from Grimshaw, one rather less wholehearted from Honeychurch.

"Here's Garside who knows his wife's been on friendly terms with Sandeman, and maybe he might even have an idea Sandeman could have been somehow to blame for her killing herself. He's all set to give the blighter what's coming to him, but there's this American trip coming up, and he needs time to think; so he goes off, after he's told Rutherford what's on his mind. Rutherford's got good reason to hate Sandeman too, and he isn't averse to putting the chap out of the way without running too great a risk. There's the Bannister boy—what could make a better cover for the murder than a kidnapping—but what are they to do with the boy afterwards? Shall they dump him and hope it'll be put down to a panic or a change of heart? It doesn't ring true. And anyway, Bannister's child would know Garside by sight. But Tom Bryant wouldn't, and you know the rest of that argument. All right so far?"

Honeychurch shook his head very slightly. The movement was ignored.

"The night comes. Rutherford has fixed the note. He calls Sandeman into hospital, but for some reason he can't kill him on the way in—perhaps because Garside won't have been able to get down from London by that time, and the child must be off the balcony and out of the way before Rutherford attacks Sandeman. I should think Garside most likely uses Rutherford's car, takes the child to some prearranged spot and leaves him. Then he drives the car back and goes down to the town himself in time to give the appearance of having come off a later train. You've got a photo of Garside on that group, haven't you?" he demanded of Grimshaw. "You'll have to get on to the guards and ticket collectors on the train he said he came on and one or two before or after. There's a chance someone might have recognised him: he'd have travelled first-class."

"A chance he would no doubt have taken into account," Honeychurch suggested mildly.

"No doubt," said Burnivel and frowned, but briefly, seeing that a digression here would lead him into deep water. "Where was I? Oh, yes, it's all over, and Garside suddenly sees he's in clover. Rutherford pinched the book, Rutherford actually killed Sandeman, and if he's caught and says Garside put him up to it, would anyone believe him? And because he knew the child better than anyone else, Rutherford is the only one of the lot who *could* have done the thing single-handed. So everything's set fair for Garside to rat on his accomplice, and he's doing it already. He's shoved a spoke through the whole kidnapping yarn; he forestalled any risk of our hearing about his wife and Sandeman from anyone else by being ever so frank about the whole thing. The only snag from his point of view is that the child might have seen him when he was supposed to be miles away. If I were Dr. Garside, I'd have shut his mouth permanently while I had the chance."

He sat down, overcome by the vehemence of his own peroration.

"It won't do, you know," Honeychurch said gently.

"I know it won't," Burnivel said; he seemed surprisingly light-hearted at the rebuff. "There are half a dozen loopholes in it; you couldn't tell me any I haven't spotted myself." He held up a hand and marked off points on his fingers. "First, Garside needn't have told us it was Rutherford who suggested to him that Sandeman was going the wrong way. Second, if Rutherford had been hanging around the place waiting for Garside to return his car, he'd have taken care to have a real alibi for that period, even if it did mean barging in on young Crisp and his nurse. Third, as you remarked, Garside would never have risked coming by train at a time where there aren't all that many passengers and he might have been recognised at the station."

"And fourth, fifth, and sixth," Honeychurch generously supplied, "there's a tremendous fallacy at the very root of the thing. I just cannot see a man plotting revenge while he goes off to the United States, leaving someone else to work out the details for him and keep him posted on progress by airmail. And it's one thing to help a friend in trouble, but whatever sort of mistaken loyalty would

133

drive a man like Rutherford to commit murder just out of goodwill and a little personal resentment?"

"It's a pity," Burnivel said. "It was a nice high-flown theory—should have suited you down to the ground." He added wistfully: "I don't mind admitting I'd like to think Dr. Garside was capable of a bit more than a lot of fine talk."

"Oh, but he is," Honeychurch said with conviction. "Decidedly he is. Most men who act a part so blatantly do it to hide a mere regrettable vacuity within. But Garside does it to disguise a very considerable intelligence, and—unless I'm mistaken—a fair amount of anxiety."

"Anxiety!" Burnivel clutched at this straw with avidity. "What's he anxious about?"

"Exactly what you think," Honeychurch said and rose. "He knows that his friend's position is equivocal; and he is quite prepared to throw a little sand in your eyes if he thinks it will make Rutherford appear less of a sitting bird for you than he does at this moment. Does he impress you, Burnivel, as the sort of man to admit to total strangers that his wife was unfaithful to him? I think his whole elaborate performance just now was designed to gain a little time; he does not know whether Rutherford needs it, but he is quite prepared to give a friend the benefit of the doubt."

He paused at the doors.

"And he succeeded in arousing you to suspicion, which was what he no doubt intended. I believe I rather admire him."

The door opened and closed behind him. A swelling rush of sound, many voices commingled in greeting, many shoulders receiving a hail of well-meant slaps, many neatly shod feet progressing down the corridor beyond, burst in upon the silence of the lecture theatre.

"The ruddy meeting's begun," Burnivel said. Then, with a sudden outraged flare of his sense of what was decent and fitting: "The way they're going on you'd think nothing ever happened in this hospital they wouldn't be told about."

"You don't think"—Grimshaw sounded worried—"they'll be told about what we've just been saying? I mean, Professor Honeychurch wouldn't be likely to talk to anyone?"

"Wouldn't matter much if he did," Burnivel snarled. "It can't be any news to Rutherford that he's got to watch his step, and Garside's not the sort to cut and run; it wouldn't be showy enough. Now, let's do some work. Pair them off, Grimshaw." Seeing his colleague looking nonplussed at this order, he said not unkindly, "Start with them one at a time if you like, and then we'll put them in pairs and see where we get."

"Pemberton," Grimshaw began, licking his lips nervously. "He hasn't any motive as far as we know, and he seems to be about the nearest thing to a friend Sandeman had. He had an opportunity, though not much of one, just ten minutes in the course of the evening—unless he crept out again later when Honeychurch was asleep. And his wife, of course. But he couldn't have pinched the book."

Burnivel nodded. "Go on."

"Ainsworth could have pinched the book. He had plenty of time to kill Sandeman or nab the child. He didn't like Sandeman, but there doesn't seem to be any more to it than that. Rutherford—"

"You can skip Rutherford," Burnivel said, "except to remember that he's the only one who might have done it all by himself, including the kidnapping note. And we can add one more thing to his account—" He showed Grimshaw the photograph he had found in Sandeman's flat. "God knows why Sandeman had it; but put it together with his big bank account and it might spell blackmail. And to make things more difficult we can put down blackmail as a possible motive for every one of these people now. Carry on, my boy; you're doing fine."

"Garside had a motive: we don't know whether he had an opportunity or not. He couldn't have got *Kidnapped*."

"Do you know anything about his wife's suicide?" Burnivel asked. "There wasn't anything queer about it, was there? I mean, he couldn't have pushed her off the platform himself?"

"Oh, no. I was at the inquest. I knew this morning I'd heard the name somewhere. No, he wasn't on the station—he had to be fetched down to the infirmary."

Burnivel had the grace to look a little ashamed. He said brusquely, "Let's go on."

"I can't think of anyone else."

"You've left Henchard out," Burnivel reminded him.

"He knew the child and Sandeman, and we don't know what he was up to late last night."

"He couldn't have pinched the book," Grimshaw said.

"That's true enough. Well, let's put them in pairs."

"Rutherford and Garside," Grimshaw began.

"That's the most likely," Burnivel agreed, "though it has to be a bit more subtle than I made out. What about Rutherford and Ainsworth?"

"Ainsworth wouldn't keep shoving Rutherford forward if he were really his accomplice," Grimshaw said uncertainly. "Unless he meant to leave him holding the baby."

"Anyway, it's quite a possible combination. Pemberton and Rutherford as a pair doesn't make sense; nor does Pemberton and Ainsworth. Pemberton and Garside is out because of the book. I can't fit Pemberton with anybody."

"Henchard doesn't fit either," Grimshaw said. "He doesn't know any of these people."

"Well, could *he* have managed alone? Or could Pemberton?"

"I shouldn't think Henchard could. He's pretty old to go lugging a big child about. And there's the book, of course. Pemberton's tall and looks in good shape, but he couldn't have got the book either, and he wouldn't have had time to get rid of the child if he killed Sandeman while Ainsworth was with Professor Honeychurch."

"No," said Burnivel, and was silent for a moment. Then, as if he had suddenly made up his mind, he went on, "And we'd better not forget Professor Honeychurch, either."

"Honeychurch!" Grimshaw looked taken aback. "But that's impossible! He's been so helpful...." His voice trailed off.

"That's no reason," Burnivel said. "It might suit him to find out which way the wind's blowing. He admits he hated Sandeman, he turned up in a queer way last night, he noticed the postbox at the gates—and he could have slipped out of Pemberton's house when they were all asleep, easier than Pemberton himself could, being downstairs."

"But he couldn't have done it by himself," Grimshaw protested. "There's the book, to start with. He wouldn't have known the Bannister child was in the hospital, so he couldn't have come with the note prepared, and he couldn't have disposed of Tom Bryant if he'd kidnapped him."

"All right," Burnivel said. "Let's give him an accomplice too, while we're about it. Pemberton might do; it doesn't solve the book part of the problem, though. And he didn't know any of the others before last night. No, I don't think we have to worry about him after all. Now, let's look into their horrible pasts and see if any of them looks like fair game to a blackmailer."

"They're as dull as ditchwater," Grimshaw said with regret, "on the surface anyway. Except Ainsworth, who seems to have got around a lot of places in the States."

"Ainsworth: I'll have to see him." Burnivel made a note. "He had supper with Sandeman a couple of nights ago. Drat! There's someone at the door. Tell them to go away."

But it was Pemberton, and he would not go away. He had, he insisted, matter of the utmost importance to divulge. Matter, he said, on which the whole case might hinge. Grimshaw let him in.

FOURTEEN

Honeychurch, drifting along a covered passage on a babbling tide of paediatricians, soon discovered that ill news had travelled both fast and far; and had undergone a little distortion in the process, as is the way with all things moving rapidly through space if the newer physics is to be believed. This passage led—so said a number of nicely stencilled signs—to a clinical demonstration in the Outpatient Department, but it would have surprised none of these urgently mobile, largely talkative persons if it had ultimately debouched at the foot of a scaffold—so alive with the anticipation of unspeakable disasters was their present mood. Tuppenny blood runs in their veins, Honeychurch thought with foreboding. Perhaps the direction of so much professional acumen to the needs of the very young tended to keep his colleagues permanently at the mental level of a bright child—a Bryant, say, or a Bannister—with a hankering after crude violence hidden insecurely in the background. Voices familiar to him, and voices entirely unknown, subdued or strident, knowledgeable or enquiring, replete with information or hungering after recondite details swelled into a steady hum as if a monstrous swarm of bees had here elected to follow out their matriarchal rites.

"—suppose you've heard about Sandeman?—"

"—in the shrubbery, they tell me—"

"—with the back of his head in a horrid mess—"

138

"—confoundedly slow about making an arrest as usual—"

"—apparently there's not much doubt about *who*—"

"—you saw the bobby at the gates?—"

"—naturally they aren't taking any chances—"

"—some boy or other, a juvenile psychotic, they say—"

"—went for the ward sister with a penknife—"

"—emptied a bottle of lead lotion into the ward maid's tea—"

"—bashed Pemberton's brains out with a bedpan—"

"—a dagger—"

"—a shotgun—"

"—perchloride of mercury—"

"—a heavy blunt instrument—"

"—curare. Terribly dangerous things these modern drugs. Two-edged swords—"

"—a two-edged sword they keep for the older boys to play with—"

"—terribly dangerous—"

"—a great loss—"

"—a sacrifice on the altar of science—"

"—and the place is absolutely crawling with plain-clothesmen. Look, there's one—"

Honeychurch, thus embarrassingly singled out as being a minion of the law, had to admit the fairness of this arbitrary pigeonholing. A plainclothesman was what he had most surely become in the crowded hours since he had risen unwillingly from Pemberton's camp bed: one who assumes the simplest and most deceptive form of camouflage and stalks about unnoticed in the hope of garnering a little knowledge from the incautious or candid. He subjected himself to a species of examination. Had he taken advantage of his protective coloration to extract confessions from others of his kind? No; everything he had learnt had been freely volunteered. Had he handed over to the police such snippets of information as had come his way? No, or only if he were fully persuaded that to do so would be in the informant's best interests. Had his presence, in short, perceptibly altered the odds against Sandeman's murderer? He thought not. Was he on the side of the police? Did he wish justice to be done?

He stood still and thought deeply. No, the pursuit, the capture, the punishment of the guilty by due process of law were all alike indifferent to him. But the failures of justice, the rare but possible miscarriage, the hasty word, the telling circumstance—these were his prime and immediate concern. It mattered less that Sandeman's murderer should hang than that the innocent should go free.

Honeychurch moved on, confounding the gapers and eyebrow-raisers with his sleepy, amiable smile: over their shoulders he had glimpsed a possible ally. Henchard's head, shining like a good deed in a naughty world, signalled the proximity of a mind nicely attuned to his own. But the chaste, rosy cupola was well in front of him, was already passing through open doors into the wider spaces beyond. A moment later Honeychurch also achieved this desirable goal: he looked round, but the psychiatrist's head was no longer to be seen. When Honeychurch eventually picked him up again, he was talking to Pemberton with every appearance of polite affability. Honeychurch turned away, found a quiet corner, and took a broad survey of the feast prepared, the table spread.

Off the central hall opened a number of consulting rooms, a casualty department, a suite of offices for almoners and the like. The consulting rooms, like so many booths at a bank holiday fair, housed exhibits ranging from the mildly disordered to the frankly grotesque. Over each door was a placard announcing what might be found within; the stout and voluble Porter lounging under a notice bearing the evocative word GARGOYLISM needed only a megaphone to assume the full glory of the itinerant barker.

Honeychurch had long passed that stage of his career when nature's grosser ineptitudes held any particular charm for him. To this exhibit he nevertheless made his way: and expressed a polite interest in the cases displayed. Porter blustered, shuffled, and swallowed like a bear offered a currant bun on the end of an umbrella. Good-natured, rather diffident, and possibly a coward, Honeychurch decided. Transparent into the bargain, and no murderer.

Latter-day Odysseus, he lumbered heavily on. At the next door, the sirens sang most winningly. Peebles lurked in the farthest corner of the room, his hands full of papers, his brain full of the most recent work. The demonstration was well arranged; his cases were well chosen, dwarfs of the pituitary type, fragile exquisite little creatures of a miniature physical perfection. Honeychurch felt the stirrings of an old interest and talked to Peebles for some time—heard the reluctant admission that the graphs, charts, and diagrams had taken him the best part of a month's work, culminating in six hours' grind the night before, with his wife in tears and his baby howling. Honeychurch expunged this name too from an unwritten list; so much industrious worthiness, such patient ephemeral toil, could not go hand in hand with that inexplicable mixture of impulse and calculation that seemed the hallmark of Sandeman's murderer.

Exhibit number three was surgical; in the fourth and last room on this side of the hall were dermatological conditions of a rarity so compelling that Honeychurch felt obliged to accord them a swift scrutiny. Saturated with the appearances, naked-eye and microscopic, of epiloia and the still more remote horrors of xeroderma pigmentosum, he returned to the central hall in time to hear Ainsworth's penetrating yelp of laughter from the door opposite. He was talking to Garside, and Garside was obviously regaling him with an account—slightly heightened, no doubt, for greater effect—of his recent skirmish with Burnivel. Honeychurch threaded his way towards them and passed Henchard, released now from Pemberton and making at top speed for the room Honeychurch had just left. They exchanged smiles and greetings. In such a crowd and at such a moment, more was impossible. It was equally impossible to talk to Garside: he was displaying some of Sandeman's cases with an offhand authority that failed to disguise an obvious distaste for the subject—helminth infestation.

"This year's star attraction," Ainsworth explained. "This way to the tomb, or—their worm dieth not. Can we sell you any information on the higher parasites?"

Honeychurch shuddered and moved away. "*Really* drastic purgation," Garside's voice murmured behind him, discussing therapy with an ardent seeker after truth. "Rhubarb is useless, quite useless...jalap...scammony ...the leaves of the bastard fig tree..."

At last he saw what he had been looking for. Beyond the title LIPOIDOSES Rutherford was sitting over a microscope and talking to an earnest Indian. He looked up as Honeychurch came in and smiled—rather perfunctorily, Honeychurch thought; indeed, his whole manner was absent, as if since the morning circumstances had weighed heavily upon him. His three cases were by any standards interesting: at the Indian gentleman's request he launched out into a demonstration of their clinical features and a close discussion of the disorders of lipoid metabolism. Honeychurch asked to look at some of the specimens and watched Rutherford extracting the slide and replacing it with another, moving the new one under the low power of the microscope in search of a truant group of cells. Absorbed, lost to his surroundings, he expounded the mysteries of fat storage in the tissues, and Honeychurch listened as if it were all quite new to him. Capable—decidedly capable, he was thinking. How unfair that one should be surprised at meeting a man with a generally developed mind—and what a comment on our age of glorified technology! But his chain of concentration was broken, his attention strayed—fatally, in the event. His eyes wandered down over Rutherford's shapeless white coat, past a breast-pocket bristling with fountain pens, propelling pencils, rulers, and torches, to a second and even more distended pocket. Here a stethoscope, a patellar hammer, a pharmacopoeia, a pocketbook, and a tuning fork found room and to spare; and amongst them was another object, and one by no means so well-suited to the time and the occasion.

Honeychurch was not accustomed to minor criminal practices. It was therefore all the more remarkable that on this occasion he put out a large but always gentle hand, allowed his fingers to close lightly on the thing he wanted, and withdrew it quickly and with minimum of fuss. Belatedly he looked behind him. The three children on their couches were all remote in the inarticulate world of early infancy; the nurse in charge of them was showing their notes to the Indian. There was no one to give him away. He hid his ill-gotten gains swiftly in his own capacious pocket and tried to attend to what Rutherford was saying. He was amazed at himself; he might even have replaced the little book if Rutherford had not at this moment slid off his stool and offered him the microscope.

Honeychurch too his place. He heard himself say—a

142

little abruptly, perhaps, since Rutherford was looking at him in some wonder: "Have many people been in here this afternoon?"

"A fair number. There's a rather ghoulish concentration on what should have been Sandeman's exhibit, and I seem to be running it a close second. I suppose the bulk of the visitors have been in and out."

"Pemberton? Or Ainsworth, or Garside? Or Henchard? Or Crisp?"

Rutherford was staring at him now in complete bewilderment. The Indian had left them.

"Who's Henchard? Oh, I know, the psychiatrist. I wouldn't know him if I saw him. Yes, all the others have been in. Why?"

"Were any of them alone with you?" Honeychurch demanded.

"Pemberton was—for about ten minutes. And Ainsworth helped me carry the slides over from my room. We were in here for twenty minutes or so before the other people started coming. Garside only slipped in for a moment—he had to read up something about Sandeman's worms rather quickly."

There was someone else in the room. Not a paediatrician, not a parent: not anyone accustomed to the inside of a hospital: someone who regarded patients and microscopes and doctors alike with steady and ill-founded suspicion. Rutherford addressed him with a perceptible trace of defiance.

"These cases illustrate two different types of disturbance of lipoid metabolism. The little girl has Letterer-Siwe's disease—the twin boys have an ill-defined type of xanthomatosis."

The man shifted his weight uneasily from one foot to the other.

"Is one of you gentlemen Dr. Rutherford?"

"My name's Rutherford."

"Would you mind coming with me a moment, sir? Inspector Burnivel would like a word with you."

"He can come and see me here," Rutherford said quietly.

"Inspector Burnivel thought you might prefer to see him privately," the man said, plainly embarrassed. "It's a bit difficult, you see, sir. Just one of us coming down here, as it were me, might pass for any sort of a visitor; but people do talk so, and if the inspector himself were to come—"

Rutherford smiled as if this example of Burnivel's elephantine tact somehow touched him. He turned to Honeychurch.

"Would you mind very much, sir, asking Ainsworth if he'd take over?"

They were gone. Honeychurch, deeply disturbed, stood a moment by the microscope, looking down at the discarded slides without seeing them. Then he went in search of Ainsworth, his fingers still curled round the adventures of David Balfour and Alan Breck.

FIFTEEN

"Quite a crowd you've got here to-day, sir."

"Quite a crowd."

"Very seasonable weather for the time of year."

"Very."

Conversation languished; it could hardly do otherwise. Rutherford was preoccupied and his escort oddly bashful. They walked side by side up the long covered way that joined the new building and the old. Cypresses to the left, a creamy tide of apple blossom to the right, followed their progress through window after window. The passage was paved with stones: Rutherford found himself reverting to a childhood habit, taking elaborate precautions to avoid treading on the lines between them. If he went the whole way without taking a false step, Burnivel merely wanted to ask him a supplementary question or two; if he slipped up, then this was a shallowly disguised arrest, and shortly a number of new and upleasant experiences would lie in wait for him. There would be—presumably—newspapermen, warnings, statements, fingerprints, lawyers, even in due course prison and a trial. He shook his head with a sudden spurt of impatience: these things simply do not happen. There is *habeas corpus*, there is the elementary right of any man to be considered innocent until proven guilty, there is—there was the plainclothesman looking sideways at him, his face the very picture of mournful concern. It needed only this to precipitate him for a brief moment into a species of panic. His mind, racing past possibilities, saw certain chances—a half-open door leading to the orchard, a corridor connecting this one to the dispensary. In any sort of chase he would have the advantage; he knew every confusing detail of the hospital's topography, and his escort would hardly be likely to whip out a gun and take a potshot at him between the apple trees or over the medicine bottles. But the moment and the temptation passed. If the plainclothesman had had any suspicion of what was going through his charge's mind he did not show it: instead, he opened the door of the lecture theatre.

Burnivel and Grimshaw, officers of the law, occupied the lecturer's dais and achieved a certain awfulness merely by virtue of its height. But Burnivel got up, came round the bench, offered Rutherford a cigarette, puffed furiously at a pipe himself. Not thus do inquisitors behave; Rutherford lurched once more out of threatening fantasy into a reality not much more reassuring. He waited, refusing the cigarette. Silence seemed likely to be protracted, and at last he broke it himself, seeing no reason why he should be further unnerved by a useless suspense.

"You wanted to see me?"

"It's a bit difficult," Burnivel admitted with heartwarming frankness. "Fact is—we've been told—look, will you turn out your pockets for us?"

Rutherford looked at him blankly.

"I can't make you do it," Burnivel said, "without making a charge, which I'm not prepared to do; I can't compel you to show me what you've got—let alone submit you to a proper search." He paused, breathing heavily. "You can see it puts me in a very awkward position."

"What am I supposed to have in my pockets?" Rutherford asked mildly.

"A copy of *Kidnapped*," Burnivel said. "Robert Louis Stevenson's book."

"Well, I haven't. I don't possess such a thing. Still, if you want to be sure—"

He took off his white coat and began to unload it on to the bench. Then he glanced at Burnivel and emptied his other pockets as well. Burnivel pounced upon the pocketbook and the pharmacopoeia, only to discard them as peremptorily. There was nothing else to claim his attention.

Rutherford picked up his possessions one at a time, lingering over it, because he wanted to think. Behind this apparently pointless demand there must be some glimmer of purpose; he had a right to some explanation.

"Perhaps you wouldn't mind telling me what all this is about?"

Burnivel sat on the bench and swung his legs with a cheerful ferocity. He picked a fragment of card from the odd papers around him and handed it over. It was the kidnapping note. Rutherford read it.

"I still don't see."

"I'll tell you some of it," Burnivel said obligingly. "You see the word 'kidnapped' on the card? It's been cut out of the page heading of a book. A copy of *Kidnapped* has been missed from one of the wards. You and Mr. Ainsworth and Dr. Sandeman himself are the only people who went in there about the right date. And someone told us you were going around with it in your pocket."

"But that's fantastic; if I'd made up that message, I wouldn't carry the thing about with me."

"You aren't carrying it about," Burnivel pointed out. "I suppose you won't tell us where you've dumped it?"

"How can I? I haven't had it."

"Good." Burnivel was almost aglow with satisfaction. "Morgan"—he turned to the plainclothesman—"go back to wherever you found Dr. Rutherford, will you, and have a good hunt round."

Morgan left them.

"You're wasting his time," Rutherford said. "I've told you I never had the book. I suppose I'm not entitled to ask who gave you your information?"

"I have to protect my witness." Burnivel said.

"Then you really believe that I—" He stumbled on the words and looked away.

Burnivel relented; he could afford to be generous.

"It wouldn't be right for me to tell you, though I don't think you'd be likely to go off and do the party any harm. After all, he's not your real enemy."

"Stop talking in riddles," Rutherford said. "What do you mean, my real enemy?"

"If you and our witness are both speaking the truth,

147

somebody must have planted that book on you." Burnivel spoke with a kind of deliberate half-regretful contempt.

Dimly, Rutherford recalled something that had happened not long ago, not far away—Honeychurch for some reason abandoning a discussion of the lipoidoses to ask whether anyone had been alone with him. *Honeychurch.*

He said wildly: "Then somebody must have taken it away again; I tell you I don't know anything about it."

Burnivel shook his head.

"It's no use our arguing and losing our tempers. I can't prove anything and know it. If you'd had the book on you, I'd have had to charge you, though"—he permitted himself a grin—"God alone knows what with. Pinching it from the ward, I suppose. Well, that wouldn't have done us any good."

"I don't see that it would have done you much harm," Rutherford said, with only the barest hint of sarcasm.

Burnivel glanced at him sharply.

"I want something better than that. How long have you been wearing that white coat?"

"Since Thursday morning. I didn't put it on till after lunch today, though."

"Could anybody have got at it?"

"Well, yes—I suppose so. I left it on the door of my room over the way when I went to the library last night, and for quite a long time this morning there was nobody in there."

"Did you look at the pockets when you put it on?"

Rutherford thought a moment.

"No; I don't think so. I was in a hurry. I doubt if I'd have noticed one thing among so many."

"So it might have been there hours," Burnivel said, "or it might have been there just a few minutes."

"Or it might not have been there at all."

"It was there," Burnivel said. "Who's been in that room with you this afternoon?"

Rutherford told him what he had told Honeychurch, and added Honeychurch himself, after some hesitation.

"Well, that doesn't get us anywhere," Burnivel said. "Stand still a moment." He got off the bench, drew a wallet out of his pocket and walked round behind Rutherford. "Did you feel anything?" he asked.

Rutherford shook his head, and wondered if his person

148

had been similarly violated once or even twice before; the thought repelled him.

"Of course, I'm pretty good at this game," Burnivel admitted. "Still, it's quite possible that one of the people you mentioned could have done it. Well, if they were trying to pin something on you, they've failed, so far. That means they may try again. And that'll give me my chance."

"Forgive me if I seem obtuse," Rutherford said slowly and handed back the wallet. "Do you intend me to act as the bait in the mousetrap while the murderer tries to make it look as if I killed Sandeman?"

"You catch on quick," said Burnivel. "Of course, it may not work out like that. I can't say. But if the idea is to let you take the rap, there's a fair chance he'll have another shot at it. People like that won't leave well alone."

"Look, do you mind leaving me out of this? I can't very well prevent whoever it is from leaving his visiting cards on me, but it's another thing to put myself out deliberately to be framed—is that the word? Suppose your murderer did the job properly next time? I've no alibi, and some people seem to think I had a motive—a few more scraps of circumstantial evidence, and I can see myself being in for a very embarrassing time of it. I've no doubt about what the outcome would be, but I'd rather not go through the preliminaries."

Burnivel shrugged his shoulders and lit his pipe again. "You've no choice. You don't have to do anything except go your own sweet way. If anything happens, one of my men will be there to watch you, that's all."

"You're going to have me followed?"

"It's for your own good," Burnivel said tartly. "Why should he get away with it? It was his idea in the first place, wasn't it?"

Rutherford had been standing, absently replacing odds and ends in his pockets without noticing what he was doing: now he sat down. Meeting Burnivel's narrow mistrustful eyes on the level was not so easy; these were eyes that were trying to read conspiracy and collusion into his own. I have nothing to fear, he told himself; but since he suspected that he had a good deal to fear, this inner voice was wonderfully devoid of consolation.

149

Against his will he asked: "Whose idea? Who's trying to get away with what? Or mustn't I ask that either?"

But Burnivel was not to be put on the defensive in any fight carried out on his territory and with his own weapons. His counterattack was clearly planned with an eye to the strategic value of surprise.

"Why did Dr. Sandeman have a photo of you hidden in his room?"

Absurdly, he heard himself repeating, "A photo? Of me? I can't imagine"—and indeed he could not.

"Dr. Sandeman had a great deal of money in his bank account, money that can't be explained."

"Well, it didn't come out of mine. Registrars are hardly paid enough to make them a standing temptation to blackmailers."

"Who said anything about blackmail?" Burnivel seized his advantage.

"It's the kind of activity Sandeman would have indulged in," Rutherford said promptly—too promptly.

"H'm. Why did Ainsworth have supper with Sandeman three nights before he was killed?"

If this were a question at random, it was a singular chance that sent it at such a moment. And if it were not, Burnivel must be even more competent than he had feared. Was it necessary, he asked himself, to protect Ainsworth to the point of severe personal discomfiture? Not, clearly, if he could make himself believe that Ainsworth had devised this clumsy attempt to incriminate him: and paradoxically, it was his conviction that the American was innocent of this lesser misdeed that finally assured him that he must be equally innocent of the greater. He fell back upon a useful and genuine ignorance.

"I didn't know he did. Ainsworth doesn't discuss all his affairs with me. Hadn't you better ask him?"

"Don't worry, I will. Did you know that Garside's wife was Sandeman's mistress? Or doesn't Garside discuss his affairs with you either?"

It was as well for Rutherford that Morgan came back at this moment to report his failure. For after his first startled exclamation—remembering Sandeman, remembering Helena, he could hardly help being startled at so improbable a suggestion—he needed desperately an interval of peace; peace to decide whether this hotch-potch of demands represented a conscious effort on Burnivel's part to confuse him—or whether Burnivel too was blundering about in a mist of conjecture, trusting to luck that the right path would magically appear before him if only he tried every point of the compass in turn. But to be compelled to fence, to hedge, to wonder if a sincere reaction of surprise appeared exaggerated and false, this complicated and futile exercise fretted him to a point where he could almost have welcomed a hand falling on his shoulder, an official warning in his ear.

"I understand Tom Bryant was your patient?" Burnivel had dismissed Morgan with the curtest of nods.

"Yes." Rutherford unkindly avoided the appropriate start of guilty astonishment. "Have you found Tom? Or had any news of him?"

Burnivel's face was sombre.

"Nothing's come in yet."

"You've searched in all the obvious places? Because, of course, he hasn't been kidnapped, has he?" He looked quickly at the inspector. "You didn't fall for that story for a moment. What do you think has happened to the child?"

Burnivel said with absolute finality, "He's dead; he has to be dead. He knew who nabbed him, or enticed him out, whichever it was. It wouldn't be safe to leave him alive. We'll find his body in a day or two."

Rutherford repeated the word "enticed" slowly to himself as if he were trying out the sound of it, but this was not what he was doing. He had seen at last what Burnivel was getting at, and the sight appalled him. By the merest chance Tom had been in one of his beds; by an etraordinary distortion of their fortuitous relationship Burnivel was suggesting that without resorting to brute force he, Rutherford, might have extracted this child from a bed on the balcony and carried him off—a trusting and unwary victim—to wherever he could most conveniently dispose of a small body. He shivered as if a chill wind were blowing about him.

"So in addition to bashing Sandeman's head in, I lured a child out of the ward and killed him in cold blood—is that what you think?"

"No; I don't," Burnivel said with finality. "You wouldn't have done that. You're not the kind."

151

"Thank you," Rutherford said. This time there was no irony whatever in his voice.

"But someone did it. Now here's my point. If you killed Sandeman and someone helped you do it by faking up this kidnapping business, this someone—"

"Let's call him my 'accomplice,'" Rutherford said. A sort of illogical calm took him in hand now that the words had finally been spoken.

"Your accomplice, then," said Burnivel, "isn't as well disposed towards you as you think. He's seen all along that things could be so arranged as to make it look as if you'd engineered the whole thing yourself. There's only one other person who knows he's involved, and that's the child. So the child dies—in cold blood, as you say." He spoke earnestly, tapping his pipe on the bench to emphasise his argument. "That wasn't what you'd intended. And now he's trying to fix it so you carry the can for both murders. Wouldn't it make things easier if you told me everything?"

"You're wasted in your present job," Rutherford said and meant it. "You should be a writer: you have an amazingly vivid imagination."

"I know." Burnivel crumpled suddenly, sadly. "I haven't a shred of proof."

They sat in silence, looking at each other. Burnivel began to suck his knuckles abstractedly. The action must have reminded him of something; reinforced as it were by reminiscence, his customary truculence returned.

"You can go now. I don't want to keep you hanging about. You might let us know," he added hopefully, "if anything queer happens. If that book turns up, for instance."

"Would it be in my best interests to tell you?" Rutherford asked. He stood up, smiling ruefully. "I'll make a bargain with you if you like. If you tell me who told you I'd got that book, I'll let you know if it turns up."

Burnivel gave the quick, odd grin that made his face suddenly benevolent, like the fox at the beginning of a fable.

"All right. I'll tell you. We'll be keeping an eye on you, so you won't have much chance of getting at him. It was your own dear professor."

"Honeychurch?" said Rutherford with a sinking of the heart.

"Pemberton," said Burnivel.

He had forgotten about the clinical demonstration; even if he had remembered, it was doubtful if he would have gone back. Such satisfaction as he might have got from watching Pemberton's reaction to his safe return could be left for some other time. His immediate need, now that a closed door intervened between himself and Burnivel, was to be alone for a time. He crossed the orchard: at the door of the Department of Child Health he paused for a moment and looked back. Morgan dodged ineffectually behind a tree and froze into immobility. Rutherford waved to him; they might have been playing grandmother's footsteps.

He made for his own room, heard voices behind the door, and was suddenly very angry. But the habit of anger was alien to him: if there were people there, presumably they had some reason to offer for their presence and would leave if he asked them to. He turned the handle and went in.

"Hallo, Bill," said Garside. "You've come at exactly the right moment. Professor Honeychurch has succeeded in convincing me that you ought to be dead. I was beginning to be quite worried."

SIXTEEN

Honeychurch said, "I found this in your pocket. I should have left it there."

Rutherford took the book and flicked the pages over absently.

"It seems rather silly to thank you—" he said at last.

"There is nothing to thank me for. I acted on impulse, and I should have governed the impulse. I thought I should be saving you a little trouble, and now it seems probable that my thoughtlessness has merely lifted you out of the frying pan and into the fire."

"Whatever the fire's like, it can't be worse than the frying pan."

Honeychurch looked grave.

"It was as bad as that?"

"Bad enough. . . . Burnivel thinks if he gives me enough rope I'll hang myself and save him the trouble. If I'd had the book, he'd have arrested me."

"It might have been better if he had," Honeychurch said. "At least I should not feel myself to blame if anything happens to you."

"I don't understand—"

"Sit down," Garside said. "We've a good deal to tell you. Have you any tea over here, Bill? I had a very early lunch, and it must be nearly four."

"No tea; there's some coffee on the shelf, if you want

it. But there'll be some sort of tea in the refectory, won't there?"

Garside and Honeychurch exchanged glances.

"Do you really want—" Garside began with some hesitation.

"To show myself in public? Yes, I think I do. I want to see Pemberton's face."

Again Garside looked at Honeychurch, this time in open triumph. It was left to Honeychurch to ask what especial pleasure Rutherford could anticipate from the sight of Pemberton.

"He told the police I had this in my pocket." He tapped *Kidnapped* gently.

"It looks as if my guess were right," Garside said.

"Do you think Pemberton murdered Sandeman and tired to incriminate me?" Rutherford was clearly startled.

"That wouldn't be nearly subtle enough," Garside said. "Perhaps the professor ought to explain. It was his idea in the first place. I just happened to drop in at the same moment. Look. I'll make some coffee."

"If you want to." Rutherford hoisted himself up on to his bench and bent over to fill a beaker with water from the tap.

Honeychurch began to tell his story; it was straightforward enough, beginning from his moment of inspiration by the microscope: "When it occurred to me that if someone had put the book where I found it, someone must bear you considerable malice. And then I hazarded a guess."

"He guessed," Garside said, applying a match to the Bunsen burner, "that whoever killed Sandeman probably meant to kill you."

Rutherford looked from òne to the other.

"Surely one wouldn't make a mistake about a thing like that?"

"The drive would have been in heavy shadow last night," Garside said. "Someone waiting for you might have pitched on Sandeman quite easily. You and he were much the same height: at night, it wouldn't have been so obvious that you're dark and he's fair."

Rutherford still looked sceptical.

"But the single fact most in favour of your being the intended victim is the kidnapping note and the rest of it."

155

Honeychurch nodded. "Yes, indeed. If anyone planned to kill Sandeman, the kidnapping hoax would be entirely redundant. We know that there are a large number of people here who hated Sandeman and whose presence would keep the issue confused; the murderer has been able to arouse a fair amount of suspicion towards you with no great difficulty. Why should he embark on so ambitious a plan when something simpler would do? But now look at it in relation to yourself. You have no personal enemies except Sandeman—if you were found violently dead, Sandeman would have been the most likely suspect. The only way to kill you without his being implicated would be to make your death appear quite irrelevant to the situation inside the hospital—hence the kidnapping scheme. You were to be the victim of a gang of criminals; nothing would have seemed more natural than that you should have attempted to intercept them."

"We will spare your blushes," said Garside kindly, "but without any false modesty, you can hardly deny that you would be a little more likely to tackle a job of that kind than poor Martin."

"Would I?" said Rutherford. He considered a moment as if the point were of great importance to him. Then he met Honeychurch's eye levelly. "You think that Sandeman himself planned to kill me?"

"Exactly so," Honeychurch beamed. "The coffee is just to the left of where you are looking, Garside."

"And there's a bottle of milk behind the centrifuge," Rutherford said, without turning his head. "Still, Sandeman can hardly have committed suicide; so he must have had an accomplice who killed him by accident and kidnapped Tom Bryant instead of Teddy Bannister. It all sounds rather—well, careless, doesn't it?"

Honeychurch shook his head and explained why there need have been no error in the abduction of the Bryant child. Meanwhile, Garside poured out the coffee and distributed the cups.

"Yes; I see that." Rutherford was as ready to accept Honeychurch's explanation as Burnivel had been. "That makes sense. But who's supposed to be Sandeman's accomplice? It's a sobering thought that a man never knows his own enemies until a multiplicity of them try to do him in."

"The thought doesn't seem to be sobering you unduly," Garside pointed out. "As a matter of fact, you seem to be getting more cheerful every moment. I can't imagine why."

"Can't you? Wait until Burnivel tells you you've arranged to hand a child over to his murderer: after that almost anything comes as a relief. I'd got used to the idea that Sandeman hated me quite a time ago; it doesn't even surprise me very much that he was prepared to go that far. Who else besides Sandeman?"

"Pemberton," said Garside promptly.

"I wouldn't have thought he disliked me that much."

"I'm quite sure he doesn't," Honeychurch said with decision. "Garside thinks it was professional jealousy."

Rutherford laughed outright. Even Garside smiled, though unwillingly.

"Sandeman and Pemberton are both good enough at their jobs, but you'll be better one day, and they know it. Sandeman would loathe to think that you of all people would beat him at his own game—"

"Bloody nonsense," Rutherford said amiably. "I'll never be any good at research, you know that as well as I do, and so does Pemberton—and Sandeman told me so often enough. You're altogether too hopeful, Julian."

"No, seriously"—Garside sounded genuinely angry— "why depreciate yourself? You don't shake in your shoes every time Pemberton raises his voice or walk on air when he deigns to tell you you've done something right once in a way."

"I don't have to," Rutherford said. "I'm leaving at the end of the month." He got off the bench and poured the remains of his coffee down the sink. "No," he repeated. "I can believe that Sandeman might have wanted me killed—but if he did, I bet it was for some quite ordinary reason. And you don't give Pemberton credit for any sense at all. He'd be as pleased as Punch if he discovered an infant Fleming: think of the credit he'd get for it." He looked at Honeychurch, nodding his full acceptance of this estimate. "Only he hasn't a Fleming; he hasn't even a Sandeman now. One ought to feel decently sorry for him; he's probably the only person in the world inclined to shed an honest tear over Martin's grave."

"Well, that's true enough as far as I'm concerned."

Garside sounded exasperated. "And it's simply confirmation of what I've been saying. Sandeman could have made Pemberton do anything."

"Not murder." Rutherford was unexpectedly obstinate.

"I agree," Honeychurch said. "Thank you, not a second cup. But unfortunately there is something else besides personal feeling involved in this affair. It may be that Sandeman's accomplice felt no animosity towards you at that stage."

"That's reassuring," Rutherford said, and added quickly, "I didn't mean to be sarcastic; I'm sorry."

"Ah, but you don't know all we know," Garside said. "I shouldn't know it, but I do."

Honeychurch looked worried.

"I fear I have been guilty of a breach of confidence. You see, I happen to know that Sandeman had a very large sum of money in his possession—so large a sum that it is difficult to see how he could have come by it at all honestly."

"So Burnivel told me."

"Did he? It is tempting to think that he was a blackmailer. And it may be that he could have used his power over some unfortunate person to compel him to commit murder. Towards you, Sandeman's creature—I use the word, of course, in its archaic sense—need have felt no malice whatever."

"But if that's true, why should I be in any danger now? If this hypothetical person hoist Sandeman with his own petard he ought to be sitting pretty by now. Why should he try to get me into trouble with the police?"

"It mayn't have been as simple as the professor makes out," Garside said. "Myself, I don't believe any man would commit murder just because another man told him to. I should think Sandeman must have persuaded this chap that you knew his awful secret too. Then the murderer might have taken it upon himself to get rid of you both at one stroke—a blow on the head for Sandeman: a judicial hanging for you."

"I don't think so," Rutherford said. "Nobody could have believed a jury would convict me on the strength of that book."

"Nobody capable of thinking clearly could believe it:

158

but if you really represent a threat to the murderer, if you know something to his detriment without your being aware of it, he may be in a state of mind to try any method of getting rid of you, however risky. I repeat, Dr. Rutherford, you are in grave danger."

Honeychurch sat back, a capacious and well-meaning oracle. Rutherford picked up *Kidnapped* from the bench and for a moment held it above his pocket as if he were going to put it in. Then he changed his mind and handed it instead to Honeychurch.

"I'm going to break a promise," he said. "I told Burnivel if I came across that book I'd let him have it. But I'm not taking any chances now. I won't give him an excuse for arresting me."

It was at once evident to Honeychurch that something more than what he and Garside had suggested was in Rutherford's mind at this moment—and if he chose after their outspokenness to withold his confidence, Honeychurch might feel regret, but could not fairly blame him. He put out his hand for the book, hardly aware that he shook his head as he did so. Rutherford caught the movement, looked for a moment as if he might explain, and then thought better of it. He only said, "I shall tell Burnivel I've seen it if he asks me. He can make what likes of that," and then turned and went abruptly from the room.

Garside looked at Honeychurch, who returned the look without being at all aware of it. "Do you think—" they began simultaneously; stopped and rose as with one accord.

"One of us," Honeychurch said diffidently, "had better pass the fruits of our discussion on to Burnivel."

"It had better be me," said Garside. "Not that he'll thank me for it, I fear. But I can avoid all mention of your nefarious doings if I set my mind to it, and you could hardly manage that yourself."

"Thank you. I hoped that you would see it in that light. May I join you at tea? First of all I have to dispose of this incendiary little volume."

"Tea?" Garside said absently. "Oh, yes. The annual broadside. Meringues, éclairs, bridge rolls oozing mustard and cress. If Burnivel can find no excuse for detaining me, I shall be happy to join you in the refectory in, say, ten minutes' time."

"That should be ample."

There were two doors beyond Rutherford's on the ground floor. One was labelled PEEBLES the other GARSIDE. Having performed this elementary piece of investigation and correctly placed Pemberton's room round a bend in the corridor, Honeychurch remembered that it was at a first-floor window that he had seen Sandeman the night before. He looked covertly towards the staircase, and caution immediately if grotesquely justified itself. Footsteps could be heard descending, followed a moment later by the feet that made them just visible beyond a corner. Honeychurch squeezed himself into the recess in the wall that held Peebles's door and wished himself smaller by several inches in all dimensions. But the man coming down the stairs went straight through the door opposite them, conveying most unfairly the impression of being not only in a hurry, but in a furtive hurry. The habit of melodrama, Honeychurch reflected drily, is rapidly acquired. There had been in actual fact nothing suspicious or secretive about Ainsworth taking the steps two at a time and bolting through the door as if he had been shot from a gun; but Honeychurch, ascending at a more becoming pace, had much ado to avoid a Burnivellian grin of satisfaction—a grin, as he told himself, in the worst possible taste, and based on nothing that could afford a reasonable man just cause for mirth.

The second door was Sandeman's. It was correctly closed. The interior was as correctly bare. The scavenging police had cleared up after themselves with the most scrupulous care. If Ainsworth had indeed been in this room—and what grounds Honeychurch produce for this formidable assumption?—he had disturbed it not a jot. And that seemed unlike Ainsworth, who to be consistent should have scattered a wreckage around him as profuse as his own exemplary candour. Yet this inconsistency warmed Honeychurch's heart. He had early discovered, or so he fancied, depths to Ainsworth totally out of keeping with his ingenuousness, his breezy, noisy sentiment: allow the depths to be a little murky and the sea-bed treacherous, and might not this man pass for a false friend, one with a tiresome secret, a guilty itching that Sandeman had diagnosed correctly and treated with a loathsome circumspection?

Thus far gone in meditation, Honeychurch stood on the threshold, wondering what Ainsworth had come here to find, and whether he had found it. Some moments elapsed before he recalled his own purposes: here, bent on a poetic justice of the most blameless order, he had determined to hide the book. He looked about for a suitable spot and picked upon the filing cabinet, twin brother to Rutherford's own, as being none too subtle and therefore kindly to his conscience. What odd phonetic bias of the mind attending upon what careless prompting of the ear led him to open the "C" drawer to receive *Kidnapped* rather than the "K" one he would never be able to understand. Yet this he did; and he pulled the contents of the drawer forward and pushed the little book well down behind them, his hand encountered another book, larger in outline, slighter in bulk. He brought it out, dimly apprehending that he had succeeded where Ainsworth had failed. For this was a copy of the Cornell students' yearbook for 1944. It fell open in his hand to a page evidently much frequented: a photograph looked up at him, exposing Ainsworth for what he had been eight years earlier—a nice-looking boy, lightly clad for some bizarre variety of sport, leaning towards another youth of less decisive feature and robust frame. And it was this weaker vessel that was labelled Philip Ainsworth by a considerable caption. Sandeman's likely murderer was here identified as Peter Anderson.

Honeychurch took the book with him and went off to make a telephone call.

SEVENTEEN

If the proper study of mankind be man, then no one could have been more properly occupied during all his waking hours than Francis Henchard, a person much given to gentle observation of his fellow beings. If he chose to indulge this foible at the expense of his host of the afternoon, Cyril Pemberton had only himself to blame: offered so much absorbing clinical material, no psychiatrist worth his salt could have resisted. Henchard accepted the gift thrown in his lap with thankfulness; for at least a brief period a close inspection of Pemberton might hold at bay the turmoil of anxiety within him. About the boy Tom Bryant he scarcely dared to let himself think. The first shock of the child's loss had been bad enough: and now, if rumour were to be credited—and he had spent a considerable part of his visit listening to rumour—the police were beginning to assume that Sandeman's murderer had also done away with Tom. Henchard was perhaps the only person in the hospital who believed Tom to be still alive, and he would have found it difficult to declare on what grounds he based his opinion. He knew well enough that anything might happen to a small boy caught up in an adult intrigue—the very helplessness of the child could serve as an invitation to malignant mischance or deliberate cruelty. And this was one to whom he had stood in a special if unsatisfactory relationship; a refractory, a tantalising, a problematical boy, who had not after all been abducted by a number of criminals—rumour insisted that the police had discarded that notion once for all.

So he watched Pemberton moving about the refectory: a man doomed to reduce to uncomfortable silence nine tenths of those he approached, while the remaining tenth assiduously gaped, applauded, and bent a spiritual knee. The pity of it was, Henchard reflected, that so much useful work had to be traced to this man's industry; he well remembered this hospital ten years before Pemberton's arrival—a drab hole with a dingy reputation. Pemberton had swept the place clean, imported a new and efficient nursing staff, collected men of promise, lured Sandeman away from London, had even in a moment of rare insight imported one Rutherford, a young man whose career seemed likely to be brought to a premature close, since unflagging tireless rumour had it that on him the eyes of the law were sternly fixed. Meanwhile, Pemberton, conscious of having done his duty by society, did it most admirably by his guests: conversation openly excited in tone, frankly conjectural in tendency, melted as he drew near into a confused murmur of appreciation regarding the afternoon's arrangements. To Henchard alone had Pemberton divulged his own part in the day's undercurrent of drama: had singled out this studious male wallflower abstractedly sipping tea in a quiet corner to mention that he had found it necessary to inform the police of something that he feared was to Dr. Rutherford's discredit; under the slightest of pressures he had even disclosed exactly what information he had handed on. He had left Henchard bewildered, wondering if this constituted in the professor's own eyes a sort of grown-up equivalent of telling tales out of school, wondering too how much or how little remorse the man would feel if thanks to his agency a shameful injustice should be perpetrated. So much sense, so little sensibility, he thought, and derived a small familiar pleasure from the consciousness of a phrase well-turned.

"I have just made a telephone call."

Ainsworth, chewing rhythmically upon a currant bun, assumed the look of noncommittal interest that Honeychurch's statement seemed to require and proffered a plate of weary sandwiches.

163

"Thank you, no. An extremely expensive telephone call." Honeychurch paused. "I spoke to Eric Ziedermayr."

Ainsworth put down his bun as if it had bitten him, and looked round swiftly to satisfy himself that he alone had heard.

"Why did you do that?"

"I saw a copy of the Cornell students' yearbook for nineteen forty-four. It was in Sandeman's room. You didn't search carefully enough, Mr. Ainsworth. It must have been a very unpleasant surprise for you to find Sandeman working here, for of course he was in the States that year. No doubt he recognised you."

"What are you going to do about it?" Ainsworth asked. Cornered, he was unblushing, even perhaps indignant.

"I shall have to tell the police, unless you prefer to go to Burnivel yourself—"

Ainsworth laughed shortly and bitterly.

"Oh, I wouldn't deny you your big moment. Though I can't see what business it is of yours."

"What business!" Honeychurch was taken back by this effrontery, but only for a moment. "Of course it is my business. I thought it reasonable to warn you of my intentions; but conceal evidence of this sort I can and will not. You may not be altogether to blame for your part in Sandeman's murder, but there is no conceivable excuse for an attempt to throw suspicion on one who believes you to be his friend."

"So help me," Ainsworth said, "I haven't a clue what you're talking about. What's my shady past got to do with Sandeman's murder? Who's this friend I'm supposed to be throwing suspicion on?"

"Can you deny that Sandeman used his knowledge to force you into carrying out his orders? Didn't you visit his flat only three evenings ago?"

"Sure I did. What does that prove?"

"It proves nothing, except that your relationship to him was hardly as superficial as you would have us believe."

"Sandeman and I were buddies, is that what you think?" Ainsworth's face split into an ill-timed grin. "Well, maybe we were at that. Leastways he seemed to think so."

"He revealed his plans to you that evening," Honey-

church said severely. "I hope you were suitably horrified."

"I was *surprised*," Ainsworth corrected him. "Horrified would be pitching it a little too strong. I guess I'd
have refused if I'd had the chance, but he had me where
he wanted me. Anyway, as things turned out I had a swell
time last night."

Honeychurch found himself floundering in incredulity.
Could murder, even in these circumstances, be so lightly
underwritten? Were confessions of guilt commonly
couched in such artless terms? Was Ainsworth—a hateful
thought—perhaps insane?

He said carefully: "I am not sure we understand each
other. What proposal exactly are you referring to?"

"But I thought that was what you were getting at. He
asked me to join him in the bar at the Grand after dinner;
he said he wanted to make a night of it. But he never
turned up, so I went to the movies instead."

An overflow from the unusually munificent tea provided for the visitors had found its way into the small
lecture theatre. Grimshaw experimented thoughtfully with
a cream bun, unwilling to break into Burnivel's mood of
ferocious abstraction with the sort of conversation sacred
to this hour of the day: the great man himself had already
drunk off three cups of scalding hot tea in rapid succession, wiped his moustache, abandoned an éclair after a
single bite, and returned to a close and cheerless perusal
of his notes. Grimshaw sighed, assured himself that teapot
and hot-water jug were empty and debated whether to
arouse the contemplative Burnivel and tell him so.

"Halfhearted."

"I beg your pardon?"

"Halfhearted." Burnivel turned upon him a look of
unmistakable contempt. "Not a fool, but a bungler.
Uncertain, halfhearted."

Grimshaw, no coward soul, rose manfully to his own
defence.

"I thought I had carried out your oders satisfactorily,
Inspector Burnivel."

"Oh, not you," Burnivel said impatiently. "You're all
right, bless you. Not but what you and he haven't got a
good deal in common. You're both inexperienced at this
job. That's probably why he likes you."

"He *likes* me? Do you know who killed Sandeman?"

"Yes; I know." He leant forward: he had found a piece of pink chalk and used it to punctuate his words with a series of staccato raps on the bench. "Who," he said, "knew Sandeman before any of the others? Who made friends with the Bryant child in a few minutes and Rutherford just as quickly? *Who*"—he broke the chalk against the bench—"shouldn't have been here at all last night and was? I wish I didn't see it this way," he went on with a kind of baffled rage, "but there it is, I do. And Sandeman must have supplied all the malice behind this murder; that's the thing to hang on to, though it won't make our job any easier."

"Then you think Dr. Garside was right, and Sandeman meant to have Rutherford killed?"

Burnivel nodded briefly and blew chalk dust off his sleeve. "It's anyone's guess why—jealousy, I should think; couldn't bear to have a chap around everyone else liked. He meant to use the professor for the job and cash in on the Bannister boy's presence in the ward. So he prepared the kidnapping note himself—he could have got the book, remember—and sent it to Honeychurch to post once the job was done. Honeychurch was to ring up Rutherford, who wouldn't know his voice, and call him into hospital. Then he'd climb over the balcony and make friends with the Bryant boy. When Rutherford came up the drive Honeychurch was to bash his skull in, and make off with the child—"

"How?" Grimshaw asked. Burnivel waved an irate hand.

"If he couldn't get him to come away of his own free will, he could have overpowered him easily enough. But, anyway, it all went wrong very early on. Honeychurch rang Rutherford's place and didn't get an answer. He concluded he was in the hospital already and decided to carry on with the plan. So he climbed over the balcony and saw what was going on in the ward. I'd guess he realised from what he saw that Rutherford hated Sandeman as much as Sandeman hated Rutherford. And that gave him his idea." He paused triumphantly. "Why not kill Sandeman—who'd been blackmailing him—with Rutherford's help, using Sandeman's plan?"

He was talking so fast now that Grimshaw could hardly follow him.

"He got Rutherford to take him over to Pemberton's house, though Sandeman offered to accompany him—that was Crisp's story, wasn't it? On the way, he told Rutherford to meet him in the drive; when Pemberton had gone to bed, Honeychurch joined him and told him the whole plan. One of them—Honeychurch, it must have been, that's why the operator didn't recognise the voice—went to the nearest phone box and rang Sandeman. He probably told him the thing was done and he could go home now. Sandeman came out, they killed him and stowed his body. Then there was the child to deal with, and they had Rutherford's car. I should think they drove him up on the moors and got rid of him."

"Killed him?" Grimshaw said. "No. I don't believe it."

"I don't like it either," Burnivel said. "More likely they chloroformed him while he was asleep so he didn't get a look at either of them."

Grimshaw sat back in his chair and appeared to think. He was not in fact thinking. He felt benumbed at the duplicity of his fellow men; at Burnivel's calm acceptance of this duplicity; at the astonishing resource concealed behind Honeychurch's kindness and Rutherford's candour.

"It doesn't leave many loopholes," Burnivel said; it struck Grimshaw that his tone was almost apologetic. "And it explains one or two things that I can't explain any other way. Sandeman's having Rutherford's photo, for instance. He would have sent a copy to Honeychurch so Honeychurch would know his victim when he saw him. And it wasn't any news to Rutherford that Sandeman was a blackmailer. And Honeychurch is an older man who's probably made a lot of money in his time, and that's not true of any of the people here."

"What do we do next?" Grimshaw asked, hoping for a chance to feel the ground firm under his feet again.

"Did you notice how rattled Rutherford was when I suggested he might have turned the kid over to his murderer." Burnivel sounded suddenly excited. "I think that's the answer. I'd bet Rutherford drove the car, but Honeychurch actually got rid of Tom. And if Rutherford could be made to believe that Honeychurch killed the child, then maybe he'd turn Queen's evidence: it's worth trying. We won't trip them any other way, Grimshaw. They've stuck together like leeches so far. It's obvious that Honeychurch took the book away before Morgan got there."

"The book—" Grimshaw caught him up. "If Sandeman pinched the book and made up the note, how did it get into Rutherford's pocket?"

"Sandeman put it there himself. It wouldn't have suited his book to have Rutherford die a hero—he'd never have heard the last of it; but if that book was found a few days afterwards, when everyone was weeping and wailing, can't you see what would have happened? A dirty little rumour would have gone round that he'd been the inside man himself; to be disposed of when the kidnappers had no further use for him. I can just see how that would have struck Dr. Sandeman." He sounded so vicious that Grimshaw felt momentarily sickened. "You know, this case gets my goat. Doesn't seem right that anyone should hang for that blighter. Pour me out another cup of tea, will you?"

"There isn't any more. Shall I ring?"

"No." Burnivel stood up. "Let's go and mingle with the nobs."

And now I know, what am I going to do? Rutherford asked himself. I ought to tell Burnivel. But I don't think I shall. Why should I do his dirty work for him? It isn't as if Sandeman's murderer has done me any harm—he's more to be pitied than blamed. He even saved my life in a way, would have saved his own skin without doing me any substantial harm if Honeychurch had let things be, would surely never have killed the child if he had dared let him live: only that's past forgiveness. If they catch him, they catch him; but I want no part of it.

I suppose he did plant that book on me? Could anyone have taken such a chance? Supposing, he thought, I'd looked round just as he slipped it in? Still, no one else could have done it: except Sandeman.

He sat back, pushing the lecture notes away from him on the table with a gesture of such vehemence that they might have been Sandeman himself and his legacy of slander. On the far side of the library Morgan browsed self-consciously over a journal, his downward gaze devout as any student's. Rutherford said, "I'm going now," because it seemed rude to ignore the man. He picked up the papers and waited for Morgan to replace his journal in the rack. Killing me wouldn't have been enough for Sandeman, he was thinking: I owe his murderer more than silence.

"I want a word with you."

With such scant ceremony, Pemberton detached Garside from Peebles, Porter, and a plate of bridge rolls. Garside smiled upon him with great and ironic charm, having learnt by experience that this method of handling senior members of his staff came so naturally to Pemberton that protest would have been useless as well as embarrassing.

"Will you read Sandeman's paper after tea? Rutherford won't be able to."

"Won't he?" Garside raised his eyebrows. "Would it be out of place to ask why?"

"He's got himself involved with the police," Pemberton said brusquely. "I don't know what he's done with the notes. Perhaps you can find out."

"Wouldn't you rather ask him yourself?"

"I haven't the time."

"It shouldn't take very long," Garside murmured. "He appears to have brought them with him."

"Here we are again," said Burnivel with a horrible assumption of jollity. "Regular slap-up tea they do here, don't they? Is it always as good as this, Mr. Ainsworth?"

"No," said Ainsworth concisely.

"Do I see Professor Pemberton over there, talking to Dr. Garside?"

"You do," Honeychurch said.

"Let's join them," Burnivel said, conveying under his air of arch conviviality a set determination. "Pemberton looks like seven wet Sundays. I wonder why. Oh, that's it! He's just seen your friend Rutherford." He chuckled. "I'll bet he thinks I've been neglecting my duty."

Unwillingly carried along by his momentum, escorted by a mentally panting Grimshaw, Honeychurch and Ainsworth—an ill-assorted couple—forced themselves upon Pemberton and Garside just as Rutherford also reached them. This little condensation of people mutually antagonistic succeeded in clearing a space for itself; from its midst Burnivel's voice delivered a penetrating greeting to Garside.

"Well, you're still in the running," he announced fully aware that he held the attention of everyone in the room. "Our men checked up and no one remembers seeing you get off the train."

Garside flushed and might have protested had Burnivel not turned immediately on Pemberton.

"You needn't think your afternoon's work has been wasted. Rutherford here will tell you I did my level best to trip him."

"And but for a brilliant display of his customary guile," Garside said with an edge to his voice, "he would now be cooling his heels in a Black Maria."

"Fortunately," Honeychurch appended, "no guile was necessary. No explanations were necessary. Circumstances forestalled explanation."

"Circumstances also render apologies superfluous." Garside had recovered himself. He muted his voice to a sepulchral kindliness. "You may consider yourself well out of it, Pemberton."

Ainsworth looked from one to the other, a man patently bewildered, as even Honeychurch had to admit. Still, bewilderment at consequences did not automatically confer innocence of causes. And Pemberton also looked confused.

"Do I understand—Has there been a mistake? Could I have been misled?"

"You were not misled," Burnivel said.

"You can trust the evidence of your senses," Garside said.

"You were absolutely right," Honeychurch said, "only you failed to allow for the operations of time."

"Not of time only." Burnivel fixed Honeychurch with a boldly questioning stare.

"Not, as the inspector remarks, of time only. Between the moment of your discovery of the book in Rutherford's pocket and the moment of his apprehension by an officer of the law, some agency, human or divine, had seen fit to remove it."

"What book?" Ainsworth was impatient, furious. "What the hell are you all talking about?"

"Walk aside with me," Garside said, "and I will tell you."

"Sandeman's talk," Rutherford said, holding out the file to Pemberton. "Do you still want me to read it?"

"If you wouldn't mind, Rutherford." Pemberton's tone was almost humble.

"It's all right," Rutherford said. "You did what you thought best. I don't like you any the better for it, but you needn't let that disturb you."

"That's the spirit," Burnivel said heartily. "No hard feelings, no recriminations. Best let bygones be bygones and bury the hatchet." As if aware that this was an unfortunate figure of speech, he went on quickly, "What's become of the Bannister child?"

"He went home at lunchtime," Pemberton said, clutching at this lifeline with gratitude. "Sister tells me there was quite a scene. He refused to go with his father at first, said he wanted to stay until Tom Bryant came back."

"The whole thing must have been a nasty shock to him," Honeychurch said thoughtfully. "One can only hope it won't have made any lasting impression."

"One can hardly imagine that it would fail to do so." A quiet voice at his elbow announced the presence of Henchard.

"Well, that's all in your best interests, Dr. Henchard." Burnivel seemed bent on dispensing general sweetness and light. "Where would you psychiatrists be if things didn't upset people? You tell me that."

Henchard looked understandably offended.

"It is most unfortunate that he should have undergone such an experience in his present perturbed emotional state. It could do him untold harm."

"What about Tom Bryant? What sort of harm will it have done him?"

Henchard turned to face the questioner, heard Honeychurch murmur a name in his ear, and saw Rutherford, around whom rumour had crystallised into an ugly assumption of guilt.

"It's difficult to say. Tom was in many ways a child unlikely to be much impressed by unusual events. He had so extreme a power of fantasy that any reality in the way of violence would probably take its place alongside his own imagined adventures. A more stolid child, curiously enough, or a much younger one, would be more likely to suffer permanent psychological damage."

"It's a good thing that Tom's parents are in no position to worry themselves into a frenzy over his loss," Pemberton said. "We have that much to be thankful for."

Rutherford said sharply, "We were his parents for the time being. If we aren't in a frenzy over it, it's nothing to be proud of."

"You are being unfair to Cyril," Honeychurch suggested. "He only implies that a great deal of adult suffering has been avoided—and adults after all have a right to some consideration."

"Some, but not much, in this context," Garside said. "Isn't it precisely the fact of a child being used as the raw material of such a scheme that really shakes one?"

"Worse still, when one allows that two children have been involved, however unequally. James's turn of the screw, in fact."

"Who's James?" Burnivel looked at Honeychurch with sudden mistrust.

"No. No, that's wrong." Rutherford cut across Honeychurch's attempt to explain with sudden intensity. "Not James. Herbert, perhaps."

"Herbert?" Burnivel and Honeychurch spoke in a ridiculous, chiming unison.

Rutherford was looking at Honeychurch and yet he was not speaking to him. Honeychurch could have sworn that this abrupt reversion to last night's brief moment in the orchard was not for his benefit alone.

"'When boyes go first to bed, They step into their voluntarie graves.'" He had quoted that, and now Rutherford was repeating it, glancing from Garside to Pemberton, from Pemberton to Henchard, from Henchard back to Honeychurch. "Their *voluntary* graves," he said again. "We've all been talking about Tom as if he were a babe in arms to be picked up and put down anywhere at any time. But he wasn't that sort at all."

"You don't surely mean that he left the hospital of his own free will, knowing what he was doing?" Henchard sounded appalled.

"I mean he didn't need to be trussed or drugged. He went out to meet somebody, to keep an appointment."

A silence full of scepticism greeted his words.

"Isn't it just what you would have expected of Tom?" Rutherford appealed to Henchard. "Suppose you or I or any of us proposed an adventure to Tom, wouldn't he come? Provided it was someone he trusted, wouldn't he leap at the chance?"

"No murderer could take a risk like that," Burnivel said.

"This one did," Rutherford told him.

"Grimshaw," Burnivel said, "you and me's going to get some medical education. Come along, my boy."

Grimshaw looked at him with a mixture of wonder and suspicion.

"Do you mean we're going to hear Dr. Rutherford's lecture?" he ventured.

"We are," Burnivel said, "and it's the last he'll be giving for some time."

Grimshaw kept his mouth shut on the obvious question. They were walking side by side up a flight of stairs in company with the unknown and the famous: the landing, when they reached it, was crowded. Swing doors gave on to a lecture theatre much larger than the one handed over for their use. Burnivel glanced to left and right, then pushed his way through the crowd to the doors. Grimshaw saw that his lips were tightly compressed.

"There's another way out." Burnivel jerked his head towards the far end of the hall. "Any idea where it leads to?"

"There's a fire escape," Grimshaw said.

"I'll say this for you—you do use your eyes. Get a man to keep a look-out down there, will you? Tell him not to let anyone get past him."

"I have," Grimshaw said, with modest self-satisfaction. "I put Morgan on to it just after tea. I thought there wasn't any point in his hanging on to Rutherford's tail while we were keeping an eye on him."

"Good for you. Soon be over now. Looks as if I were right, doesn't it?"

Grimshaw nodded unhappily.

"Though I don't know why Rutherford couldn't have told me instead of spouting a lot of poetry to Honeychurch. Must want the old chap to give himself up, I suppose. Anyway, once this talk's over I'll charge them both." With a sidelong look at Grimshaw, he said defensively, "There wasn't any point doing it earlier. They don't want the meeting spoilt. This way it won't look so bad."

"There's Honeychurch," Grimshaw said, "sitting next to Ainsworth, and Garside's just in front of him. I suppose there's no chance of his trying to prevent Rutherford spilling the beans? I mean, he wouldn't take a potshot at him, would he?"

"Use your head," Burnivel said with a return of his old contempt. "Committing murder in front of three hundred people wouldn't help him much. Still"—he relented a fraction—"it's just possible. If he has a gun, which isn't likely. It won't do any harm to let him see he wouldn't have a chance to get away if he tried anything on. Is that Pemberton on the platform? I'll just go and chat to him for a moment. That should do the trick."

He walked up the central aisle.

PART THREE

CREPUSCULAR

...indeed, I've slept
With mine eyes open a great while.

JOHN FORD: *The Broken Heart*

ONE

"There is about this lecture hall," Garside remarked over his shoulder, "what an experienced journalist would probably call an atmosphere of hushed expectancy."

Honeychurch leant forward and murmured in his ear: "Would you say that these people are expecting something to break—as your journalist would put it?"

"I would say they undoubtedly are. But how they should have got wind of it is hard to understand."

"Burnivel," Honeychurch said sombrely, "has stationed Grimshaw at one side of the door and himself at the other: and I took a short stroll after tea and noticed an absolutely transparent plainclothesman standing at the foot of the fire escape—indeed, for one moment I actually had the curious sensation that he was watching *me*. Supposing"—he paused for a moment on the threshold of imponderabilities—"supposing our man should be foolhardy enough to make an attempt here and now, it would seem impossible for him to get away."

"It would be an uncommonly stupid thing to do," Garside said.

"It would indeed."

Honeychurch sat comfortably back in his chair, overhanging the aisle on his left and Ainsworth on his right. Garside's hush had begun in his ears also to acquire the character that Garside had ascribed to it. So might a Roman crowd have awaited the gladiators: so might a mob collect at a lynching. Honeychurch took himself firmly in hand; this was to attribute altogether too sinister a significance to the undefined suggestion of tension in the audience— an eagerness quite out of proportion to the legitimate interest of the programme for which they were assembled. It was only to be expected that some of the gathering should be well enough informed to derive an ignoble satisfaction from their presence at this curious session where a man, possibly a murderer, was to read the last words of the man he might have murdered. Honeychurch sighed, and his sigh had the force of a prearranged signal: for it was at this moment that Burnivel, a step or two in front of Rutherford, walked up to the platform and spoke to Pemberton in an undertone made audible by the sudden absolute silence. Then he retreated to the back of the hall.

Rutherford rose to speak in a quiet that famous orators might have envied. His unemphatic voice would have had little power against an audience disposed to fidget and whisper; but this one hung on every word with a concentration that should have been unnerving. That Rutherford was not unnerved was shown by his even conversational pitch; but the sources of his present confidence eluded Honeychurch, who waited, hoping for enlightenment.

He listened, but his attention drifted away by degrees from Sandeman's dry authoritative account of the genesis of the pethidine experiment and the properties of the drug; that aspect of the case seemed to him disappointingly barren. He thought instead of what had been said at tea-time, and why it had been said: for he could not overcome a feeling that Rutherford had spoken with a purpose when he suggested that Tom Bryant had gone voluntarily to his death. He had suggested a relationship of trust between the child and the murderer; had been concerned, it seemed in retrospect, to impress upon them—who hardly needed impressing—the element of personal betrayal. But Burnivel's objection, short and cogent, echoed in his mind— no murderer could take a chance of a child's conveniently behaving as one would wish him to behave when life and death were quite literally at stake. Rutherford must be wrong.

It was at this point that his ear picked up a word dropped casually, as it were, from the remote heights of Sandeman's pharmacological exactitudes. For a moment Honeychurch swore at the discrimination that offered him an idea only to let it escape; he could not even recall the word, let alone ascribe to it any special meaning. He tried to think that whatever he had singled out as important was nothing but a familiar name, an anticipated reference, but his instinct to listen as if his life depended on it was a flat denial of any such slight association. Rutherford read on, sentence after sentence of seemingly interminable discussion: the action of pethidine on the ciliary muscle, the biliary tract, the central nervous system. And here Honeychurch pressed his palms together with a gathering premonition of what was to come.

"We were led to consider the use of pethidine for paediatric purposes by a comparison of its hypnotic effects with those of the other powerful analgesics. The relative duration of hypnosis—I mean, narcosis—"

His voice trailed off. Another ear, Honeychurch thought grimly, at least as sensitive as my own. He looked up and caught Rutherford's eye over the twenty intervening rows of expectant listeners; and as he caught it, Rutherford turned away as if in search of some elusive member of the audience. Then three things happened at once. Rutherford laid down his notes and was out of the door by the platform before Pemberton saw what he was about: Honeychurch got to his feet faster than he would have believed possible and shouted surprisingly, "Stop him! Don't let him go!": Burnivel disappeared through the swing doors at the back as if this moment had occurred in answer to a prayer.

There was a confused and angry murmur as of bees disturbed. Three hundred paediatricians lulled into somnolence by too much tea and too much Sandeman woke with a start to the fact that here was the news breaking, the whole outrageous drama enacted under their very noses. To a man they rose, to a man they surged forward or sideways in a vague general pursuit. Honeychurch found himself once more swimming against the current. We are going to be too late, he thought—too late to stop him and avert the consequences. How could I have been so blind?

They were out of the hall, they were on the stairs: on the next landing more swing doors led to the operating theatres. Burnivel was just ahead of them, so close now that Honeychurch could touch him on the shoulder. And—

"He's coming this way!" Burnivel shouted. "Look out, Grimshaw!"

Poor Tom's a-cold, Rutherford said aloud, fantastically poised at the top of a fire escape; and in these simple and clamant terms the problem continued to present itself as he bounded down the first flight of metal steps pursued by an uproar of voices and a thunder of feet; as he looked through the fenestrated treads to see the plainclothesman in a new and enlightening perspective; as he flattened himself into the first-floor doorway and groped behind him for the handle. The head below tilted in response to the astonishing noise above and began to move inexorably upwards. At the same moment the door gave and Rutherford slipped through—led by a vision that pointed downwards, unlike most visions, at bare feet, at thin pyjamas. Poor Tom's a-cold; had been cold for many hours, and not with the final chilliness of death, either; and spurred by the knowledge that he and no other was responsible for what happened to the child, Rutherford tore across a room where two anaesthetists blandly sipped tea, acknowledging his flight with the most urbane of smiles as if it were something to which they were by long experience inured. But a moment later he heard their voices lifted in protest behind him as he whipped round the corner into a passage between the theatres. His white coat, his familiar face had conferred upon him a sort of diplomatic immunity, and this immunity the plainclothesman most blessedly lacked.

Professional snobbery was a curious ally, but he thanked appropriate deities for the few seconds' grace as he half ran, half slid along the stone floor: he had long enough to reach the double doors at the end and confront Burnivel at the foot of the stairs opposite him, Grimshaw barring his way at the head of the next flight, and both bellowing loudly as they sprang towards him. He backed through the doors and left them massively and dangerously swinging; a theatre trolley stood against the wall, and he set it in erratic but effective motion: on the glassy surface of the polished stone it gathered a desperate momentum, bucketing heavily between the walls and swerving towards the door of the anaesthetists' room in time to knock the faithful Morgan headlong to the floor. Rutherford was already halfway across the theatre, digging a mask out of his pocket as he ran—so strong and so irrational is the force of training—was in the sterilising room, where an autoclave absurdly offered concealment, a trolley piled high with dirty instruments offered weapons. Beyond the autoclave an open window gave on to the orchard: Burnivel's voice behind him was raised in a yapping triumph. How he got through the window he did not stop to consider, nor how he swung without grace or enthusiasm from a convenient branch below until it most unkindly snapped. He picked himself up and ran again, and the air around him was convulsed with wrath and purpose. He thanked God that the British police carry no firearms as he rounded the end of the building, heard the crunch of gravel under his feet, saw beyond the gates Garside's grey car, and was somehow in it and turning the ignition key. There were no other cars at the gate: with any luck the car park would be full, and Burnivel might be held up indefinitely while owners were traced and impediments shifted. He had a lead, and a good one, and he would need it.

"Blithering idiot!" and "Blithering blasted idiot!" Burnivel cried, stamping his foot absurdly on the gravel as he watched Garside's car vanishing up the road. Lumbering heavily up to join him, Honeychurch assumed that it was Rutherford he apostrophised in these unflattering terms: but Honeychurch was wrong. It was not Rutherford, it was not the sweating Grimshaw, mopping himself at his side, nor the absolutely transparent plainclothesman panting apologetically in the background. It was Burnivel himself that Burnivel berated, and with reason.

To be so nearly right, to be so utterly wrong! What excuse could he conceivably make for this fiasco, this bungling prelude to carnage? He glared this question at his followers, he saw the gleam of understanding sympathy in Honeychurch's eye, and that was worse than Grimshaw's blank incomprehension or Ainsworth's frank incredulity. The American raced up with Garside on his heels, and Burnivel rapped out, "Where's your place?" to Garside, and to Grimshaw, "Get my car—you know where I left it," while on Honeychurch he turned a look of baffled ludicrous despair. And before Garside could answer, he had gone tearing on, "You'd better drive; it'll be quicker," and to Honeychurch and Ainsworth in an inclusive loud statement, "You can get in the back. If we're in time, which isn't likely, it'll help to have a few reinforcements."

Garside said, "Do you really trust me, Inspector? Isn't it quite likely I'll drive you in the opposite direction?"

"Oh no, you won't," Burnivel said. "Not if you know what's good for you. And what's good for your pal, come to that."

Ainsworth looked from one to the other; he was very pale.

"Look, I don't understand. Where's he gone? What's he gone for? Does it mean—?"

"It means Dr. Rutherford is a sadly impetuous man," Honeychurch said.

"It means he knows where the child is," Burnivel said, "and he knows the child is still alive. Let's hope the child stays alive, that's all."

Ainsworth looked back at Honeychurch, who nodded his head. Burnivel peered down the road as if looking for his car would make it get to him sooner. And perhaps he was right, for in another minute Grimshaw drew up at the kerb and got out. Garside replaced him at the wheel with Burnivel at his side in a matter of seconds; Ainsworth and Honeychurch crowded into the back. Leaning out, Burnivel addressed Grimshaw.

"Find another car: beg, borrow, or steal it, and say I told you to. Bring Morgan along with you and don't waste time."

"Pitts Leighton?" Grimshaw asked Garside. Garside nodded bleakly; the car moved off, the hospital receded. Streams of traffic separated them from Rutherford and ten minutes of precious time. It was useless for Honeychurch to beg a suspension of the laws of nature enabling the car to soar over the city and be wafted like a bird to its destination—or, since suspension of the laws of nature might be too much to ask, a mere revision of civil law permitting them to take the wrong side of the road despite Burnivel's official presence. But even as he wondered whether to broach this idea would make matters worse, the idea itself became a lost hope. Traffic that had piled up behind a signal or a policeman now flowed turbidly past them as well as with them.

Garside swore, took out a cigarette, tried to light it, then craned round to look for Grimshaw; but the solid press behind them defeated his intention. On the way back his glance took in Ainsworth, and he smiled.

"Cheer up, Philip. There's nothing for you to worry about. Why, only half an hour ago the professor would have bet his last sixpence you were the murderer. Isn't that so, Professor Honeychurch?"

A transient awkwardness rendered Honeychurch speechless.

"I wish to hell I had been," Ainsworth said. "I wish I'd put Sandeman under the ground before he ever started this lousy racket."

"Which lousy racket?" Honeychurch emphasized the words with gentle distaste.

"The pethidine racket, of course," Ainsworth said.

T W O

Tom rowed wearily across enormous expanses of ocean under a blazing sun. He had already rowed 7,463 miles, and he was getting very thirsty. He passed his parched tongue over his cracked lips and muttered hoarsely to himself. Then he shaded his eyes with his hand and looked for clouds and the promise of rain; but it was the dry season; the blue vastness of the sky touched the blue vastness of the sea all the way round him. He pulled in his oars and looked and looked at his horny, callused hands. Then he got out of the zinc bath and took a second drink from the tap on the garage wall. The water tasted as brackish and horrible as before, but he swallowed it. After a brisk battle with a shark whose teeth flashed hideously at him through the glassy surface he got back into the bath, feeling exhausted—as well he might, after all these gruelling weeks alone on the Pacific, or in the Pacific, whichever it was. He strained his eyes looking for a sail on the horizon or a tiny feather of smoke from the funnel of a steamer plodding between Sydney and the Panama Canal. Since his own sloop had been sunk in an encounter with a Portuguese man-of-war (which Tom had seen depicted in a book as an oddly futuristic craft with a top like an umbrella and a lot of propellers under the water) and he had been cast adrift in an open boat, he had twice been deceived into thinking help was at hand: but each time the car, or van, or lorry, or whatever it was (a frigate or

184

a whaler, he told himself) had gone by and nobody had heard his eager call. He was getting sick to death of the sea.

He had stuck to *A Passage to India* for an hour or more, turning over page after page in the firm belief that the next would bring a tiger hunt or a snake-charmer or a child brought up by wolves or an elephant running amuck. None of these things came. There were some promising caves; but after reading this sequence twice through Tom was at least as uncertain as Miss Quested must have been as to what exactly had happened to her, or even if anything had happened at all. Hope deferred maketh the heart sick: Tom closed the book and bent over the steering wheel. He hurtled off into the night, pursued by cops who didn't know the rear seat was loaded with dynamite; he touched ninety over the Yorkshire moors while the bullets of robbers splintered the rear window; he skidded down the Great North Road while cops and robbers alike battled to stop him getting through. The cops mined the road ahead of him, the robbers trained machine guns on him from the bushes. He drove on, wounded though he was. A Sioux arrow, poison tipped most probably, had got him in the arm: he glanced sternly at the pale woman at his side, a baby on her lap. She whispered something, and he looked back and saw the great canvas roof of the wagon ablaze: he tightened his lips grimly and urged the flagging horses on. Through the stormy night rushed the stage-coach, bearing its load of rescued aristocrats in retreat from the Terror, the great blood-dripping knife of the guillotine, Sir Thomas Bryant holding the reins in his hands of steel. Past a million scurrying fishes, past monstrous presences of whales and porpoises, rose the submarine. From the conning tower he discerned a destroyer skimming murderously along the Channel. "Dive!" he instructed his second-in-command. They dived. "Avast, belay there!" he shouted into the rigging. "Reef the tops'l! Scupper the main mast, you landlubbers, or I'll keelhaul you! There, there, there she blows!"

The man-of-war, looking like a Jules Verne project, loomed into sight. Tom's crew mutinied to a man—otherwise they would have sent the Portuguese to Davy Jones. They had cast him adrift with jeers and yells, and ten minutes later he had watched them walking the plank, for of course the whole thing was the basest treachery.

By this time he was sitting in the zinc bath: he had moved it into the vivid parallelogram of sunlight on the floor and picked up two bits of wood to do duty as oars. Squinting down at his thin white chest, he had to acknowledge that the tropical sun had scarcely the strength one would have expected: he immediately saw himself richly bronze with a fuzz of dark curly hair on his chest and a thick stubble around his determined chin.

Another sail, another plume of smoke, offered him a tantalising hope of rescue. He ran to the doors and shouted over and over again, but the sound of the car faded into the distance. Tired, discouraged, and completely himself again, Tom returned to his bath. Listlessly, he picked up the oars; then with a sudden burst of impatience and rage he threw them hard against the wall, and went to look at the clock. It was ten to six.

Then he heard a new noise—a soft recurrent noise, a tapping noise like someone knocking ever so gently, like someone not expecting an answer really but just trying.

He crossed swiftly to the doors: there was no doubt about it. He could hear breathing, a more sustained, an even gentler sound than the quiet persistent knocking. Something moved beyond the door: there was a brief flash of light on something rather above Tom's head, on a pair of delicately gold-rimmed spectacles.

Tom stood still, but his mind was racing. For this he knew he had seen before, very recently, last night, only it was moonlight then, and at the time he hadn't really realised what he had seen. If only he had, he would have known what to do. He would have told Dr. Rutherford as soon as he got in the car and they'd have caught him together. And by now it would all be over; he would be safe and a hero. He might still be a hero, but he wished with all his heart he was sure he would be safe.

A voice, barely louder than the soft breathing, said surprisingly close to his ear:

"Tom? Are you there, Tom? Are you all right?"

He wouldn't say anything: he would keep absolutely still.

"Tom?" said the voice again; but perfunctorily now as if it had lost interest. Footsteps, muffled, faded on the grass. Tom put his eye to the crack between the doors. The man had gone to the right or left: at any rate he wasn't retreating down the drive. That meant he wasn't satisfied. But Tom took comfort from the knowledge that if he couldn't get out, the murderer couldn't get in: not unless he had a key to the padlock or knew how to force it. And as yet he didn't know that Tom was in the garage.

Tom whirled round. Tapping had again caught his attention: this time it was more definite, high-pitched and peremptory. The knocking was on glass now. In the same glance Tom saw his undoing and his undoer. Through the grass-green letters, his useless signal to the indifferent trees and the hill beyond, Henchard's face with its mild look of anxiety peered into the dark interior.

Tom cowered automatically into the space between the back of the car and the door, but he knew the action was wasted: whether he could be seen or not, the word on the window gave his presence away—that, and the locked door. The face had gone, the footsteps returned, and shortly the clipped, diffident voice produced its now familiar question.

"Tom? Are you there, Tom?"

"I'm here all right," Tom said bitterly. "You know I am."

"How long have you been locked up?"

"Wouldn't you like to know!" He was saying the first thing that came into his head.

"Thank heaven I've found you," Henchard said. He sounded as if he meant it, and well he might, Tom thought savagely. "We'll get you out of here in no time."

"No, you won't," Tom said. "Go away, or I'll shout till someone comes."

"Tom, my dear child," Henchard was remonstrative, "you've had a terrible shock, I know, but you're safe now."

Tom said thickly, "I'm not your dear child. I hate you, you beastly old goat. I thought you were going to take me to my mum and dad and you didn't. I saw what you did, and I'll tell everyone. I'll tell the police and they'll hang you."

There was an agitated dance of light outside; the man was shaking his head.

"Tom, Tom, you've made a dreadful mistake. You've

187

had a nightmare and imagined all sorts of things. It wasn't me you saw."

"Yes, it was." Tom was shouting now at the top of his voice. "I know it was you."

"Listen, Tom." Henchard's voice was unimaginably tired. "Dr. Sandeman was killed last night about the time you left hospital. The police think Dr. Rutherford killed him. You must get these silly ideas out of your head before I take you back, or you'll be getting yourself into trouble."

Tom sniffed loudly and with intentional rudeness; beneath the surface assurance he had caught the accent of pleading, and was merciless.

"Get you into trouble, more like. What'll they think when I tell them it was you that told me to come out of the ward when I heard the owl hoot and get into your car?"

There was a long silence. When he had had as much of it as he could manage, Tom said loudly, "And I'll tell them about the other times when I came to see you and you thought I was asleep and you told me I'd go and open the door five minutes after I woke up or eat an apple or do something daft. But I wasn't asleep, I never went to sleep, not once."

A sighing intake of breath like resignation itself came from beyond the doors, then more footsteps. He's going away, Tom thought, poised on the brink of laughter. I've scared him stiff and he's going away. Then doubt assailed him; would anyone give up so easily? He went back to the zinc bath, moved it into the peripatetic sunlight and stood nudging it with a toe grimy from walking on the concrete floor. His brow was tightly puckered with the effort of concentration. It was easy enough to imagine things for himself, but more difficult to do it for someone else. If he were Henchard and Henchard were he, what would he do next? Undoubtedly, he, Tom, would make some effort to kill him, Henchard. But that meant getting into the garage and he had no key.

But Dr. Rutherford had a key, and some time or other he would come home, and perhaps he would have Garside's car and bring it up to the garage, and that would be Henchard's chance to get at Tom. He heard himself sob. Kid stuff. He had never felt so decidedly a kid in his life. Wearily, without quite knowing why he did it, he

188

carried the bath over to the window, turned it upside down, and climbed up. The light lay tenderly along the grass, painting shadows that were themselves luminous where little hillocks and tufts of weeds disturbed the plushy surface. On a circular seat under a plum tree sat Dr. Henchard, his eyes closed, his head bent forward as if he were listening intently, his hands folded tidily on his lap, over a short iron bar.

The road was crowded: it was the trunk road connecting Leeds to Bantwich and carrying on to Doncaster. Until he reached the turning off to Pitts Leighton he would have to crawl carefully along hemmed in by buses draining off spectators from the Saturday football match, Saturday afternoon shoppers in cars, Saturday trippers on bicycles panting along in search of fresh air on the darkening moors. The trams mercifully clanked to their terminus a mile beyond the hospital, but even when they were left behind speed was out of the question. Sandwiched between two lorries which effectively prevented him seeing the police behind or Henchard in front, Rutherford gave himself up to thought—infinitely vexatious thought that painted for him a uniformly dark picture of his own monumental stupidity, his blind underwriting of a proposition that had no weight but that given it by Burnivel's dogmatism. Burnivel had said the child must be dead or the murderer could not consider himself safe: and Henchard had spoken of Tom as alive with simple conviction. It was Rutherford's own wish that had run the two ideas together and made him believe that if Henchard had not yet killed the child, he would never do it, because he could somehow achieve security without a second murder. Rutherford himself had shattered that security when he told Henchard that Tom had known what he was about: the suggestion must have created havoc in that quiet man's well-ordered mind. The child he had hypnotised into performing minor acts had most audaciously played a part, probably even taken a pride in his own resistance: until finally his general boy's instinct of curiosity, his particular instinct to accept the role of hero in any adventure, had led him at close quarters and in three dimensions to the things he had only known printed on the pages of comics or flat on the screen of a cinema. He had witnessed murder and blindly fled, cho-

sen between two cars and plumped for Rutherford's own—
which made Rutherford incontrovertibly his abductor;
worse still, his goaler. It was bad enough to have shown
Henchard so startling a glimpse of the truth; to have so
arranged matters that Tom was trapped and helpless was
unbearable. He glanced at the clock on the dashboard—
if Henchard had left the hospital when the others went to
the lecture theatre, he had the best part of forty minutes'
start: perhaps the unfamiliarity of the road would cut it
down a little.

What had possessed him, he demanded fiercely, hoot-
ing a useless defiance at the lorry in front as it grated to
a dismal standstill, what had possessed him to take so
blind a risk? In the last analysis the thread Tom's life hung
by was his own pride, his lunatic pity for Henchard, his
lunatic certainty that the man would give himself up when
his bluff was called. The lorry jerked into motion, Rutherford's foot hazardously pressed the accelerator and the
bonnet of Garside's car escaped mutilation by inches which
would have been the end of all . . . the end of all, the pop-
pied sleep; wherein lay the key to Sandeman's concentrated malice towards himself, the callousness of his earlier
attempt to discredit his junior, the more controlled intention that shaped a timely finish for him before today's
meeting when the paper had to be read and Sandeman's
outrageous alterations in the figures exposed to Rutherford's absolute scepticism. So insatiable an appetite for
pethidine—and at the crudest computation, the haul must
have run into thousands of grammes—was in one man
unthinkable. Therefore there were others, others who
bought destruction at whatever price he cared to name.
But one does not offer drugs of addiction to casual
acquaintances or peddle them to children. A paediatrician
would be in the most disadvantageous position for dis-
posing of such wares, but not so a psychiatrist. Who better
than a psychiatrist could select those patients feverishly
determined on escape from intolerable burdens of anxiety
and feed them coveted poison while trustingly they paid
larger and larger fees? Between them over the last few
months Sandeman and Henchard must have amassed a
small but useful fortune with little chance of discovery
until the results of the experiment had to be produced.
And even then they would have been safe enough without

Rutherford's opposition. Who else would have known that the figures were falsified? Ainsworth might have guessed, but Sandeman could have silenced Ainsworth. What moral blinkers he had found to calm Henchard's apparent timidity into keeping on so perilous a course, Rutherford could only surmise—but Henchard had vindicated himself in a way. Whether mistakenly or deliberately, he had destroyed his familiar daemon instead of the unsuspecting stranger presented to him as an easy target with no more right to consideration than a face on a photograph.

He turned off on the Pitts Leighton road; for three clear miles he could race homewards. Now his mirror showed him a black car diminishing the distance between them, though still too far off for him to be sure that Burnivel was in it. If there had ever been a time to demonstrate or explain, the time was past. There was no chance of convincing Burnivel without the lecture notes he had carelessly thrown down; an outburst of recriminations at the roadside would only make matters worse. Plant-blurred red brick appeared against the blue bulk of the hill a couple of miles ahead. To the right heather and gorse sloped steeply away down to the main road: beyond the house the slope achieved a dizzy verticality, plummeting a hundred feet into lush green meadows freckled with sheep. The sort of place, he reflected, where movie villains struggle with movie heroes before diving to a neat but nasty quietus. And even as he rejected this romantic concept as irrelevant, a suspicion of its absolute relevance struck him with overwhelming force.

Not until that moment had it occurred to him that he shared Tom's danger: he had measured his own risk entirely in terms of a battle of words with Burnivel and a stinging rebuke from the coroner if the darkest of his fears proved true. As an alternative to probable death, mere social embarrassment took on an unwonted attraction, and Burnivel's menacing hoot behind him had something appealing in its invitation to surrender while the going was good. It would be so easy for Henchard to kill both Tom and himself, to thrust him over the crag, perhaps, and lament his destruction while appending a pious regret that this justifiable defence of self had not sufficed to preserve the child he had attempted to rescue. Could it be done? Could

Burnivel be hoodwinked? Emphatically, yes. His own conduct, his unreasoning panicky flight, would lend credence to the lie, and the wish to believe could blind Burnivel as effectively as anyone else. To lose Tom, to lose his own life, to lose that curious commodity reputation—it seemed a high price to pay for a moment's impulse of pity.

How soone doth man decay: Herbert again. A quotation for every occasion, he thought, and wondered if this constituted one of the more esoteric benefits of Honeychurch's liberal education. Physic himself must fade, All things to end are made; he watched brightness fall from the air in little puffs of pink cloud far away to the west. Now more than ever seems it rich to die, he proclaimed to the windscreen wiper, but without conviction: and a moment later simple fact announced itself in a barely perceptible shiver, a dampness of the hands clammily adhering to the steering wheel. *Timor mortis conturbat me*, he admitted.

But a struggle above the cliff, a ludicrous unarmed combat, would give him a reasonable chance—he was younger and heavier than Henchard, and these unfair advantages could be used to the full if Tom were dead and himself in the last extremity of danger. Unfortunately, no such open battle was likely. Henchard also could guess at the probable outcome of so unequal a contest, and to Henchard was the choice of weapons. Something in the nature of a trap or an ambush would be more in his line. And he had had time for the baiting and setting, time to arrange the fuses, time to adjust the delicate machinery of his own conscience to the need for continued vigilance, continued violence.

"Now we can get going."

Garside said nothing, but the car jerked forward: the main road was behind them and a long way ahead against the hill the convolutions of the Pitts Leighton road were dazzlingly white on the grey-green of turf and heather. And a long way ahead too light flashed momentarily and tellingly against moving glass, the window of another car. And—

"There he is!" Honeychurch and Burnivel exclaimed in unison. Garside remained obstinately silent; Ainsworth also, after the fragmentary excitement had wrung a cry from him, lapsed back into a dull, vacuous misery. Honeychurch felt disposed to offer him comfort, but he could think of nothing to say: facile optimism was out of place; commiseration would, he hoped, be premature. To strike a balance between the two in his present perturbed state was too difficult a task.

Cautiously he said, leaning forward between Burnivel and Garside: "Have we any chance at all of catching up on him?"

Garside emerged reluctantly from taciturnity. "This road's not bad. I can keep up a steady seventy; but about a mile on we have to turn off on a rotten little lane that's not much better than a farm track."

"I don't believe it," Ainsworth said suddenly and loudly.

That Garside's revelation of the local topography should arouse such a vehement protest seemed improbable. Honeychurch framed a question, but Burnivel asked it.

"What don't you believe?"

"He couldn't do it—kill the kid, I mean. Not even if it meant hanging else. You"—he turned to Honeychurch—"you can't believe he's that much of a rat? Even if he killed Sandeman, even if he were helping Sandeman to peddle dope, I'll bet Bill never meant to do anything to the child." His voice suddenly touched a pitch of frantic accusation. "If he does it," he told Burnivel, "it'll be your fault. You'll have driven him to it."

"Shut up," Burnivel said. *"Shut up!"*

It was Honeychurch's turn to be bewildered, to be doubtful. Had he jumped ahead of reasonable conjecture into sheer guesswork? Was his interpretation of Rutherford's flight merely an illusion conjured up by his own unaccountable bias? No: he dismissed the idea at once, and without hesitation.

But before he could speak, Burnivel again cut in on him: "Who said I thought Rutherford was going to kill the child? I've made a mistake all right, but not the mistake you think. It's Henchard we're after, not your precious pal."

"You knew it was Henchard?" Honeychurch tried to keep the note of mild jealousy out of his voice; at such a moment the intrusion of such a petty emotion seemed unforgivable.

193

"When did you know?" Burnivel demanded.

"When Rutherford tripped up on the word 'hypnosis'. That was when I realised what he was trying to do at teatime."

"But why?" Burnivel said. "Why did he let Henchard know that he knew?"

"There used to be a convention," Honeychurch said slowly, "in rather sentimental plays written about the turn of the century, you know, that if an officer did something dishonourable, say, he was left alone with a loaded revolver."

Garside said, twisting dangerously round, "You mean Bill wanted him to get away?"

"Not to get away in the sense you mean. He wanted him to realise the game was up."

"I don't understand a word of it." Garside's driving had become hideously erratic—they were turning a corner, the surface of the lane was pitted and scarred: they were going as fast as they had gone on the better road, bounding over crevices in a new and thoroughly alarming manner that buffeted the breath out of Honeychurch and precluded any further explanations. They were gaining minute by minute on the other car; and in the mirror over Garside's head Honeychurch saw Grimshaw in a convertible not a hundred yards behind. Burnivel looked round at him; the light of battle was in his eyes.

"I hope to heaven we're in time—"

"We're in time," Ainsworth said. "Look there—"

They looked there: Burnivel's fingers grasped the handle of his door, Honeychurch lowered the window and thrust his head and shoulders through, trumpeting a warning yet hardly knowing whom he warned—the injudicious Rutherford or Henchard, least vindictive of murderers?

A bend in the lane concealed the house at the end of the long climb. He rounded it, and there was no car parked at the gates: he wished this meant something, but knew that it didn't, for only fifty yards further on the lane swung round another turning, and there was a wide grass verge above the precipice beloved of itinerant Bantwich families toying with the pastoral in terms of ham sandwiches and thermos flasks. Rutherford debated for a moment whether he should drive on and see for himself, but time was all-important. If Tom were still alive, he owed his survival to the padlock on the garage door; given even that the chain were strong and the respectable Henchard unlikely to be versed in the skills of illegal entry, time might still be important.

A chilling thought came to him as he began to slow down. Why should Henchard exert himself to get into the garage? He had only to wait. Sooner or later Rutherford would turn up, as he was turning up now: sooner or later the hum of a car engine would announce his arrival; two birds might as well be killed with one stone, or if murder bred true, with one iron bar. The trap was baited, and somewhere behind the house or in the coal shed Henchard would be biding his time, meek, patient, meditative.

The car slid to a standstill. The gates were closed as he had left them. At a quick glance there was no one in the garden and no evidence that anyone had been there. Henchard might merely have bolted, he told himself: Tom might be somewhere else: the whole complex structure of his thought might be hopelessly faulty. But he was not reassured; he knew that for the first time in his life he was mortally afraid.

And after all, there was no need to walk into the trap. He could stay where he was until Burnivel came. There was no need for him to leave the car's protection, to open the gates, to run up the path, to fumble for a key ... so he left the car, opened the gates, ran up the path, felt for the key: there was no choice after all. As the last throb of the engine died in his ears over and above his own hurried breathing he heard the rasping sobs of the child to whom a sanctuary had become a snare: sobs that grated to a crescendo and were replaced by a frenzied and imploring cry.

"Go away, go away!" the child was screaming. And then on a sustained quivering note of fear, "Don't let him get me!"

Rutherford's hands were damp and unsteady; nevertheless the key turned, the chain slid free, the doors gaped, and Tom threw himself—dirty, flushed, and shaking— into his arms. Rutherford held him, spoke to him without knowing what he said; and then heard the other car, heard Honeychurch's voice shouting indistinguishable words. He turned towards the gate; the blow that should have sent him to join Sandeman in the shades glanced sickeningly off his shoulder and forced him to his knees, still grasping the child, idiotically thinking: This'll teach me to mind my own business. "Only you are my business," he said aloud, waiting for the next blow to fall. "Don't cry, Tom. It's all right now."

Miraculously, it was all right. There was no second blow. Instead, there were shouts, footsteps, the harsh metallic clank of something dropping on the path. Rutherford turned his head and saw the little man taking off his glasses, trying to wipe them with a hand that shook as uncontrollably as Tom's whole body, while hopelessly and terribly tears streamed down his cheeks and his mouth made small silent explanatory grimaces as if he were trying to say that he was sorry.

THREE

"They won't like this at the Yard. They won't like it at all."

As epitaphs and obsequies go, Honeychurch reflected, it was as satisfactory as most, better than some. It suggested a flurry, questions asked, opinions strongly given: and what more could Henchard ask for, lying pitifully and painfully dead at the foot of the crag, a narrow black shape appropriate curved into a note of fruitless interrogation?

"Your interrogation has not been fruitless," he said to Burnivel, with a vague idea of administering comfort. "You will return with a solution, if not with a prisoner. Surely that should appease the statutory powers?"

Burnivel shook his head.

"They won't like it at all," he repeated. "And the newspapers will lick their lips over it. I shall get poison-pen letters from all over the country telling me I've hounded a poor innocent fellow to his death. Death—the universal white-washer, isn't that what Garside called it?"

He looked as if he would like to spit.

"It didn't whitewash Sandeman," Honeychurch reminded him.

"Nothing would have made that blighter out any better than he was." Burnivel turned abruptly on his heel and flung back over his shoulder, "I can see Grimshaw and Morgan coming. About time, too."

They panted up, apologetic, explanatory.

"I took the first car I found," Grimshaw said between gasps. "We ran out of petrol half a mile down the lane."

"It doesn't matter," Burnivel said.

He walked slowly to the edge and looked over again. They followed him, shaping expressions of wonder and dismay.

"Yes," Burnivel said; "he got away. Now go down and fetch him. No; wait a bit. I'll come with you."

"If you think I might be of any use," Honeychurch offered, "professionally, I mean—"

Burnivel's grin was lopsided. "He's too old for you, Professor. Boys up to ten, girls up to twelve, isn't it? And he's finished anyway. I can feel a pulse that's not there as well as you can."

Boys up to ten, girls up to twelve; Honeychurch watched them walk along the edge, gingerly picking their way among stones, tufts, clumps of heather, doubtful sandy ledges. Then there was a way down, precarious for the first twenty feet but easy enough going after that. One at a time they let themselves down, shifting their footholds from rock to rock, and gaining a gentler slope without difficulty. Honeychurch heavily sighed. The sun had gone down, a cold breeze stirred the grass around his feet. Like a gramophone record with the needle stuck in a groove, the absurd phrase maddeningly reiterated: boys up to ten, boys up to ten, boys up to ten.

"He couldn't do it. When it came to the point, he couldn't do it."

"All right. Take it easy. They'll probably pin a putty medal on him before they hang him just to show how glad they are he didn't kill you too. Not to mention the child. Look, keep still, will you? How d'you suppose I can tell what's wrong when you keep shifting around?"

"What the hell does it matter?"

"Not much, by the looks of it," Ainsworth admitted. "You'll have a bruise the size of a saucer, but that's all. What d'you use for padding? And keep your hair on. I'm only trying to be useful. Look, I'll fix you a sling."

"I don't want a sling. Where's Honeychurch? Where've they all gone?"

"It'll probably take all three of them to put the handcuffs on that dear old gentleman. Here's the prof, anyway." Ainsworth had discerned a figure looming beyond the hedge. "Say, something must have gone wrong: he looks like a funeral. You don't suppose they've let him get away, do you?"

Honeychurch, opening the door, looked indeed like a funeral. He answered Rutherford's question before it was asked.

"He threw himself over the edge. He must have died instantly."

"Threw himself over—!" Ainsworth was incredulous. "How in the name of heaven? How come Burnivel let him slip through his hands?"

"He was never in his hands." Honeychurch lowered himself into the nearest chair. This must be, he decided, looking round, Garside's library. And that, his eye told him, falling on Rutherford's bare shoulder, would be Ainsworth's sole contribution to the day's events. So much for Honeychurch the master detective, supersleuth and arch-Holmes. "Where's Tom?" he asked.

"In the kitchen with Julian, eating sardines on toast," Ainsworth said. "But, look, you haven't told us—"

"I can't tell you," Honeychurch said. "I don't know. One moment Burnivel and I were at the gates, then you pushed past with Garside, and Burnivel got hold of Tom: I don't recall what happened after that. I saw Henchard was going to make a dash for it, and I suppose I meant to intercept him. I think I knew what was going through his mind. He got through a gap in the hedge and I was"— he paused: the triviality of the obstacle seemed to him so bitterly apt—"I was too big to follow him. I had to go back to the gates. He had quite a start and he was desperate, whereas I was only doing what my social conscience told me I should. I can't say I chased him with any conviction."

Ainsworth, helping Rutherford back into his shirt, looked as if he could have spoken volumes, and all of them condemnatory.

"I know." Honeychurch bent and stared at the carpet. "I know. But when so ludicrous a difficulty as a gap in the hedge that's too small stops one—What's the use? In any case, it seems irrelevant. He is as harmless now as he would have been behind bars. He has always seemed to me a remarkably harmless individual."

Rutherford said, "Where was Burnivel all this time?"

"He is a family man," Honeychurch said, as if this accounted for everything. "Naturally, his first instinct was to make sure the child was unharmed. Didn't you realise it was he who took Tom away from you?"

Rutherford shook his head.

"Too many things happened too quickly."

"Exactly." Honeychurch pounced with thankfulness on the phrase, so commonplace, so explicit, so reassuring. That was all: too many things had happened too quickly.

"By the way"—it was Ainsworth speaking—"what are you going to do about my skeleton in the cupboard? Are you going to tell Burnivel? It's all right. Bill knows. He's been covering up for me all day."

Honeychurch frowned, recalled thus truculently to the exigencies of the moment.

"It will only make confusion worse confounded if I tell him. But naturally I must stipulate for your ceasing to pull the wool over everyone's eyes. Deliberate imposition—"

"What else could I have done?" Ainsworth said reasonably. "I'd been qualified two years. I was the young hopeful of my generation at Cornell. I did all the interneships I wanted, and then Ziedermayr told me to go off somewhere where I'd have to make my own decisions for a bit. Like a fool, I did."

"That wasn't particularly foolish," Honeychurch said. "A young surgeon needs to acquire self-confidence."

"Yeah, I know," Ainsworth said with scant patience. "Only I got so darn self-reliant I bit off more than I can chew. Then one day I did a therapeutic abortion when the gynaecologist was on leave—leastways, I thought it was therapeutic." His voice acquired an unaccustomed hardness. "Local society decided it was criminal. My name was deleted from the Register. That should have been the end of me."

"It was the end of Peter Anderson," Honeychurch observed gently.

"True enough. Phil Ainsworth was a quiet type who went off to the Philippines directly he qualified, to be a missionary with his old man. I figured it would be safe enough to borrow his name. At first I had to forge my testimonials, but later"—he sounded triumphant—"I got

Ainsworth some pretty smart ones in his own right. Then I got too big for my boots. I risked doing a job at the Mayo Clinic: and of course they held a surgical get-together there and I walked slap into Ziedermayr first day."

"Ziedermayr is a very fine person," Honeychurch said.

"He is indeed. He looked straight through me and out the other side. Later I got a note from him. He said he'd keep his mouth shut if I got out of the States. You know the rest."

"You got a travelling fellowship," Honeychurch said. "You thought you were safe. And as luck would have it, you ran slap into Martin Sandeman."

Ainsworth put the finishing touches to Rutherford's sling.

"He was an expert in his own line. He played with me like a cat with a mouse. He used to get me up to his room and ask me what I'd advise him to do—should he tell the prof or save time by going to the police directly? He'd ask me what I thought would happen—extradition? A prison sentence? Real blackmail was too honest a game for Sandeman; if I didn't kill him, it's only by the grace of God. I've often enough wished him dead. But why he ever pitched on that tomfool idea of asking me to go on a binge with him—"

"It was to provide him with an alibi," Rutherford said.

"To provide *him* with an alibi? What did he need an alibi for?"

They told him.

Garside came in with a bottle of whisky.

"Where's Tom?" Honeychurch said, feeling comforted in the depths of his soul by so timely a ministration. "And how's Tom? For really that's more important than his mere corporeal whereabouts."

"He's in bed," Garside said. "I've put him in your room, Bill. We'll make up an extra bed later. God only knows if there any sheets aired, but we'll hope for the best. If you like to take the risk, sir"—he smiled at Honeychurch with so outrageous a charm that Honeychurch immediately thought of Burnivel and was grateful for his absence—"we should be very happy to put you up for the rest of your stay. I gather you had a rather hard time of it last night?"

"The use of the word 'hard' is apt," Honeychurch said reminiscently, accepting a glass with thankfulness. "Thank you. Your invitation lifts a great weight from my mind. And are we to understand that Tom is really asleep?"

"I should hate to commit myself," Garside said. "He is in bed, he has a pile of books and magazines, and I have left his light on. He was nodding a little when I came away, but he probably has remarkable reserves."

"I wonder—" Honeychurch began and stopped as the handle of the door began to turn synchronously with a terse peremptory knock.

"Well, he's dead," Burnivel said.

"What have you done with the—" Honeychurch started to ask, but—

"Grimshaw's taking care of the body," Burnivel went on. "I told him I still had work to do."

The phrase was ominous; the tone in which it was spoken yet more so. The room darkening into a restful sober light was full of things as yet unspoken. Honeychurch hoped with all his heart that they would never be spoken; but it was no use asking for miracles, no use attempting to deflect Burnivel, sore, cheated, full of righteous wrath.

"Have a drink?" Garside said.

"Thanks; I don't need stimulating," Burnivel said. "And there's some things I want straightened out."

He walked to the window and turned round. Deliberately or not, he had contrived to get his face in shadow; they could only guess at his expression. A fixed scowl most probably, or perhaps that peculiarly mirthless grin. Ainsworth struck a match; the little noise was startling. He bent down and held it to the unlit fire. In a moment flames appeared, consuming paper, licking wood.

"There isn't one of you," Burnivel exploded, "who hasn't lied to me."

"Oh, come," Honeychurch murmured. "Perhaps there may have been a little prevarication, but hardly actual lying."

"I'm not clever like you," Burnivel said, with acid in the words. "I call things by their common names. If you don't like what I say, you can blame yourselves for it. Perhaps I pitched it a little too strong. You—" from the angle of his head he was picking out Rutherford—"you only suppressed the truth. I suppose that isn't so bad. Didn't any of you stop to think what you were playing at? If you'd only left that confounded book alone"—his wrath swerved to include Honeychurch—"I could have put Rutherford out of harm's way; but that would have been too tame for you or too embarrassing for Dr. Rutherford."

"You cannot possibly reprimand me any more severely for what I did than I have berated myself," Honeychurch said gravely. "And you must remember that we had never considered Henchard as a possible murderer. Garside here had picked on Pemberton: I was"—he stopped in deference to Ainsworth's presence and ended lamely—"just as wrong. And I might have known. I remembered when we saw the photograph you took from Sandeman's flat that someone had said something to me about Rutherford that sounded odd; it was Henchard, of course. He said he'd never *spoken* to Rutherford where the natural thing would have been to say he didn't know him."

"Yes," Burnivel surprisingly agreed. "I should have made that photograph spell Henchard, but I let it spell Honeychurch." He paused, and a faint note of amusement crept into his voice. "With Rutherford's help, you could have done it, you know. I knew it was Sandeman planted the book; then there was an unexplained telephone call to Sandeman late at night in a voice that the operator didn't recognise—Honeychurch again, I thought. But there wasn't a shred of evidence, so I didn't make too much of a fool of myself, thank God. It was all right for you"— even in the darkness Honeychurch could tell his expression was withering—"to make clever guesses and to act on them. Guesses don't go down well with a judge and jury. But if you'd told me the truth, Dr. Garside, you'd have put a link in the chain for me. You knew dam' well your wife never had a love affair with Sandeman, didn't you?"

"Yes; I knew." Garside spoke softly. He reached behind his chair and switched on a standard lamp. The glow was gentle, yet they blinked and rubbed their eyes. "Helena took pethidine; I knew Sandeman got it for her. Some time before she killed herself he refused to let her have any more. I tried to get her some, but it wasn't so easy. Sandeman kept it all in his laboratory. And I thought she was safe enough. Pethidine withdrawal isn't so serious a business as morphine withdrawal, you know. Usually addicts only feel ill for a week or two and then get over it." He paused, and ended flatly, "Helena was exceptional, I suppose."

Honeychurch said cautiously, "Would this information really have been of so much use to you, Inspector?"

"Not this," Garside said, "but something else. Helena was Henchard's patient for a while. He gave evidence at her inquest—said she was emotionally unstable and so on. He didn't mention that she'd been on pethidine. I thought it was out of deference to my feelings."

"You see?" Burnivel said. "It wouldn't have proved anything, but it would have helped. Well, Dr. Garside, why did you lie to me?"

"Damn your eyes," Garside said amiably. "I'd just come back from the other side of the world, and the first thing I knew I was being told it was common knowledge that Bill Rutherford had finally got his own back on Sandeman. That seemed unlikely: I decided it would be a simple act of charity to throw a little sand in your eyes. I picked on adultery because I thought you'd like it better than drugs. I'm sorry; I shouldn't have pandered to your baser instincts."

Burnivel looked his opinion and left his look to speak for itself.

"Now it's your turn, Dr. Rutherford. Why in heaven's name didn't you tell me why Sandeman wanted you killed? You knew at teatime: you deliberately tried to provoke Henchard into giving himself away."

"Did I?" Rutherford looked up, surprised evidently at this interpretation of his conduct. And then, as if it had ceased to matter much, "Perhaps I did. I don't know."

"It had something to do with Sandeman's paper, of course," Burnivel said.

"Why?" Ainsworth demanded.

"What linked Sandeman and Henchard?" Burnivel countered. "Pethidine, of course. If Rutherford was any danger to them, it must have been because of the missing pethidine. Well?" He turned to Rutherford. "What was it? And why didn't you tell me?"

"Sandeman had altered all the conclusions in the experiment to make it look as if pethidine was going to be really useful. At the end, he suggested he should go on with the work for another year." He went on slowly. "I don't know why I didn't tell you."

"Perhaps you thought you'd play a little game all by yourself," Burnivel said. "Not even two at a time, like Dr. Garside and the professor: you thought you'd just let slip a hint to Henchard that you knew what he'd been up to."

"I didn't know till I was reading Sandeman's paper aloud. Then I slipped on the word 'hypnosis'. And then I saw what he must have done, and realised Tom was still alive. And I guessed he was here, because this was the only place he could be."

"I don't see," Ainsworth dared Burnivel's eye manfully. "What's all this about hypnosis? What have I missed?"

"I thought Henchard had made an arrangement with Tom—told him to be at the gates when the moon came up, or something—"

"When an owl hooted," Garside supplied. "That's what Tom told me."

"But if he'd done that, he would have had to kill Tom later or he'd be given away. That was all I meant"—he glanced at Burnivel—"when I let slip a hint, as you call it. Afterwards I saw that you were right; no murderer could take such a chance. He meant to make use of hypnotic automatism to get the kid out of the way—to drive him up on the moors, perhaps, or leave him in an empty building. Tom wouldn't know what had happened when he woke up. Then I suggested Tom had walked out voluntarily, and he guessed what had happened."

"What on earth can Henchard have felt like," Garside said, "when he found he hadn't got the kid after all?"

"He wouldn't have been too worried. If Tom was walking about Bantwich in his sleep, he wouldn't have come to any great harm, and the rest of the plan would still have held together. No; I imagine Henchard was hardly bothered about Tom at all until he thought I knew what had happened. He had other things to worry about."

"He still had to solve the problem of preventing you reading the paper and letting the cat out of the bag."

"He must have been on tenterhooks until he heard that Pemberton had told me about the book," Burnivel said. "Funny he didn't tell me himself."

"I don't think he knew," Rutherford said. "I hope he didn't. I'd much rather think that was entirely Sandeman's own idea. Anyway, he was an intelligent man; he would never have believed that I'd be convicted on such a flimsy scrap of evidence. Perhaps he hoped that there'd be enough fuss for the pethidine experiment to die a natural death."

"Well, that's that," Burnivel said. "And I hope you're satisfied with yourself, Dr. Rutherford. If you'd come straight to me—"

"Oh, Lord Almighty!" Ainsworth turned to him. "What are you getting at him for? He saved Tom's life, didn't he?"

"Tom's life would never have been in any danger if he'd put a curb on his tongue," Burnivel said with searing emphasis. "Herbert!" He added his scorn, his indignation reverberating from the walls. "James and Herbert! A bloody fine pair, whoever they were. As for you, Mr. Ainsworth, don't you imagine you're out of this. What were you doing spending an evening in Sandeman's flat? I thought you and he were at each other's throats."

"Sandeman wanted to get things on a better footing," Honeychurch said before Ainsworth could open his mouth in reply. "He simply invited Ainsworth along to talk things over. I believe he even ended by asking Ainsworth to go out with him last night. No doubt that was to provide himself with an alibi for the time of Rutherford's murder: it must have been most galling for him to be called into hospital by Rutherford himself."

"It must have been," Burnivel said. Then he swore scabrously, fully, and without reserve, and when he had finished swearing he laughed—sitting abruptly on a sofa with his hands on his knees, he laughed till he shook.

"I'll say this for you: you certainly stick together. A pack of kids scrumping apples couldn't stick any closer. I wish you luck at the inquest, that's all. Though that won't bother you, seeing the coroner's an old friend of the family."

"It's difficult," Garside said, ignoring the provocation, "to see Henchard as a murderer. He seemed so, well, mild. So ineffective. Not that I knew him well."

"He didn't need to be any sort of villian," Honeychurch said. "Nor was he in the last analysis. Standing directly behind Rutherford and knowing his only chance was to kill him and the child before we got to them, he still couldn't do it."

"It was your shouting that distracted him," Burnivel said; "and Rutherford's turning his head. Don't you go making out that he was overcome by his better feelings, Professor Honeychurch. That sort doesn't have better feelings."

"I wonder. It was Sandeman after all who drove him to this. Henchard was no murderer, and he never wanted to kill Rutherford; even if everything had gone according to plan and he had been able to summon Rutherford to hospital at the right moment, he would never have killed him. There was only one man in the world he was capable of murdering, and that man presented himself at the right moment."

Burnivel made a gesture of the purest negation. "Of course he would have killed Rutherford. There were shadows, his eyesight wasn't good, he knew Rutherford only from the photo Sandeman showed him, and he must have been in a fine state of nerves. He killed Sandeman by mistake."

"Mistake? Yes and no. Henchard may have told himself, as Sandeman certainly told him, that Rutherford's existence threatened his security, but somewhere at a deeper level he knew better. He killed the man he knew deserved to be dead."

"All right," Burnivel said gruffly, "he was more sinned against than sinning, if that's how you like it. I shouldn't think Dr. Rutherford looks at it that way. When you know a chap's had a go at bashing your brains out, I shouldn't think you feel so calm and forgiving."

Rutherford seemed not to be listening. Honeychurch was filled with compunction. Pain and fatigue impose their own rules, and Burnivel had no right to infringe them. He said, "Thank God he's out of it now," because it seemed to him that that was what everyone but Burnivel was thinking. He may have been right.

At the head of the stairs they parted—Garside taking Honeychurch off in search of a long-disused guest room while Rutherford went to his own bedroom to find pyjamas and a toothbrush. He could still hear Ainsworth and Burnivel in the hall arguing furiously and uselessly as they

207

had argued all through dinner, all through the evening. He yawned, leaning against the doorpost, and then he pushed the door slowly open. Tom was still awake, sitting up in bed, writing something on the flyleaf of a book. Rutherford smiled at the child experimentally: Tom's answering look was neutral, thoughtful, but not positively haunted.

Obscurely encouraged, Rutherford crossed the room and sat on the foot of the bed: said (and was aware that Tom must have heard the words many times before): "Why aren't you asleep, Tom?"

"I didn't feel sleepy. I haven't done anything all day except sit about and make things up. Now I'm writing it all down."

"The things you made up?"

"No; what really happened. When I got back there"—whether by "there" he meant the home or the hospital he left conveniently vague—"they'll never believe it. Unless I get my pictures in the papers, of course. Do you think I will?"

"No," Rutherford said without hesitation.

"Well, then; I thought if I got it down, just like it really was, you could all sign it and that would prove it was true. Then they'd have to believe me."

Rutherford was silent: it was the silence of a growing respect for Henchard, who had evidently known his job.

"Do you think *he'd* sign it if I sent it to him? Are prisoners in the condemned cell allowed to get letters?"

"I don't know," Rutherford said. And added in as matter of fact a tone as he could muster: "He won't be in a condemned cell, Tom. He's dead."

"Dead!" Tom sat up and stared. "Did you string him up?"

"No, we didn't. There's a sort of cliff a little way up the road. He jumped over: that's the last you'll hear of him."

Tom considered it in silence and dejection. After all, he's not yet ten, Rutherford thought, panic-stricken in the face of this appalling self-possession; and it's not as if Henchard or Sandeman meant anything to him.

He said, "Did the day seem very long? You must have been hungry."

"I ate your chocolate. I'll buy you some more. I read your diary, too."

"You shouldn't have."

"I got fed up. Anyway, there wasn't much in it."

"No; I don't suppose there was."

"You put my name down once—Does your shoulder hurt much?"

"Fair to middling. It's all right when I remember not to move it."

"Lucky it wasn't your head, like he meant it to be. I think you should have put up a bit more of a fight."

"How could I?" Pardonably nettled at this thankless disparagement of his recent conduct, he looked at the child with a gathering frown. "You were hanging on to me like a limpet. There wasn't anything I could do."

"All the same—" Tom sighed. Then he brightened. "When I write that bit, I'll make you out braver than you really were."

"Thank you. Only if you do, I shan't be able to sign my name to it."

"I suppose not." The point was by now clearly irrelevant. Tom's head had found the pillow, his eyelids were already drooping, his hand curling under his cheek. Rutherford stood up and put out the light. Crossing the room with unusual care, he heard an odd sound in the darkness behind him. He turned sharply.

"Go to sleep, Tom. It's very late."

"I am going to sleep...." The voice was convincingly drowsy after all. "I was just thinking.... I'll get Professor Honeychurch to sign my book, and he's much more famous than you are."

Rutherford shut the door and stood for a moment on the outer side, listening—as only twenty-four hours earlier Honeychurch had listened—to the soft regular breathing. He had forgotten to collect his pyjamas, he had no idea where he was meant to sleep; he did not know, he did not care. There was a couch before the dying fire in the library: he stretched himself on it. Stripped of infamy as of heroism, no longer a crook or a superman, he slept. Upstairs Tom slept, and Garside, and Honeychurch. And Henchard slept for ever.

ENVOI

Magnanimously enough in the circumstances, Pemberton drove Honeychurch to the station on the following Tuesday. The morning had been devoted to the double inquest: the inquest had been admirably stage-managed by Garside's capable friend, the coroner, and now the prolonged weekend could finally be allowed to close.

Honeychurch leant out of the carriage window, collecting smuts on a pocket handkerchief.

"I ought to thank you, Cyril. I have had a most diverting weekend."

Pemberton produced a smile, one kept ready to hand for such occasions—a smile with a distinct odour of camphor to it.

"It has been most successful altogether," he admitted. "The cases on Saturday were well presented, I feel, and my talk on Sunday seemed to arouse some interest."

"It did indeed," Honeychurch said; and wondered whether Pemberton's equal existed in the universe. To prick the bubble of so bloated an indifference was irresistible. "Such a pity," he murmured, "that Dr. Rutherford found himself unable to finish Sandeman's paper. That particular session lacked the completeness of the others."

Pemberton shook his head sombrely. "Some of our juniors are frankly unpredictable. They'll grow out of it, no doubt. A year or two in my department seems to knock the corners off them." He grew suddenly confiding. "Now, take Ainsworth—not that he's really any concern of mine, fortunately. This morning he came to me and asked me how to set about getting a British qualification—said he didn't want to go back to the States, he'd prefer to practise here. I can't understand these young men. Anyone would think they had eternity before them."

"So they have," Honeychurch said and added with a little malice: "You'll be losing Rutherford as well, won't you?"

"I hope not." Pemberton was non-committal. "I think I shall be able to persuade him to stay on now that Sandeman has left us."

"I doubt it," Honeychurch said. "I have advised him to apply for my clinical assistantship in a couple of months' time."

"He's not ready for that sort of thing yet," Pemberton said; it was obvious that he was annoyed. "He will never make a really good research worker."

"You would be surprised to find how entirely he agrees with you on that point."

"He lacks application," Pemberton said loudly. "He fritters his time away. He is quite unable to see the point of routine consolidating work. Now, Sandeman—"

"Even Sandeman," Honeychurch suggested, "allowed his attention to wander on occasion. I thought that point was rather nicely brought out at the inquest."

He felt immediately ashamed of the easy gibe, for Pemberton had visibly if unexpectedly crumpled.

"If there has been one thing in this whole wretched business," he was saying, "that really disturbed me more than all the rest, it was finding that Sandeman—of all people—had falsified his results: I can hardly believe it even now. I can hardly bring myself to think it of him."

So this, Honeychurch reflected, is the ultimate tragedy for Pemberton. It is a good thing that he too should see cause for regret in this sorry affair—and how admirable of him to see it on so large a scale, beyond the simply human, the pettily personal!

He felt the train beginning to move over the rails and said aloud, competing with the gathering roar: "Not all of us have your integrity, Cyril. If you have a fault, it is that you expect too high a standard of your fellow men."

Like the bad fairy in a pantomime, Pemberton was extinguished in a puff of steam, waving a stiff farewell, arranging his formal smile. He had not heard Honeychurch's small tribute.

He was beyond small tributes, Honeychurch suspected.

MYSTERY
in the best 'whodunit' tradition...

AMANDA CROSS
The Kate Fansler Mysteries

Available at your bookstore or use this coupon.

___**THE QUESTION OF MAX**   31385 2.50
An accident...or foul play? Amateur sleuth Professor Kate Fansler attempts to discover the truth about a former student's death...and her elegant friend Max.

___**THE JAMES JOYCE MURDER**   30214 2.50
When her next door neighbor is murdered, Kate Fansler must investigate. Every guest in her house is a prime suspect, as she puts aside sorting through James Joyce's letters to his publisher to find the guilty party.

___**DEATH IN TENURED POSITION**   30215 2.50
Kate Fansler must get on the case when her old friend and colleague Janet Mandlebaum is appointed first woman professor in Harvard's English Department and then found dead in the men's room.

 BALLANTINE MAIL SALES
Dept. TA, 201 E. 50th St., New York, N.Y. 10022

Please send me the BALLANTINE or DEL REY BOOKS I have checked above. I am enclosing $ . . . . (add 50¢ per copy to cover postage and handling). Send check or money order — no cash or C.O.D.'s please. Prices and numbers are subject to change without notice.

Name_____

Address_____

City_____State_____Zip Code_____

Allow at least 4 weeks for delivery.

Attention Mystery and Suspense Fans

Do you want to complete your collection of mystery and suspense stories by some of your favorite authors? Raymond Chandler, Erle Stanley Gardner, Ed McBain, Cornell Woolrich, among many others, and included in Ballantine's new Mystery Brochure.

For your FREE Mystery Brochure, fill in the coupon below and mail it to:

Ballantine/Fawcett Books
Education Department — MB
201 East 50th Street
New York, NY 10022

Name_____

Address_____

City_____ State_____ Zip_____

12   TA-94

MEAN MORE

e. More people who care.

*Gulf Canada Limited registered user.

TH LITRE BEATERS

70995 78049   00200

✂

Gulf LITRE BEATER

$2.00 Off Gas Coupon!

One coupon per minimum
25 litre fill-up or more.
Redeemable at any Gulf
Retailer in British Columbia
or Alberta. Offer expires
September 30, 1985.

Gulf
*

GULF MEANS MORE

Gulf Canada Limited Registered

By TERENCE ROSS
Staff Reporter

The two-year-old sensatio Proctor seeks his fifth straight tomorrow in the $100,000-guar Jack Diamond Futurity at Exh Park.

King Proctor, by the Kentuck Proctor and out of Clayton T mare Sifting Sea, didn't look world beater when he made his debut back in May.

It took the colt five starts to his maiden July 7, but since th has won the Blue Boy, New Wes ster and Stepping Stone.

King Proctor, who will be ridd usual by Buford Mills Jr., has a m running style for a horse so yo He's not a speed horse; he comes off the pace and in the Aug. 31

Fogh second in soling

SARNIA, Ont. — Dave Curtis of Marble-head Mass., moved up a notch in the standings to take over first place after an eighth-place finish yesterday at the 15th World Soling championships. Olympic bronze medallist Hans Fogh of Toronto finished second in the race, to move from fourth to second in the standings.

Equestrians brave weather

CALGARY — Ronnie Freeman of Laguna Hills, Calif., and Paul Schockemoehle, the European champion from West Germany, won yesterday's international classes during the weather-plagued second day of the Spruce Meadows Masters show jumping tournament.

Clubs will have to allocate half their ground space to membership card-holders. The edict comes in the wake of widespread violence at matches last season.